Rachel

Phoenix Burn

Phoenix Burn

Laci Maskell

Also By Laci Maskell

Still Life Moving
So . . . That Happened

Phoenix series:
Phoenix Born

To my mom, who has suppported me in this journey from day one. You always believed in me. Words cannot express my deepest gratitude for you. You've seen me at my best and my worst and always been there for me. I couldn't have done it without you.

One

I twitch my nose up and down, back and forth, like a rabbit. My thumb and index finger form a trail from the top to my nostrils. After two months it still feels wrong. Looking in the mirror I can't tell that it was broken, but somehow my nose knows. Like I betrayed it by letting it get broken.

I had hoped I might regenerate like I did when Nash and I crashed his bike, or when Xander stabbed an ice knife into my chest. No such luck. I had to go back to school with a broken nose and cuts and scrapes all over my body. Tucker suffered a blow to the head, but that wasn't so noticeable to the student body like a broken nose.

But getting attacked in downtown Cedars, Nebraska was noticeable to Tucker. Things like that don't just happen here. Tucker has been very suspicious the past two months. Logan and I told him several times that we were mugged, that he got knocked out first, that one of the guys broke my nose and knocked me out, and that Logan fended them off. Tucker believed it at first, when he couldn't remember much. But the more time that passes, the more things he remembers, and the more suspicious he gets.

I've never had to lie to my best friend before, but now the lies keep piling on top of one another like a messed up version of Jenga. I have to tell him the truth. I want to tell him the truth. The whole truth. But there are things, people, who would hinder that. Logan, for one. Xander, though I haven't talked to him since that night. My father, the biological one, would also stop me from telling Tucker the truth.

My father. Now, he is a whole different story. He may be my father, but biology doesn't mean much when the man has been absent my entire life. He claims he didn't know about me and Nash, but honestly, how could you not know you had not only one, but two kids, for sixteen years? Especially when you happen to be a mythological creature who can hear heartbeats and just altogether knows things others don't. Let's just say I haven't warmed up to him yet. I have a dad. I've had a dad my whole life. A dad I love very much. One I'm not looking to replace.

My father claims he is not here to replace my dad, but why else would he be here. Oh wait, he's here because he happens to be the leader of a race of people and wants me to fight in his war, and take over for him if anything should ever happen to him. No pressure right. I've known I am a phoenix

2

for a total of four months, but apparently that is long enough to take over an entire race if need be. Yeah, right.

I wasn't even given time to adjust to being a phoenix, time to process just how I might feel about it, but that didn't stop everyone from thrusting me into this world. I did ask Logan to teach me the ways of being a phoenix, but the way he imparts his wisdom is a process I can handle. He helps me understand without throwing too much in my face, but without dumbing it down to me. The only throwing he does with me is to throw me to the floor in one of our sparing matches. He may be gentle when he gives me knowledge, but when it comes to fighting, gentle is not in Logan's vocabulary.

I twitch my nose one last time before making my way to the kitchen in Logan's house. I take a bottle of water from his fridge then stare at the door of the fridge once it's closed. The picture Logan took of the two of us is the only thing that adorns the door. Other than the picture of me and my three best friends Xander gave me for Christmas, which now sits in my closet, it is my favorite picture. Logan and I are so opposite in looks it's almost comical. Logan with his dark skin, darker hair, and flaming blue eyes, and me with my fair skin, platinum blonde hair, and dark, dark eyes. We look frightfully opposite, but our differences complement each other, and we look like we might belong together. Just might.

I am caught in my revere when Logan's arms wrap around my waist from behind. I smile and rest my head back against his hard chest. He kisses the top of my head and hums his contentment into my hair. I love him as I have never loved any one before. And although the past two months have been two of the best months of my life, they have also been two of the strangest. While Logan is the most loving boyfriend when we are together, in school, and anywhere away from my father, he is distant and formal when my father is anywhere near. Yet another reason why I am not my father's biggest fan.

"I love this picture," Logan says, his deep voice rumbling in his chest.

"Me too," I tell him.

"I love you, Casslyn."

I stiffen in his arms and I know he can feel it. He turns me around so I am facing him. The look in his eyes, that dejected, worried look, tears me apart.

I try to smile and play it off by saying, "Why don't we go downstairs so I can kick your butt?"

His eyebrows join together. His shoulders shake like he is trying to fight the urge to roll them back. "Casslyn?" he asks, clearly hurt.

I've told him I love him before. I'm not sure why I can't say it now. But the more Logan loves me, the closer we get, I feel myself pulling back. I've wanted to be with him for months and now that we are together I'm the one messing it up. But I am too aware of the fact that the hardest day of loving someone is when you lose them. I found that out when I lost Nash. I'm sure people would tell me, in fact Tucker has told me several times, that because I could lose him I should love him harder. But I loved my brother as much as humanly possible and I still haven't recovered from losing him. I'm afraid loving Logan with all I have, and losing him, might kill me. But I don't want him to use kid gloves around me like Tucker and Xander did after Nash died. So I keep it to myself.

As if he knows what I am feeling, and understands, he takes my face in both of his massive hands and leans down to kiss me. It is a kiss that melts my heart and makes me weak at the knees. "It's okay, love."

He rests his head against mine and we breathe together. I love him so much. Why can't I just say it back to him? If I can't say it to him, maybe I can show it to him. I take his face in my hands and lean up to him, planting my lips to his. It is a slow burn, but a fire starts nonetheless. The kiss deepens. Logan picks me up by my hips and places me on his kitchen counter. My breathing becomes erratic, my head foggy. His scent, pure rain, becomes so strong I can almost taste it. His thumbs run under my shirt, along the edge of my shorts, making me shiver. I wrap my legs around his waist and pull him closer. He makes a noise deep in the back of his throat and it goes a long way to undo me. I do love this man.

Logan pulls away. Breathing heavily, he says, "Before you kick . . . my ass. Maybe we should run."

I smile and tease, "You don't think those kisses were cardio enough?"

He grins his wicked grin and says, "Close but no dice. You can't get out of your run. It is part of your training."

"I'm not trying to get out of it," I say, because it is true.

"I only thought we could do a bit of substitution."

He laughs, while shaking his head, and pulls me off of the counter.

***

The air rushes out of my chest as Logan throws me to the ground. He hovers over me with a hard look on his face.

"Do you ever get tired of that?" I ask, catching my breath. "I mean, the whole domestic violence thing has got to get old," I say, laughing on the last word.

Logan holds his stare for a moment longer then starts laughing with me. "Not funny," he says.

"It won't be when I'm strong enough to kick your butt," I say.

Logan laughs harder and rolls off of me onto the floor. I lie beside him and watch his chest rise and fall with his laughter. It is rich and comes from deep in his chest.

I move quickly and roll on top of him, straddling him, and staring at him. In a voice that is barely harsh I say, "Are you laughing at me, Logan Rivers? What? You don't think I'll be able to take you on when I age?"

"Sadly, I do not, love. I am simply too manly and brute for you," he says, snark lacing his voice.

"Ha," I laugh.

Slapping my hand down on his chest, I stand and get in the fighting position. I'll show him how funny he is.

"Get up," I bark at him.

Logan continues to laugh, but stands up and readies himself in front of me.

"Are you ready for an ass whooping?" I ask him.

"Bring it on, love," he says, that damn grin plastered on his face.

I rush at him, forgetting everything he's taught me about patience, and let out a fierce battle cry. Logan side steps me and kicks my legs out from under me saying, "Wrong," as he does so.

I get right back to my feet and ready myself. I attack again, this time without the battle cry. Again he bats me away like I am a pesky fly.

"Have you learned nothing I have taught you? Come on, Casslyn. You know this stuff."

I glare at him but say nothing.

This time I wait. I wait like a hungry but patient lioness. I *will* make my kill. Logan taught me to wait, to watch, to listen.

So that is what I do.

I wait for Logan to attack. I can be patient.

I watch his body language, paying attention to any ticks or clues his body may give away to his intentions. Does he look right? He might attack right. Does he look at my arms or legs or stomach? He might focus his attack there. Does he favor one side more than the other? He might have a weak side.

Then I listen. Is his breathing heavy? He might be worn out. Are his footsteps heavier or lighter on one side? He

Phoenix Burn

might be injured.

Of course, Logan is in perfect health so none of this applies, but I will not always be fighting him and will need to know these things to defeat my enemies.

I don't have to wait long. I watch Logan's right shoulder shift and am able to dodge out of the way before he throws his punch. Good thing too, because as it sails past my head I know it would have been a hard one.

"Good," Logan says before he changes his position and throws another punch. I am not quick enough to avoid the hit to the gut, but am able to move so it doesn't hurt as badly as I know it could.

I recover quickly and throw a right hook of my own. Logan deflects easily but I surprise him with a spin move and a kick to the side. He deflects it but the surprise and pride are written on his face. I mistakenly allow myself a second to celebrate. Mistakenly because Logan uses my distraction to lower himself to the floor and use a spin move of his own to take my feet out from under me. I roll over as soon as my back hits the floor, waiting for his next attack.

"Good," Logan says again. That's the most I ever get from him. When we train he is not my boyfriend. When we train, Logan is a soldier. An instructor.

I contemplate taking my shirt off and continuing in my shorts and sports bra. It works every time. Logan may be a hard core soldier, but he is first and foremost a guy.

Logan stands above me and looks down. He pauses for a moment, so uncharacteristic. I dare to make a move and pull the hem of my shirt up an inch over my stomach.

"What are you doing?" Logan asks me.

"I just thought it was getting a little warm in here. Don't you agree?" I ask inching my shirt up just a like more.

Logan closes his eyes and says, "Don't, Casslyn." His voice is even deeper.

I pull my shirt up a little farther. Just to see what he will do. And in a flash, Logan is on top of me, pinning both of my arms above my head. I lean my head up, to kiss him or to head butt him, I'm not quite sure. Logan's head moves to meet mine and as our lips touch I savor his taste and his scent before I bite his lip, roll us over, and pin him to the ground.

"That was dirty and underhanded," he says, his chest bouncing with laughter underneath me.

"Anything goes, remember."

Logan grins and says, "I've taught you well."

"Letting my daughter get the best of you, Mr. Rivers?" Logan's and my head snap towards the stairs and the sound of my father.

"No, sir," Logan says, boyfriend gone, soldier returned, as he rolls out from under me. "I was demonstrating the technique of escaping when pinned down, sir."

I roll my eyes as my father says, "Very well, Logan."

Then he turns his attention to me. "I trust your training is going well. My idea for this-,"

"This was my idea," I say, cutting him off.

"Yes, well, I trust that you will continue-."

Again I cut him off saying, "And I trust that you will

leave now."

Logan's head snaps my direction and without looking at him I can feel the disapproval radiating off of him.

The man in front of me, the one who calls himself my father, takes my comment with a grain of salt. I guess you don't become the leader of an entire race by being a softy or vulnerable to the words of a rash teenager.

"Logan, may I have a word?" My father asks.

"Of course," Logan says, rushing to his side.

There are many things about their relationship I find bothersome. Logan is far too eager to please him. My father is far too eager to order Logan around. Logan forgets he has any attachment to me when my father is anywhere in the general vicinity. Logan forgets he has any emotions at all when my father is anywhere in the general vicinity. Logan's fondness for my father seems less than normal. The list goes on. I'm sure I'll add to it the more time I see them together. It's not exactly something I'm looking forward to.

The urge to eaves drop is powerful. I'm more than positive they are talking about me and I feel as if I should be part of the conversation.

For months after Nash died Tucker and Xander would talk about me like that, huddled, in hushed tones. It is unnerving to say the least. They thought they were saving me by not telling me what they were talking about. They were wrong. It only made me feel less like they were looking out for me and more like I was an outsider. Xander and Tucker have since learned their lesson.

I asked Logan a few weeks ago if he would tell me what they had discussed. I thought maybe, since I am his girl-friend, the one who kisses him, he might tell me. But no, he told me anything my father wasn't comfortable discussing in front of me, would not be divulged to me by him, that he would not betray my father's trust. Needless to say, I really don't like the relationship they have.

"Enough already," I say aloud to them. "You're cutting into my training time. You can talk to your precious soldier another time."

Logan turns and gives me a stern look. Too bad it doesn't work on me. I'm passed giving a shit if I insult my father. I'd say he deserves it.

"We were just finishing," my father says.

"I don't care," I tell him.

"Logan, Casslyn, I will see you later," my father says, walking up the stairs that leads to the basement.

I've since stopped listening to him.

Logan walks over to me, his brows furrowed. He rolls his shoulders back. I know I'm in trouble now.

"Not only is that man your father," he says. He takes a quick step towards me, drops down, circles with his leg out, and takes mine out from under me. I fall back hard and hit the back of my head on the mat. It's Logan's way of teaching me a lesson.

I move to stand back up but Logan is on top of me too quickly. He pins me down and forces me to pay attention to him.

He continues, "He is the leader of your race. You will show him the respect he deserves."

"I will show him what he deserves," I tell him, sarcasm lacing my voice. "Maybe won't be respect."

Logan picks me up by my shoulders. For half a second I think he's going to slam me down. For half a second I think he considers it. But then he lets me go and walks away from me.

Too bad I still have steam built up from seeing my father.

"If you love him so much. If you think he deserves so much respect. Why don't you be his son? You can be the next leader of the phoenixes. You can be his precious soldier. You can be the child he deserves. I don't want it."

"Casslyn, stop," Logan says, taking large steps away from me.

I can't.

"What? Is he the dad you always wanted? You couldn't make your father proud so you replaced him. Your dad didn't spend enough time with you but mine would? Am I getting close, Logan? Did your dad not give you enough love and attention, but mine would? What is it, Logan? Do you wish my father was yours instead?"

Logan's chest is heaving by the time he has crossed the basement and stands in front of me. His shoulders bob up and down. His eyes are brighter than normal. If I didn't know with every fiber of my being that Logan would never hurt me, I might be frightened.

Logan gets within inches of my face and says, "My father was killed by the griffins when I was twelve. My mother died trying to avenge him. Your father took me and my sister in when we had no place to go." His voice is deep and sad. "He fed us. He clothed us. And he trained us. I owe your father everything. And I intend to pay him back in any way that I can."

I stand my ground though I feel like a pile of shit. How could I say those things to Logan? How could I be so cruel? Why couldn't I stop myself? I love Logan with all my heart and yet I hurt him.

Logan's face is hard lines and edges. He is truly upset with me. I've only seen him this angry with me a few times. But every time, even when I think he is wrong, I feel terrible. He stares at me for a moment longer, then walks away. I flinch when I hear the front door slam.

Worst-girlfriend-ever award winner right here.

I suck in a deep breath then let out a frustrated scream. My father has messed up so much by coming here. I wish he would leave so things could go back to normal. Whatever that is.

I tape up my hands and find the punching bag. The first hit vibrates through me and loosens up some of the tension from our fight. I hit harder the second time, needing to relieve my body of its tight hold on my anger.

My parents are so screwed up. All three of them. My relationship with one best friend is all but over. My relationship with the other best friend is damaged and nearly ruined. My relationship with Logan is teetering and unstable. My brother, my confidant, my other half, is gone and never coming back. I'm part of some ancient and powerful race that I'm not even sure I want to be a part of. I have mortal enemies because of the blood that runs through my veins. An attempt on my life has been made at least three times now, that I know of. And all of this is going on while I try to navigate high school. It's more than one girl should have to handle. I'm not sure I can hold on much longer. I'm not sure I'm strong enough.

Again and again I punch the bag, harder every time until I am punching and sweating and screaming and crying simultaneously.

I'm grabbed from behind. I panic and start to flail. I need to get my arms up to I can form an attack. I fight the grasp of my captor, but it's too strong.

He leans his face close to mine. I pull back to head butt him but then his voice falls over me. "Calm down, Casslyn," Logan says.

I stop fighting him and lean into him, succumbing to his hold. Emotions too strong to combat race through me. My breaths are heavy as I try not to cry harder.

"It's okay, love," he whispers into my ear.

He sits us on the floor and cradles me in his lap. I work hard to stop crying, to calm my breathing, to do anything but act like a wuss. I'm better than this. I know I'm better than this. Logan knows I'm better than this. Sometimes I swear Logan saves me by letting me break down. And sometimes

I wish he wouldn't. If I'm going to protect myself and the people I love, I can't cry every time something goes wrong.

"I'm so sorry," I tell him, once I've got a handle on the breathing while talking thing.

"It is forgiven," he says.

He doesn't say there is nothing to apologize for. It would have been a lie. But the fact that he chose to forgive me when I was malicious to him means more to me then he could ever know.

"You've done enough training for the day. Go home, take a shower, and get ready for tonight," Logan says.

He stands and pulls me up.

"What's tonight?" I ask him.

I'm pretty sure we don't have a date planned.

He turns his head and eyes me like I'm messing with him.

I raise an eyebrow to show him I'm really not sure what he's talking about.

"It's your birthday party. How could you have forgotten?"

My hand swings up and hits me square on the forehead. Forgetting my birthday party totally deserves a little face-palm action.

But, I forgot because I didn't want to remember. I never want to remember that night. I wish I didn't still have a birthday.

Logan continues to stare at me. I'm not sure what to tell him.

"Do we have to do this?" I ask him.

"Of course we do. It's your birthday."

"Technically my birthday is tomorrow."

"Yes, but we don't want you bursting into flames in the middle of your house with a bunch of party guests do we?"

"It would be interesting," I joke. "Seriously, I don't want a party."

"It's a little late for that, don't you think?" Logan asks. He places his hands on both of my arms and says, "What's this really about, love?"

"I have nothing to celebrate. I hate my birthday."

"I thought you loved your birthday. Tucker told me about the great parties you've always had."

"Yeah," I tell him. "That was last year. And the years before that."

"Cass, it's still your birthday. You shouldn't feel bad for still enjoying your birthday."

"You don't understand, Logan," I say, pulling away from him and walking back to the punching bag. I strike it before saying, "There's nothing to celebrate. There's nothing to enjoy. It's not my birthday anymore. March 11th is now and will forever more be the anniversary of the murder of my brother. It's a date that taunts me. It screams at me. 'You're one year older, Cass, but your twin never will be'."

Again Logan walks to me and places his hands on my arms. They are warm and send shivers through my body. By now I am aware that it's not just the temperature of his skin. Logan is using his powers to send warmth into me. It's just one more thing I found out about being a phoenix. Of course I won't be able to do it, or use any other phoenix power until I come of age tomorrow. I'm not sure how I feel about it all.

"Cass, I know it hurts. I know you miss him and there is a hole in your heart. As unsympathetic as this is, I do know how you feel. That's how I also know that other people are hurting. Your mom is also dealing with his loss. Your dad. Tucker misses him too. I know you loved him in a different way than they did. I know you were connected to him in a way no one else can understand. But I also know that as much as you may need them, they also need you. If you put on a brave face and enjoy your party, if only for a couple hours, it may just allow your parents and your friends to enjoy themselves, if only for a couple hours. Can you do that? Can you put aside your pain for a few hours and help those around you heal?"

"I hate you right now," I tell him.

Why does he have to always be right and wise about everything? It's like a complex he has.

"I know you do. Now go home, shower, and get ready. I'll be over shortly."

"Yeah, yeah, yeah," I tell him, walking up the stairs.

***

The short skirts that hang in my closet mock me.

The attack from the griffins on New Year's Eve resulted in pretty significant scaring all over my body. Because it was winter I could cover it up by wearing sweatshirts and pants. Now that it is warming up, some people, meaning Tucker, have become suspicious that I no longer wear skirts. I used to wear skirts like it was my religion. The shorter the better. Now I'm afraid of the looks I'll get. The fact that I had outbursts in school after the death of Nash has caused my peers to see me differently. I don't want them thinking I've started cutting myself if they see my legs full of scars.

"Wear one of them," Logan says from behind me.

His scent fills my bedroom. I'm not sure how someone can smell like rain, but Logan does and I love it. I've been caught sniffing him a time or two.

"I can't. They will all stare at me," I tell him, still facing the closet.

"No they won't. They love you, they won't care you have a few scars on your legs."

"A few? Are you blind?" I ask, finally turning to him. "My legs are covered in scars."

"I love you, I don't care that you have scars on your legs," he says. He pulls me to him and plants a kiss on my forehead.

"I can't. Tucker is already suspicious enough as it is. Xander told him I fell on New Year's Eve. He would want to know what really happened plus he'd be mad I lied to him. I can't."

"Have it your way," Logan says.

"I always do," I say, smiling slyly at him.

He raises an eyebrow but doesn't say anything.

I grab a pair of jeans from the pile and pull them on while Logan turns away. He's seen me naked twice now but still is courteous enough to turn around while I change. I grab a fancy top off its hanger and shove it over my head already ready for this night to be over.

I look up and finally notice Logan's appearance. Let me tell you, I have a hot boyfriend.

"You look great," I tell him.

He shrugs like his appearance means nothing to him, or that it's easy to pull off. Either way I envy him.

His fitted navy blue button down and black vest show off the muscles in his chest and arms. The dark jeans he wears accentuate his long, toned legs, plus they draw attention to his tight ass. Besides the pajama bottoms he wears low on his hips, these jeans may be my new favorite piece of his wardrobe.

"I feel like I should change," I say, offhand.

"You look great," Logan says. "You always do."

"You're my boyfriend, you have to say that."

"Have you ever known me to lie to you?"

I narrow my eyes at him.

"Scratch that," he says. "But I'm not lying when I say I think you always look good."

I playfully punch him in the shoulder as the doorbell rings.

"Your dad is here," Logan says. "Correction, both of your fathers are here."

I can't wait to be able to hear everything. Seriously. I

strain my ears to see if my powers prematurely kicked in. Nothing. No such luck.

When Nash and I crashed last year my father came to the hospital and saved my life by donating his blood to me. It doesn't explain why I regenerated when we crashed, but it could explain why I regenerated when Xander stabbed me. It's all weird and messed up and not even Logan or my father can explain it to me. Logically I should have died along with Nash in the crash. Logically I should have died from Xander stabbing me. But hell, I'm a freaking mythological creature so I'm not sure logic plays into my life any longer.

"Let's go get this over with," I say.

Logan grabs my arm when I walk past him. He pulls me to him and kisses me hard. His tongue is warm when it meets mine. I'd much rather stay up here all night and make out with him than open presents and eat cake.

"Casslyn," he says once he's pulled away. My eyes are still closed from the euphoria of his kiss. "Try to have fun tonight."

"Yes, sir," I say, standing up straight to salute him.

He slaps my ass as a reprimand then follows me out of my room.

Downstairs we find my dad talking to my mom and helping her place serving dishes piled full of food on the kitchen counter. My father stands off in a corner, his arms crossed, watching them.

"Who invited him?" I ask, indicating my father.

"Your mother?" Logan asks. I'm not sure he knows why

he's here. Though any second now he will turn into my father's soldier and forget he's my boyfriend.

"I don't even know why he is here."

Logan cocks and eyebrow and looks down at me.

"Okay, sure, if it weren't for him I wouldn't be here. But, if it weren't for him and our stupid race, Nash would be here."

Logan purses his lips but decides not to comment.

Not wanting to start an argument again, I turn to the kitchen and watch my parents. I smile when I see my dad place a kiss to the side of my mom's face. They are trying to repair their relationship. When my father showed up at the hospital last year he practically ruined everything between my parents. I blame him, but I also blame my mom for keeping it all a secret from my dad. They were beginning to get along again a few months ago and I was ecstatic about it. Then my father showed up again. I was afraid his presence would bring the reunion to a halt, but it hasn't. At least not that I can tell. I know my dad doesn't like the fact that my father is here. I'm not sure if it's because he is afraid my father will try to take my mom or me away from him, or the fact that he just doesn't like him. However, my dad knows I don't really want much to do with my father, plus my mom is working so hard trying to mend everything between them, so he doesn't feel completely threatened.

"Tucker's here," Logan says.

We make our way through the living room and to the front door. Tucker walks up the front steps and waves from behind the door. I pull it open and let him through.

"Happy birthday, Cassie," Tucker says, moving the gift to one hand so he can give me a side hug.

"Thanks, Tucker," I tell him.

He pulls away then turns to Logan. Tucker eyes him from head to toe and says, "Wow."

Logan chuckles under his breath then shakes Tucker's hand. "It's nice to see you, Tucker."

"Always a pleasure, Logan," Tucker says. "Seriously."

Logan takes the gift from Tucker's hands and takes it to a different room.

Tucker mouths, "Oh my God," to me.

"I know," I tell him.

I think it's funny that my best friend finds my boyfriend attractive. I'm well aware that if Logan was gay Tucker would be on top of that in a heartbeat. I want so badly for Tucker to find someone to love. He deserves it more than anyone. With Xander and I at odds lately he hasn't gotten the attention he needs and I feel bad about that. Plus with my new relationship with Logan, training with him, and my father in the picture I haven't had a lot of extra time to spend with him. I hope to rectify that soon.

"Is Xander here yet?" Tucker asks.

"He's not coming," I tell him, afraid we're about to get into it.

"Why not?"

"I didn't invite him."

"Why?" Tucker asks, aghast, like he doesn't know our

friendship has been on the rocks for the past six months.

It doesn't help that I can't tell Tucker that Xander is my mortal enemy. I can't tell him that Xander would much rather stab me in the heart than attend my birthday party.

"We aren't really friends right now," I tell him.

"Bullshit. You can't just break up the musketeers because you aren't getting along right now. You might not be getting along, but you are still friends."

Logan stands beside me, uncomfortably shifting his weight between his feet. Logan didn't ask me if I'd invited Xander to my party, the one I'd nearly forgotten about, but he knew I wasn't about to include him as one of my guests. Especially since Xander stabbed me in the chest only a few months ago. However, Logan is aware of how close I was with Tucker and Xander before Logan moved to town. I know everything with me being a phoenix and Xander being a griffin would have come to light eventually but the thought that Logan coming to town made everything speed up has crossed my mind.

"Okay, Tucker. I'm sorry. I didn't invite him. He wouldn't have come anyway. Can we just celebrate my birthday?" I ask him. I don't want to lay on a guilt trip or incite a pity party for myself, but I'm really not in the mood for this party anyway so I'm not really in the mood to get into it with my one remaining best friend right now.

"Yeah. Sorry." Tucker looks away from me for several moments while we stand in silence. When he can no longer handle the awkward quiet, when he can't decide whether to walk away or say something, he opens his mouth and says, "So what's on the menu? I'm starving."

"Let's find out," I tell him, leading the way to the kitchen.

The three of us move into the kitchen and circle around the island counter where my mom has laid out a smorgasbord of my favorite foods.

My parents always gave Nash and I two parties for our birthdays. The first party was always with our friends and family. The second was always just us and our parents. I'm sure my parents and I will have a dinner together for my birthday but I don't see it being anything like what they were in the past. Without Nash, it won't be the same and it won't be as important.

Tucker, Logan, and I grab paper plates and pile food on them. My mom made sliders and french fries covered in nacho cheese and bacon, as well as nachos and pizza rolls. Boxes of snack cakes are piled onto each other at the end of the counter. A cooler of pop sits on the floor next to the counter. I love food. I love junk food. And I'm not ashamed of it. Now that I've got an everyday workout regimen I don't even mind stuffing my face. Not that I did before.

I grab a pop from the cooler and follow Tucker to the table, walking passed my father without glancing at him. He's my father, he's half of the reason I'm here, maybe more than half since he saved my life a year ago, so he has a right to be here, doesn't mean I want him here. I'm surprised Logan is following me around and hanging by my side with my father here. I'd have imagined Logan would be huddled in the corner with my father, keeping watch, or discussing my life in hushed tones.

I sit next to Tucker and start talking about random things. Logan told me to enjoy myself, to have fun. If I have to be here, I might as well try to get something out of it.

Some of my aunts and uncles and cousins join the party. The pile of presents grows. The air in the house is a bit tense, everyone is missing Nash. No one really knows how to interact with me and my parents without Nash. I'm sure they don't know if they are allowed to bring him up, if we are still walking on egg shells without him.

But eventually someone slips and recounts a funny story about when Nash and I were younger and the tension loosens, everyone relaxes, and I do end up having a good time.

Tucker is the last to leave before Logan. I can tell he wishes Xander was here. And if I'm honest, I wish Xander was here too. It was the first birthday party since we've been friends that we haven't all been together. But times being what they are, Xander's attendance isn't something that was an option.

Nonetheless, I did enjoy my birthday party. I didn't open my gifts while everyone was here. I couldn't. I couldn't spend my first birthday without a twin opening gifts in front of anyone. I'm not sure I'll ever open them. Tucker's will get opened. I'm sure Logan got me a gift, and though I'm sure it isn't in the pile of them, it is the second gift that will for sure get opened.

I go to bed with the intention of sleeping, but with the knowledge that I will be aging into a phoenix tomorrow. With that on my mind, there is no way I'm getting any sleep tonight.

Two

I'm pacing my room. I can't stop myself.

I couldn't get the exact time of my birth from my mom or dad but I could glean an approximate time. So, in approximately an hour I will essentially burn alive then come back.

The pacing continues.

"Casslyn?" Logan asks me cautiously. He sits on his bed watching me pace back and forth. Only his eyes move.

I ignore him.

I know he can hear the speed of my heartbeat. I'm sure it worries him. But I'm also sure he knows the reason for it. He doesn't need words to figure this one out.

No phoenix has ever regenerated before they had fully aged. I have. Twice now. What if that means something bad? What if I'm defective somehow? What if I burn and don't come back? What if I burn Logan's house down? There is a lot to think about. This is fire we're talking about.

Will it hurt? Will I be aware of everything? How long will it take?

"Love?" Logan asks again.

I shake my head at him and continue to make a path in the hard wood.

"You know you can ask me about anything you're worried about," he says.

I know I can. I should. I'm being stupid for not asking him. But it's a bit of a pride issue. Not that there's much pride left when you've paced in front of your boyfriend for two hours. But how can I explain myself to someone who was born to be exactly who he is. Who is perfect at being what we are.

Logan is no longer placated. He stands, grabs my arm in his large hand, and pulls me to him. I can feel his calming warmth spreading through me. My eyes drift shut taking comfort in it, if only for a moment.

"I'm not sure what to say to you," he says.

Like I thought. He doesn't understand because this is all he's ever known.

I turn my attention away from him to stare at the floor. I don't want to face him. I don't want to be ashamed for how I feel.

"At least let me try," he says, when I repeatedly disregard his words.

I let air fill my lungs deep and long. I hold on to it as

long as I can. Maybe I'll pass out, not have to tell Logan how I feel, then maybe miss my whole coming of age thing. The air passes out of my lungs and through my lips. Logan will keep at it until I tell him what's wrong. And it's not like we have a lot of time left.

I look into his eyes, but get nervous and look down to his nose. "Do you think I'm stupid for being scared?"

I'm not sure what I expect as his reaction. It would really hurt my feelings if he laughed at me. I might punch him if he says yes. It would totally suck if he brushes me off.

But no. I should never underestimate Logan. He's never let me down before.

Logan lifts my chin so he's staring into my eyes. The flames in them dance. I'm not sure if it's just because his eyes are so beautiful or if it is a power of a phoenix. It could just be an illusion for all I know. It's not something I've ever asked. But they are beautiful.

"No. I think it's normal to be afraid," he says, the corner of his mouth barely turned up.

"You weren't scared. I'm sure my father wasn't scared. You sister couldn't have been scared."

"That's different. I was born and raised to be a phoenix. To be a soldier. So was my sister and your father. We were all ready to transition. We all spent our entire lives preparing emotionally and physically for the day we would age. You've had a few months to think about it. Do not feel ashamed."

"Good, because I am legit freaking out right now," I tell him.

Logan's shoulders bounce as he laughs. I smile back but can't find the courage to laugh along.

"Are you ready?" he asks me.

I stop breathing for half a second then start panicking.

"No," I say, practically shouting at him. "Are you kidding me? You haven't prepared me for this. I have no idea what is going to happen. What is it going to feel like?"

"Calm down, love. You're going to be okay. I promise. You know what is going to happen. We've discussed this."

"I know."

"Why don't you lie down and get comfortable?"

I let him take my hand and move me. "What happens to people who don't know they are a phoenix and just suddenly light on fire when they age?"

"Not all of us are prepared as I was. Though I can't tell you for certain. The only phoenixes I know have always known what they are. However, there are stories of phoenixes who weren't aware of their powers and accidently light people or things on fire. It is not always disastrous, but it can be. And I believe those are the phoenixes the griffins believe are so dangerous. However, you know those phoenixes aren't the true reason they want to massacre us."

Logan leads me to the bed and helps me to lie back on the pillow. I'm not sure I could have done it myself. Not a word he said alleviated any of my nerves.

He retreats to his desk chair. My heart races in my chest. I run my hands over Logan's comforter and focus on the softness.

Sure, we discussed what will happen any minute now. But Logan couldn't really explain what it feels like for your entire body to be on fire without burning alive. He couldn't tell me what happens when your body reduces to ashes and only your consciousness remains.

Panic rises in my throat. I'm not sure I can go through with this. Though there is no stopping it.

"Cass," Logan says, trying to get my attention.

I turn my head towards him and close my eyes.

"You remember the first time you were in here?" he asks.

He's trying to distract me. I let him. It's a good memory.

"You woke up and immediately started ogling me. I knew you were awake, I could hear your heartbeat change. But even then, even when I knew there couldn't be a future for us as a couple, I wanted you to look at me."

Heat builds in me starting deep in my gut. I'm not sure it's because of Logan's words but I'm not going to open my eyes to find out.

Logan continues to speak. Continues to fill my mind with words and not worries.

"I had to stay as far away from you in that room as I could. You were naked in my bed. You have no idea what that did to me."

Warmth spreads like a thick poison through my veins.

Logan said a phoenix's fire is not surface, but comes from within. It is not separate, but a part of us. It cannot be removed or duplicated.

Sparks ignite and sweep from my core to my fringes. I feel the exact moment the first flame licks my skin. I open my eyes to see it flicker on the tip of my nose.

Logan inhales deeply. I look to him and catch his glance. His gaze is reverent and loving.

New flames overcome my body. They touch every scar Xander, Colt, and the other griffins inflicted on me. They leap to each other and connect, growing large and bright. It is beautiful and overwhelming.

Finally the flames dancing on my skin converge over the scar Xander left when he stabbed me. My eyelids drift shut when the flares covering them become too much.

I'm aware as my skin begins to blister, the flames taking more of a root.

I'm aware as my body loses its shape and slowly burns to ash.

I'm aware as my consciousness leaves my body, only to hover over it.

For as panicked as I felt going into this, I find myself still. It makes me think of my dad saying Nash and I were always so still together.

"Happy birthday, sis."

His voice fills me, warms me even further.

"Nash!" I exclaim.

"Miss me?" he asks, a huge grin on his face.

"That's not funny, jerk," I say, punching him in the arm.

We're at the park. I think back to a year ago, before everything went to hell. I remember lying in the grass with

Nash, being still together.

An ache so deep it feasts on my soul reminds me that this is a dream and this dream-Nash is not mine to keep in waking life.

"I miss you," he tells me, more serious.

"Where are you, Nash? Why can I still see you? Are you a ghost? A figment of my imagination?"

"I'm part of you. I'm in your head. And your heart. And your soul. I will be here until you no longer need me. Until you let me go."

"I don't want to let go," I tell him sitting on my favorite swing on the set. The fear of losing him, even this version of him, grips me.

"That's why I'm still here," he says, coming behind me to pull the swing back.

He let's go and I surge forward and pump my legs. Nash sits on a swing, pushes himself back with his legs, then continues to stand there.

"Anyway, this is morbid and depressing. I said, happy birthday. Now, unless you've forgotten, we are still twins. Is there something you'd like to say to me?"

The words *I'm a year older than you now* are on the tip of my tongue. But he just said we were crossing into depressing territory, and I can't bring myself to upset him for the short amount of time I have him.

"Happy birthday, Nash," I tell him. I let go of the chains and instinctively reach for my wrist and the bracelet Nash gave me last year.

When I woke up in the hospital after the accident I reached for it, only to find my wrist bare. I screamed until someone found it. I screamed for seven hours. I couldn't speak for two weeks.

"You better not give me shit about how you really are older than me now," he says.

I laugh, pump my legs harder, and say, "Never."

"You know, I shouldn't get so used to seeing you. One day you're going to realize you don't need me anymore. Then I won't get to see you."

"I'll always need you," I tell him, coming to a skidding halt.

I make him look at me then repeat, "I will always need you, Nash."

He pouts and says, "You've got Logan, and Tucker, and Xander."

"Don't you dare, for a minute, think like that. I would give anything to have you back. You know that."

"I know. It's just hard sometimes. Seeing you continue on, being the one stuck."

I don't know what to say to him. I've never seen Nash act like this. He's usually my pillar of joy and strength. I'm the moody one. I choose to ignore it.

"Hey, why didn't you tell me Ashley is a griffin?" I ask him.

"Cassie, I just told you, I'm part of you. I know what you know."

"But you've told me things that I didn't know."

Nash opens his mouth to speak, then shuts it and walks off. He sits down on one of the playgrounds tractor-like-sand-diggers.

"I didn't know she was. I'm sorry," he says and begins to dig. I watch him as he lifts bucket full after bucket full of sand. His brows are crumpled. His mouth is transformed into a scowl. I've really never seen Nash like this.

"You don't have to be sorry. I wasn't trying to make you feel bad."

"What good am I to you if I can't help you?" he asks. He digs, slamming the tractor's shovel into the sand.

I've had enough. I can no longer watch him beating himself up.

I grab Nash's arm and swing him around to face me. Placing both my hands on either side of his head, I pull him forward until our foreheads are touching. Simultaneously we press our eyes closed tight then open them, and link.

If Nash or I were ever having a hard time. If we ever fought. If one of us was out of sorts. This is what we'd do. Call it weird. Call it insane. Call it a twin thing. If one of us was ever detached, we could always press our foreheads together, stare into the other's eyes, and reconnect. I'm not sure if we absorbed the others stress. I'm not sure if we just found peace in each other. But our bond never once failed us.

Even now, Nash dead in the ground for a year, I can feel his anguish receding. I can feel my Nash returning to me.

I pull back when I know he will be fine. He doesn't say thank you. I don't say anything.

"Did you get any good presents this year?" he asks me, having abandoned the digging.

"Not really. Though any present after your dream car is pretty much worthless."

"What did Logan give you?" he asks.

"Shouldn't you already know that? Wait a second. Are you aware every time we make out? Oh, God. This is horrible."

"Calm down," Nash says as he laughs. "I'm not aware of everything. It's not like I'm a peeping twin. It's not like I can see through your eyes. It's more that I'm aware."

"I'm still not sure what that all means, but as long as you don't see me and Logan . . . together, then I don't really care."

"He really loves," Nash says. There is a sureness in his voice.

I want to know how he knows this. I'm sure he'd just say he's *aware* of it.

"Yeah, I think he does," I say.

"So, on a different note. Your body is a pile of ash right now. That's some FUBAR shit right there."

"I know. I still can't believe it. I'm not sure I believe it right now. Seriously how can I be a phoenix? This is fiction. Fiction is fiction. It's not real. How can I be fiction and real at the same time?"

"There is that saying that fiction has to be make sense. Real life doesn't. Or something. I'm not sure that makes sense."

I chuckle as he tries to sort out his thoughts.

"Are you sad that you're missing out on it? That your body isn't a pile of ash?"

"I don't know," he says, leading me back to the swings.

We always go back to the swings. Even when we were younger. There was something addictive about pumping your legs harder and harder until you were swinging so high up you thought you might go over the top. There was something about the wind rushing past you then your stomach dropping as you plummet back the way you came. I guess being a phoenix makes more sense now. Birds love to fly with the wind in their face.

"I guess I can't be upset over something I never got to be a part of."

"This is the greatest birthday ever," I say.

Nash barks laughter at my sarcasm. We both feel an ache deep in our guts. I know because I can feel it enough for the both of us.

I feel a pull on my mind. I feel my grip on Nash and the park slip. I feel like I'm about to wake up.

"Nash, I think I'm about to wake up,"

"Yup," he says.

"I don't want to go. I miss you so much."

"I'm always with you, Cassie. I've told you that."

"It's different when I can't see you."

"I know. You're going to be fine."

"You say that. But I don't ever feel fine. I go through shit, like getting the crap beat out of me, and I don't feel like

I'm fine."

I feel another pull. Another slip.

"You're going to be fine," he repeats. "Happy birthday, Cassie. I love you."

"I love you, Nash," I tell him before he's gone.

I know I'm awake. I know Logan knows I'm awake. I can hear the change in his heartbeat. But I don't open my eyes. If only to keep the image of Nash in my head a little longer.

Wait.

I can hear the change in his heartbeat?

I jolt up. My eyes snap open.

There it is again. I hear the rhythm of Logan's heart fluctuate.

I stare at his chest and listen to the beat. From across the room. I can feel him smile, though I'm not sure how, because I can't see his face.

It is only when Logan's breathing, along with his heart, becomes ragged that I realize I am sitting up in his bed, naked.

My arm is covering my chest before I tell it to. I use the other to pull up the blanket covering the lower half of me.

I look back up to Logan with rosy cheeks. When he continues to stare, as if he has X-ray vision, I clear my throat to gain back his attention. He swallows, and I can hear it. I can literally hear the noise his throat makes when he swallows.

"I covered you when you became ash."

"Thank you," I tell him. "How long was I out?"

"The first time you regenerate, the day you age, takes twenty four hours. Almost all full regenerations take twenty four hours. There are rare occasions when the process is longer or shorter. As you know, small cuts and wounds don't take so long."

"You watched me for twenty four hours?" I ask.

"It was my pleasure," he says.

Logan smiles and continues to sit back in his chair. Now that I focus on him, study him, he looks different. The Logan from the past several months, the one who constantly guarded me, protected me, worried over me, is absent. The Logan who only cared about me, my needs, my feelings, my world, who put himself second, is scarce. Knowing him, that Logan will come back, or at least always be in the background. But sitting in his chair, gazing lovingly at his girlfriend, I catch a glimpse of a new Logan, a Logan I want more of. He's at peace it would seem. He looks more relaxed than I have ever seen him. It may have something to do with me coming of age and the fact that I will no longer be so breakable. Who am I kidding, it has everything to do with that.

"You look happy," I tell him.

He smiles like I've never seen before. It's open and free. I could really get used to this new Logan. Not that I didn't fall in love with the old one.

"You look amazing," he says, a gleam in his eyes.

"Oh, yeah?"

His gaze changes into something darker, heated.

"You realize I'm coming over there, right?" he says, his

voice almost a growl.

My heart begins to jack hammer in my chest. I feel hot in different places. Swallowing becomes difficult. A need for Logan's touch spreads like wildfire across my skin.

He raises an eyebrow suggestively. I know he can hear my heartbeat. I can hear his jumping.

I raise an eyebrow back at him and say, "What's taking you so long?"

In a flash he is on top of me, his body mass a gentle weight. Heat blooms when our lips collide. My body reacts to Logan in a way it never has before. Warmth and passion and emotion pass between us, reaching a max then spilling over.

Logan's shirt finds a spot on the floor. Skin converges in sparks. His hands roam over my body. My head swims from his touch. I can't get enough.

He kisses a hot trail from my mouth to my neck and lower still. I find it hard to keep my eyes open, my lids heavy. "I love you so much," Logan says between kisses.

"I love you," I tell him, an inferno rising in my core.

My fingers play over Logan's skin, a trail of warmth left in the wake. I swear I can hear it sizzle.

My entire body is hot. I feel on the verge of combustion like I could regenerate again.

Logan pulls away but I'm in a state of bliss. I can't open my eyes. I feel on fire from his touch.

"Love," he says, breathless.

I hum to him, still unable to focus.

"Casslyn," he says.

I force my eyelids to open, though it is difficult.

"Holy shit," I yell.

Logan is on fire.

Literally.

Flames cover his entire body. His skin is actually sizzling.

Using strength I didn't know I had, I curl my legs around his, flip him over, and use the blanket that was covering me to pat out the flames.

My heart slams into my ribs. Tears streak from my eyes. I've just killed my boyfriend.

"Logan, I'm so sorry. Oh my God. I'm so sorry," I say, continuing to pat him down with the blanket.

Tears flow freely now. My brain burns in my skull. I lit my boyfriend on fire. I am the monster Xander and the griffins think I am.

Logan grasps my hands in his and stops my fire extinguishing.

"Could you take the blanket off my face please," he says from under the cover.

My chin quivers. Unshed tears form a current down my cheeks as relief floods my chest. I didn't kill him.

My wrists still clutched by Logan's hands, I move the blanket from over his face.

His skin is perfect. There is not a mark on him.

No way. I saw him on fire.

I jerk my hands from his and rip the blanket off of him.

He is as naked as I am, his jeans and boxers burnt off. But his skin is unmarred. Relief is a deluge more powerful than any hurricane wave could ever be.

Logan reaches for me but I jerk away from his grasp.

"Don't touch me," I tell him.

I run from the room and don't look back.

Turns out you can't run very far when you're buck naked.

Logan finds me, sobbing, in the bathroom minutes later.

He hands me a stack of clothes and turns around while I dress.

As I dress I notice my skin, almost for the first time. There is not a mark on it. I take my time to examine it. Every mark, every scar that has ever marred my skin is gone. The cuts left my Xander and Colt, gone. The scar on my knee from second grade bike-athon when I fell off my bike, gone. The scar on my ankle from getting caught up in a barbed wire fence when I was in fifth grade, gone. My skin is flawless and beautiful.

"I'm so sorry," I tell him.

"How do you feel?" he asks, his eyebrows furrowed.

"Horrible. I can't believe I did that to you."

"Not what I mean, love. How do you feel as a phoenix?"

I make a mental overview of my body. "Okay, I guess."

"Why don't you come out of there and we can test it out."

"How about we don't and say we did. I am not lighting you on fire again," I say, crossing my arms.

"Casslyn, don't be ridiculous."

"No. Logan," I say sharply. "I wasn't even sure I wanted to be a phoenix. I didn't have a choice in the matter. I was scared shitless. And the moment I wake up as a phoenix I light you on fire. Don't tell me not to be ridiculous."

"I'm sorry," he says, moving toward me. "I was being insensitive. Please come out and we can talk about this."

"I'd rather not," I say.

"Don't make me come in there after you," he says, putting his hands on his hips. Somehow, on him, it looks more menacing than weird.

"I'd like to see you try," I tell him, getting into my fighting stance.

Logan rushes me, catches me off guard, then throws me over his shoulder.

I could yell at him. I could tell him he's not playing fair. I could hit his back until my fists hurt. But instead I let myself be man handled and forced into something I don't want. Fighting would be futile anyway.

He tosses me onto the couch and sits on top of me so I can't make for an escape.

I raise an eyebrow at him but don't say anything, deciding rather to sit silently and pout. I make sure to keep my hands to myself so I don't accidently set Logan or the living room on fire.

"Now, I want you to focus. Pay attention. Attune yourself to your body like you've never done before. How do you feel? What do you feel?"

I scowl at him and play stubborn, refusing to do what he asks of me.

But then I get curious.

I am now a full grown phoenix. It's got to feel different then what I felt a day ago.

So I focus. I become attuned. I close my eyes and concentrate on my center.

What I find is incredible.

I can hear every sound inside this house and many outside it. I can feel every inch of Logan touching me in minute detail. I can feel the threads of his jeans, the cotton of his shirt, the heat of his skin on mine. The hum of the house vibrates in my feet and moves up. I open my eyes to see dust motes floating in the air across the room.

But, beyond touch and sight and the other senses, which I could go into, I feel something new and entirely different. I feel fire in my veins. In my bloodstream. My body tingles and jolts and feels alive and it's almost more than I can handle. I feel like a bomb that could go off any second. It's unnerving and thrilling all at the same time.

I twitch feeling power zip under my skin.

"It will settle down. You're power will settle and become second nature to you."

"Logan, I set you on fire."

"It happens. I would have been worried if you didn't."

"What if I do it to someone who isn't as flammable as you? What happens if I set Tucker on fire? I can't let that happen."

"So we train you. You didn't think your training was going to be all physical did you?"

"I can't ever hurt anyone, Logan. I can't become what the griffins think we are."

"I won't let that happen. I promise."

Logan's promise flares in his eyes. Logan's eyes never lie.

"I saw Nash, when I was out," I tell him.

He stills on top of me. I can see his jaw as well as his mind working. He worries that I can still see my twin.

"I can't say I understand this. I've never encountered it before. And I have to be honest, it worries me. But, I know how much you miss him, and I know how happy it makes you to see him. So, for now, I'm going to try to not think about it. It's not like there is anything I can do about it."

"He seemed weird."

"How so?" Logan says, shifting above me, only to stand and begin to pace in front of me. So much for peaceful Logan. That lasted a whole, what, hour?

"I don't know. Like he was sad. Lost. Troubled even."

Logan stops pacing to face me.

"Casslyn, you're going to hate me for this, but I feel like your father needs to know about this. I don't think I should be the one to tell him, but I know you're not going to."

The instant urge to argue with him, to tell him that's not going to happen, is sharp and right on the tip of my tongue. But I can't argue with Logan every time we disagree on something. As much as I like arguing with him.

"I'll think about it. It's not like I see Nash all the time. If it happens again, I'll consider telling him," I say.

Logan looks relieved, but also like he doesn't wholly agree with me.

"But, if you go behind my back and tell him before I'm ready or have agreed to it, I will never forgive you. Do you understand me?"

"I understand," he says, leaning in close for a kiss.

I revel in the flicker that spreads from his lips to mine. Then I feel a spark ignite when our tongues meet and pull back.

"Not happening. No more make out sessions until I know I'm not going to cover your body in flames."

Logan's lips juts out in a pout. He says, "That's not fair to me. What did I do?"

"Not happening."

Logan pulls his shirt over his head and leans into me. My vision goes a little cloudy. He's stealing my trick right out from under me.

"We'll see how long that lasts," he says, pulling his jeans off.

Luckily he has sport shorts underneath.

"You want to go for a run?" he asks, a smile spreading across his face. "You can't imagine how it feels."

"I'm going to beat you this time," I tell him, taking off through the house ahead of him.

He catches up quickly and says, "Not a chance."

We take off down the gravel road. I run at my normal

pace feeling the air thick around me.

"Let go, Casslyn," Logan says running beside me.

I'm not sure what he means until I push a little harder. Then I understand.

The wind whips my skin like a lash, its chill striking my hot skin in a contrast that is blinding but feels amazing. I can feel each pebble of gravel through my shoes as I run. Birds chirp in faraway trees. Deer, mice, and rabbits scurry through the growing wild grass and newly tilled corn fields.

I close my eyes and feel the world rush passed me. I have never felt so alive. I've never felt so in control before. I've never felt so powerful.

Three

Logan and I sit on his couch watching the road runner continuously outsmart Wile Coyote. Not once has the meep meep of the road runner or the never ending failures of Wile Coyote gotten old. I could spend every Sunday just like this, tucked into Logan's arms, watching cartoons.

I smile when Logan absentmindedly plants a kiss to the top of my head. I sigh contentedly and cuddle in closer to him, his arm tightening around me.

Logan and I have been training harder since I became a full grown phoenix. Harder entails everything it could, longer hours, more difficult fighting styles, heavier weights, more miles, more everything. It's been taxing, but also exhilarating. I'm putting my body through things I never would have imagined and not only is it up for the task, it is thriving.

Once I got over the scare of lighting Logan on fire I've started using my power. I never thought of myself as a pyro but I love setting things on fire. There is something majestic and powerful watching something whole, something as simple as a piece of paper, intact, then flames ignite and spread, reducing that thing to ashes and dust, to nothing. There are times when I use my power where I can see the hatred from the griffins. They are afraid of us. They are vengeful because Apollo favored us. And yet I have a strong feeling they are jealous.

I've gotten better at using my powers. It's not like I can perfect using fire after a week, but I have gotten better. Logan has started me off slowly, with small tasks. I've lit so many pieces of paper on fire I've lost count. We then went to cardboard boxes. Those are easy. After learning Logan is fire proof I wasn't so concerned about lighting him on fire. In fact he has had me practice on him a time or two. It is still nerve wracking seeing my boyfriend's entire body on fire, but at the same time he is beautiful. I wouldn't mind seeing him surrounded by flames all day every day.

The only concerning thing about our training of my powers is the fact that they don't always work like they should. My father and Logan said that no phoenix they know has ever had problems using their power, or calling upon their power. I, on the other hand, am an entirely different story. My powers only work properly about seventy percent of the time. I can always feel the fire within coursing through my veins, streaming under my skin. But I can't always call upon it. We all have our theories, most of them correlating to the fact that I regenerated in the accident that killed Nash and regenerated when Xander stabbed me. It's not the first time I've been the freak and it surely won't be the last. Being the freak is something I've gotten used to and even grasped onto. It' s something I've embraced and celebrate. If I'm to be a freak I will be the best freak anyone has ever seen.

I'm getting really sick of the phrase *no phoenix they have ever known or heard of.* It falls from the mouths of Logan and my father nearly every day. And it's always about me. And not in a good way. In most stories the phrase *the only one* concerns the chosen one, the one to save the world. In my case, I'm the only one defective as a part of my race.

Besides training my body and my powers, Logan teaches me more about the phoenixes. Before I aged, he had told me most of our history. Where we came from. What we've done over the years. And he taught me about our history with the griffins. Now that I've aged Logan teaches me about the war with the griffins. Battles, fighting styles, tactics, and so on. Logan tells me that mostly the phoenixes use their fire as their only weapons against the griffins, mostly so we can defend ourselves, but not actually kill them. I disagreed with letting the griffins live if they are going to attack us and was very verbal with it. Logan took it all in but did not argue with me. Once I'd spoken my peace he told me that there are several ways to kill a griffin but one sure way is to stab them through their two hearts. Most wounds they can heal from, but a stab to the heart is a sure death for them. I thought it was pretty obvious, but what do I know. Along with the griffins, the only way to truly kill a phoenix is a stab to the heart. However, you can't just use any old knife to get the job done. We would heal too quickly. The one way to kill a phoenix is with a blade made out of ice. An ice knife stabbed through our hearts will stop our fire from working, stop it from healing us. Logan said the griffins don't leave home without ice knives.

So we continue to train and train until the only think I know how to do is train.

But, all that training and strain on my body takes its toll and some days it's nice to take time off to relax, curl up with my boyfriend, and watch some cartoons.

It's also nice when my boyfriend decides he's had enough of the cartoons and wants to incite a make out session on the couch. I quickly put a hold on the no make out ban once I found out that I couldn't actually kill Logan by setting him on fire. Turns out, a phoenix cannot harm another phoenix with their fire.

I'm innocently watching as Wile Coyote sets a trap for the road runner, a trap that will never work, when Logan's tongue snakes out of him mouth, runs up the skin behind my ear, and his warm breath kisses it sending shivers down and up my spine. I intentionally ignore him, goad him into teasing me further, just because I know he can hear my heart rate spike, because I know he enjoys getting a rise out of me. I use it as a way to test myself, to see how far Logan can push me until I snap and maul him with my mouth.

Logan runs his hand up my thigh, squeezing as he goes. It is in part to tickle me and in part to arouse me. It works both ways. Still I ignore him, even though my heart wants to jump through my chest and attack Logan itself.

His mouth finds its way to the crook of my neck where his lips part and rest on my skin, damp and warm. My eyes flutter closed from the heady sensation. I clench my thighs together and revel in the touch of his lips playing on my skin. Never did I think in the months it took me to convince Logan to be with me did I expect being with him to be this intense.

"Casslyn, my love," Logan whispers in my ear, his hands moving to my hips. "It's about time you gave in. I want to taste your lips."

His words, whispered, his voice deep and throaty, are enough to undo me. I turn on him and push him down so he's lying on his back. I straddle his hips and lean in close enough to feel the warmth of his body. His hands remain on my hips, his fingers sinking into my soft flesh.

I lean into him, closing the distance between our mouths. He inches closer to me but I pull away.

"Not yet," I tell him, doing the same thing he did to me months ago. I waited in agony for his lips to meet mine. It's payback time.

Logan pulls back and bites down on his lower lip. It does bad things to my already wound body. I was trying to punish him, but he's making it difficult. When he traces his hand down the back of my thigh I lose my shit and clobber his mouth with my own. A laugh rattles his chest but he kisses me back as fiercely as I kiss him. I close my eyes and lose myself in the moment with him.

There are times like these where I want Logan to touch me differently. Where I need his hands to rove over my breasts, between my legs. Times where the moment is so intense, where my body buzzes so hard, I need a release. But I know he won't unless I ask, and I won't ask.

This is one of those times. A time I need things to move forward before I combust or I need them to stop completely.

Fire builds in my chest aided by the passionate need for Logan. Heat spreads through my body, synapses fire in my fingers and toes. My body is about to ignite any second. And while I know I won't harm Logan, I pull away, not willing to lose control over my power.

I hover over Logan, an inch away from his swollen lips, heavy, panting breaths colliding and passing between us. A shuddering breath escapes my lips as I push myself off of him. Placing my ass on the couch I turn away from him. My heart thrums in my ears and I will it to slow down.

Logan sits up beside me. I can feel his eyes on me. I can hear his heart beating as fast as mine. I can sense his questions.

"Are you alright, love?" he asks. His arm stretches out for me, but slowly, like he's not sure if he should touch me.

"I'm fine," I say, turning to him. I wonder if he can hear the lie in my voice.

His eyes narrow like he doesn't believe me, but he doesn't push it.

"I'm hungry. You hungry?" I ask him.

His eyes stay narrowed for a moment longer then his whole face shifts.

"Always," he says.

Together we walk to the kitchen to scope out the situation. I open the fridge and stare at nothing. Logan has a bottle of ketchup, a jug of milk, and three cans of Mt. Dew in his fridge. There is no food. From a few feet away from me he opens his pantry and studies it, a frown on his face.

"It would seem as though I'm fresh out of anything edible," he says, still staring into the pantry.

I hop onto the counter and place my elbows into my thighs, my head cradled by my hands. I wasn't actually hungry when I said I was, but with a lack of food I suddenly am. Logan closes the pantry doors and steps between my legs.

He takes my face in his hands and places a kiss on my forehead, my nose, and finally reaches my mouth.

I kiss him back but pull away before it becomes more than I can pull back from.

"How about I run to the grocery store?" I ask, needing some space from the sexual tension radiating the house.

"Let me go change and I'll come with you," he says.

"No," I say too quickly.

His eye brows furrow in concern.

"It's just," I start, wondering what I'm going to say. "For the last year I've done all the grocery shopping by myself. It's almost peaceful. I get exactly what I want and don't have to argue about anything. Plus, I could get something a little special and surprise you."

"I really think I should come. With the griffins becoming more aggressive, you should be protected," he says.

"Logan, do you honestly think a bunch of griffins are going to attack me in the grocery store?"

His look is dead serious. He does believe the griffins will attack me in the grocery store.

"Look, I promise I will back off and come home if anything at all looks suspicious."

"You swear?" Logan asks.

I pull his face to mine and kiss him deeply. When I pull away I stare into his eyes and in a baby voice, so he knows I'm serious but also playing with him, say, "I swear."

Logan lifts me off the counter and carries me to the front door. I wrap my legs around his waist and squeeze them together. I yelp and jump in his arms when he pinches the bottom of my butt. He laughs and I bite his lip when he tries to kiss me, making him laugh harder. His laugh is deep and throaty and rattles through his chest. It is intoxicating and mesmerizing.

When he sets me on my feet his gaze has turned serious. "If anything happens to you," he says.

"Logan," I say before he can finish that sentiment. "It's the grocery store. Nothing is going to happen to me. I love you. I'll come back to you."

His hands cup my face and he leans his head into me until our foreheads are pressed together. I'm really not sure what he's getting so worked up about. We haven't had a griffin attack in months. We haven't even seen evidence of them in months. Xander hasn't given us any indication of them moving on us. Plus, I'm just going to get food, I'll be back in an hour, tops. If I'd have known he was going to get this worked up I wouldn't have made such a fuss about going alone.

"I love you, Casslyn," Logan says before his lips meet mine. His fingers slip something into my front jeans pocket while our lips connect.

I pull away from him, knowing he won't do it, and wink at him to assure him everything will be fine.

"I'll be back," I tell him. "Be ready to be wowed. I'm thinking mac and cheese and hotdogs."

He smiles and chuckles as I slip out the door.

I didn't lie to Logan when I told him grocery shopping has become peaceful for me. In the beginning I would march down the aisle searching for the food I wanted, a squeaking cart wheel to distract me from the separation of my parents and the loss of my twin brother. Recently it has become a distraction from being hunted down like an animal by the griffins.

Now, I walk down the aisles and hunt for something special to make Logan. That boy makes me weak in the knees so easily it's frightening. I suddenly remember him slipping something in one of my pockets. My fingers fish into my pocket for a moment before pulling out a one hundred dollar bill. I smile down at it happy for more reasons than having money to buy whatever I want. Logan may be the first boyfriend I've had, but he may as well be the best I've ever had. I don't know what I'd do without him, now that I have him.

When I've gone through each aisle twice and thoroughly, I place my groceries on the counter, check out, and head for the car. It's not until I've got the food stowed away in my trunk and am walking back to my car after returning the cart, do I sense something off. Though I can't put my finger on exactly what it is. Without bringing too much notice to myself, I hurry back to my car, remembering my promise to Logan to flee if I noticed something not quite right. I have my purse in the seat next to me, the key in the ignition, when a dark presence hovers right outside my window. Then another outside the passenger window.

My heartrate picks up in my chest. Before I can think to push done on the locks, my door is wrenched open. I turn to see the guy who has been present at two of my attacks. Ashley's lover. Colt, I think his name is. Fear ripples through me, igniting the fire within.

He reaches in the car for me. When he places his hand around my neck I curl mine around his arms and let my power loose. Flames spread from my hand to his long sleeve shirt. I push with my power to extend the flames to his skin. He yelps and pulls back from me, his arm on fire.

I take a quick glance around the parking lot, maybe I can scream for help, but I see no one. It's Sunday, the day of rest, no one is here. No one will help me.

I try to push Colt away so I can shut the door and drive off in escape but the passenger door has opened and my car is invaded by another griffin. I reach out for him, flames covering my hands. I'll light my car on fire if that's what it takes to escape these bastards.

Fear and adrenaline course through my body, making the flames hot and unstable. The back doors of my car are opened, new passengers occupying my space. I'm grabbed around the neck from behind. I grab for his hands feeling his skin burn under my grasp. He yells from the pain but I'm losing breath, losing focus, losing my grip on my power. I keep my hold on the guy behind me. If I can get him to let me go I may have a chance.

But then Colt is beside me, his arm no longer on fire. I can't breathe. I turn to see Colt pull his arm back. The last thing I see before everything is dark, is his fist, racing toward my jaw.

***

I wake up in the dark. A dim yellow light hangs high above me. I'm in a small room with concrete walls and a metal door.

I'm hanging.

My hands are clasped in iron shackles hung from the ceiling. Dried blood is caked around my wrists. My feet barely reach the floor. I reach out with my senses to take inventory of my body.

The skin around my wrists is raw and chafed. The left side of my face is numb and bruised, my lip swollen and split open. I swallow and cringe. My neck is also swollen and bruised. I can nearly feel each finger print from the hands wrapped around me. My stomach feels like it's been used as a punching bag. There is a gash the length of a knife on my right thigh. The griffins must have gotten in a few shots after I was out. Dirty bastards.

I reach out for my power, feel out its depths within me. I call it forward, willing it to heal me as it has done before. Fire courses right under my skin. It rages and burns but it won't penetrate my skin. It won't heal me. I try instead to light the shackles binding my wrists, because I know that works. But again I am left with nothing. No fire. No healing. No escape.

My shoulders hurt from being strung up above me. My wrists ache in their tight manacles. I've got a backache from my feet not being able to support my weight. My legs are numb, my toes tingle from sleep.

If I can't heal myself or escape, I need a new tactic. I tap into my other senses and push out my hearing beyond the room I'm in. I hear steady breathing right outside the door. There must be a guard standing watch. Beyond that I can hear voices but nothing discernable.

I'm thirsty and even more hungry than I was before.

"Hey, guard," I call out. "Could I get some water? Maybe something to eat?"

I can hear as the guards head whips in the direction of the door, but I can also hear as he forgets I spoke and returns his attention elsewhere.

So much for that plan.

I think about all that food sitting in my trunk going to waste and I sit here in a cell. I think about the cartoons Logan and I were watching. I think about Logan's hands on my skin, his lips on mine. I think about promising Logan I would be fine, that I would come back to him. I wonder if he is already panicking. I wonder if he'll be able to find me. I wonder if I'm going to die in this cell. At least it doesn't smell bad.

I pull down on my shackles trying to pry them from the ceiling but without my feet firmly planted on the ground I don't have enough strength backing me. It only causes the iron to bite into my skin and rip it open, warm blood trickles down my arms. I wince when it runs into my armpits. I grab onto the chain with my hands and pull my feet upward hoping my body weight will pull the chains from the ceiling. I get halfway curled up when I lose strength and my feet crash to the floor, the momentum and weight pulling at my body and dislocating my right shoulder. I scream from the pain wishing to cradle my arm into my body, but it hangs limp, disconnected from its socket. My muscles and tendons throb around my shoulder. I bite down on my split lip trying to relocate the pain. I swallow when my mouth fills with blood. Blood from my hands, my lip, and my leg pool at my feet. I'll become concerned when the pool grows larger.

I'm spent. I really don't know how I'm going to escape now.

Realization hits me like a sledge hammer. The griffins

have me. I'm going to die this time. My parents will never know what happened to me. Logan will never find me. I won't be able to say goodbye to Tucker.

I hang my head and bite my tongue to hold back the tears. They course, bloody, down my cheeks anyway. I close my eyes and shut down my senses. I don't want to hear my death coming.

I stay that way for a long time. I try not to count the minutes passing. It does no good. The quiet is too loud. My pity party is depressing. I can't stand it. I've spent the last year pitying myself. Nash died, my parents split up, I discovered I'm this creature I'm not sure I want to be. But those things happened and I'm still here and kicking. I may have an injured body and a dislocated shoulder but I'm not dead yet.

My resolve is setting in when I hear voices outside the door. One voice belongs to a girl. Her voice alone sounds menacing. The other voice makes me smile. It belongs to Xander. I have no delusions he's about to break me out of here, but hearing his voice is enough to keep me fighting.

"She's in there," the girl says.

"Has Raphe questioned her yet?" Xander asks her, somehow, from here I can feel his eyes on the door I'm behind.

"Not yet. He thought you should be the first."

"Why?" Xander asks, his voice sharp.

"Beats me. Maybe he's looking for you to finally prove yourself," the girl says, I can hear in her voice this is a test. Xander hasn't proven himself to the griffins. That thrills me and scares me at the same time.

"I want to do this alone," Xander says.

"Fine," she says. "I'll be right here if you need me."

I hold my breath until the door opens and Xander walks in, closing the door behind him.

"Cass," Xander says. His voice is a whisper that bangs into the walls and crashes into me.

With effort I lift my head to meet his gaze.

"There's something I've been meaning to tell you," I say, my voice weak and strained. I'm suddenly so angry I can taste it. Xander is one of them. He's a part of the reason I'm in this mess. He wants me dead just like the rest of them. "I can forgive you for trying to kill me, but I will never forgive you for killing Nash."

I watch as anger surges through Xander's chest to his fist. I watch as it connects with my jaw. I know he regrets it instantly.

I cough then spit in his face. I smile as it splashes his eyes then slides down.

"I didn't kill him. You know that," Xander says. I watch as his jaw works. He wants to spit right back at me.

"You may as well have," I say, then hang my head back to my chest. This conversation has already turned exhausting.

"I'm here to talk to you," he tells me.

"So talk."

I watch him study me, his eyes roving over my body, and he asks, "How did they catch you?"

"Like you care," I say, adjusting my weight from one foot to the other. My shoulder throbs with the effort.

"Cass," Xander says, his voice contorted.

"What, Xander? They caught me. I convinced Logan I was safe enough to go to the grocery store by myself. They cornered me as I was loading the food in the trunk of my car. Happy now? What does it matter how they did it?"

"How many phoenixes are in town?" Xander asks me, changing his whole tone and body language. He's here for a purpose. They think I'll open up to him. They think I'll betray myself and Logan and my father because of my past with Xander. They are wrong.

"Oh, don't even," I tell him, jerking my body to the side to make myself sway back and forth. "Let me guess, they sent you in to question me because we've been friends forever and they think I still trust you enough to answer you. Then when you've gotten what they want they kill me. No thanks."

"Cass," Xander says. He grabs onto my arms and jerks me back and forth. "Just answer me. Do you want to answer me or them? I promise you I'll be gentler than them."

"Do what you want to me. I'm not answering your questions," I say, then surprise him by kicking his leg out from under him. It takes its toll on my body but is well worth it. If he's going to align himself with those pigs he deserves everything coming his way.

He steadies himself then slams his fist into my side. I yell out then try to pull my legs up to guard myself. I can't actually say I saw that coming.

He is fuming mad right now, though I'm not sure why.

"Where is your father hiding?" he asks.

I don't answer him. Punch.

"How many phoenixes are in town?"

Silence. Punch.

"How many are on their way?"

I stare him straight in the eye but remain silent.

Xander's breathing becomes heavy with anger and frustration. He turns away from me but turns back to backhand me in the face. I clench my teeth in anger and to keep from crying out. If I wasn't chained up this would not be a one sided fight.

Blood runs like a faucet off my lips onto the floor. I'm still not yet concerned with the size of the blood puddle beneath my feet.

Xander pauses his assault on my body to study me. Something is finally clicking in that brain of his.

"Why aren't you healing?" He asks me.

"You were wondering that too, huh?" I ask, worry overlapping the curiosity in my voice.

I can see gears working in his mind. He's wondering if I'm actually a phoenix. He's doing the math. He knows when my birthday was. It's eating him up as I watch. But his resolve is set. His faith in his people it too strong.

He shakes it off and gets back to business.

"How could you let Logan kill that family?" Xander says, surprising me with his question and the turn his interrogation has taken.

"What are you talking about?" I ask.

"I've seen the photos of the family Logan incinerated in Colorado."

"I don't know what you're talking about but Logan hasn't left town since he moved here. He's been glued to my side the entire time," I honestly have no idea what he's talking about but he's not about to corrupt my belief in Logan when I know what he's saying is a lie.

"Casslyn, I saw the photos. The family was burned alive."

"Then the photos lied. Logan hasn't killed anyone. Did he kill any of the griffins the night they attacked us? Did he light any of them on fire? No."

"What about the reports of you and Logan killing innocent people in Iowa?"

I scoff and shake my head. This is nearly comical if my life didn't depend on it. "If you truly believe that I killed someone or that I allowed Logan to kill anyone then we were never friends." I want to spit at him again. I actually believed Xander was my true friend. That even though we were mortal enemies we could somehow get past it and still be friends. I was wrong.

Xander stands in front of me. I listen as his heart stops for a mere moment and starts again. He's trying to work through the lie they fed him so easily he swallowed without question.

"You can leave now," I tell him, all but dismissing him.

Again gears turn behind his eyes. He's trying to decipher if what he believes is true, if what his people told him is true, or if what I said is the truth. Not long ago Xander confessed his love for me. Maybe that is strong enough to fight the griffins hold on him.

"Cass, if I tell you I love you right now, will you hold it against me?"

"No," I say, voice not faltering a bit.

Something in Xander shifts. He moves to me and whispers in my ear, "Let's run away together. I can get you out of here. We can forget what we are and just be together."

It's a desperate plea of a deranged man but he doesn't care. He wants me to be safe, I can see it written on his face.

"I don't want to forget what or who I am."

"But I love you," he tells me, growing more desperate by the moment. He steps away from me and forcefully runs his hands through his hair.

"Xander," I say, a smile touching my damaged lips. I know what I need to do. I know I should have done this the moment he told me he loved me. "Will you kiss me?"

"What?" he asks, not sure where this is coming from.

"Just kiss me."

He takes a tentative step towards me. He's trying to decide if this is a trap. He now knows I can't heal myself. He's trying to decide if I can still light him on fire.

One more step and his lips are an inch from mine.

He breathes out and tries to steady his racing heart. I recognize it as something I've done many times.

His hands move to cup my face. I'm in love with Logan. I could never betray him, but this needs to happen.

Trepidation causes his hands to shake but I watch as a calm settles over him, a joy and a wanting he's had for years. I wish I could fulfill everything he needs, but I'm not his one.

He places his lips on mine.

I try my best to kiss him back, to give him what he needs, to make him realize something he needs to know. That I love him, but I'm not in love with him. He's a good kisser, I'll give him that. I can taste his passion and his years of want.

His lips are soft and warm. I hum a little when my tongue meets his.

He pulls away from me a bit breathless. I'm light headed from blood loss but am holding on.

He stares at me, "That was everything I've ever dreamed it would be," he says.

"Xander, are you in love with me?" I ask him, my gaze steady, penetrating.

I watch as his entire body shifts, realization settling in, a weight lifts off.

"No," he tells me. Confusion and heartbreak color his face.

"I know," I say, a small smile playing at the corner of my lips. He's finally got it. He finally sees it's okay to love your best friend without being in love with them. I wonder if he is relieved or frightened. He's convinced himself for years that he's loved me. What is he going to do without that? I hope he can move on quickly and easily.

"How? How did you know?" he asks me.

"You're my best friend. I know you. Just like you know me."

"They're going to kill you," he tells me, the whole weight of that fact settles on his shoulders pushing him into the ground.

"I know," I say, the light in my eyes dimming. Here we were having a friendship breakthrough and he had to go and ruin it with doom and gloom.

"I'm going to get you out of here," he tells me, rushing for the door.

"Xander don't," I call to him, but he's already out the door.

"Did she give you any useful information?" the girl from before asks him.

"Not much," he tells her. "She wasn't willing to talk. I had to get rough with her."

"Good," a new voice says. This voice is scary and dominating.

My gut clenches.

"We'll make her talk," he says.

"I hope so, sir," Xander says. I listen to his pulsing heart and wonder if his people can hear it, if they know he's about to betray them.

"You've done well today, Xander. Now go home and prepare for tonight," the man says.

"What is tonight, sir?" Xander asks.

The girl says, "We're going to kill her."

"Good," Xander tells them. "We need to rid this world of as many of the monsters as possible." If I didn't know he's going to try to get me out of here I might believe him.

"I'm glad you feel that way," Scary man says. "Now go home."

"Yes, sir," Xander says.

I swallow hard when I hear him retreat up a flight of stairs. All I can do now is hold on and pray that he gets me out in time. It's one thing to know you're about to die, but to hear someone say they are going to kill you is a whole other thing. Admitting to killing someone is a scary thing. It takes resolve and determination. These people are determined to kill me. Maybe I should have taken Logan to the grocery store with me.

***

I stand it my cell listening to people crowd into the space outside it. This is the time. They are going to kill me.

"My good people," the man from before says. My throat tightens making it difficult to swallow. "Today is a day to celebrate the griffins. Today is a day to rejoice in our beliefs and what we stand for. Today is the day we kill the daughter of the leader of the phoenixes."

The crowd outside my cell shouts and cheers. I can hear some of them jump in place, their excitement palpable. My death excites them. I wonder how Xander could possibly save me now. It sounds as though there are at least fifty people out there, maybe more. I'm not getting out of this.

The girl who brought Xander to my cell and Ashley pull me from it. I'm chained and dragged. While Xander was gone this afternoon the griffins took liberties with me. They took turns beating on me. Cuts and bruises covering my body. Blood oozes from various new wounds. My lips are more damaged. The pool of blood at my feet began to concern me.

I don't know why I'm not healing. I would be nearly fine right now if I was healing.

This is going to be bad.

"This phoenix has brought a plague to our town and we must put a stop to it," Scary man says. The way he addresses the people, the way he stands before them, he has to be their leader.

The crowd cheers.

Their leader grabs my chains and connects it to hook hanging from the ceiling.

"Thank you, Ashley, Greer," he tells them when he takes my chains from them.

Greer, the griffin with Xander from earlier doesn't say anything.

Ashley, on the other hand, says, "You're welcome, father."

Holy shit. Ashley is the daughter of the leader of the griffins. I didn't see that coming. Sure she is a griffin, and sure she gets in on a lot of their action, especially when it comes to attacking me, but I did not expect her to be their leaders daughter. It all makes sense now. Why she's always hated me. Why she always went after me in school. We were born to be enemies and now I know why.

Their leader nods to Ashley then grabs my chin and makes me look at him. My eyes glass over with springing tears, my breathing shallows. I don't know how much longer I can hang on.

Whatever Xander is planning, he needs to do it soon.

"Do you have anything to say for yourself?" their leader asks me. I think I remember Logan telling me his name is Raphe.

My eyes roam the room searching for something. When they land on Xander I stare at him a moment then close my eyes. I remain silent. There may be no getting out of this but what am I going to say to a group of griffins that would do me any good. It would be a waste of breath.

"So be it," Raphe says.

The girl stands to his side a silver brief case in her hands. She opens it for Raphe who takes out the only deadly thing to my kind. An ice knife.

Raphe holds it up in front of me. I don't know if I should act like I don't know what it is, or if I'm really too weak, because I don't react. That is, until Raphe holds it up to my cheek and pulls it down. I scream, a slash opening down my cheek. The wound smolders but I still don't regenerate. There are no flames to heal the gash. Pain slices through my entire body. The fire within me rages but recoils from the cold of the ice knife. I've never known pain like this in all my life.

Raphe brings the knife down and slices my arm. I scream again but am quick to bite down on it. My breathing quickens. My vision dances before me. If I wasn't being held up by chains I would be on the floor.

What are you planning, Xander? I can't take this.

"Why isn't she regenerating?" someone in the crowd asks.

Raphe pulls back, caught off guard.

My head jerks up. I'm caught off guard. Why would a griffin come to my aid?

"Yeah," someone else says, "If she's a phoenix her wounds would light on fire and heal."

"Trust me, ladies and gentlemen, the girl before you is a phoenix. Our sources tell me she has come of age."

Sources being Xander. I'm sure everyone is aware of that fact.

"Then why are there no flames?"

Bless these people for wasting time.

"Perhaps," Raphe says, "she is defective. Maybe they have learned to control when their body regenerates to keep from being discovered. I promise you she is a phoenix."

"Then stab her and let's see her reduced to ash."

"Patience, my good people. Wouldn't you like to know if she has any information that may be important to the cause?"

"Yeah," the crowd says together, shouting their approval.

Damn them.

They are reduced to silence when we are covered in darkness.

A breath escapes me.

This has to be Xander's plan. But how could he be doing this? I can clearly see him in the crowd.

Sounds of a scuffle clatter behind me, around me. I hear flesh strike flesh. I hear bodies hit the floor.

I scream a grating, mutilated scream, as I'm stabbed in the stomach with the ice knife. Raphe has me. He's going to kill me. Whatever Xander's plan, it's not going to be fast enough.

I try to focus on the chaos around me. I try to devise any way I can get away from Raphe, but I'm losing consciousness quickly, blood pouring from my abdomen.

There is no way Xander is going to get me out.

Fists assault flesh. Bones crack. Grunts echo between the four walls. My voice cries out into the dark when Raphe holds the ice knife to my throat.

I hear Xander call for me but I know it's too late.

Then the knife is removed from my throat. I try to see in the dark, try to focus my hearing on a possible sneak attack. A punch is thrown. A grunt echoes. A body falls.

I scream when I'm grabbed by the arms.

"It's okay, love. I'm going to get you out of here," Logan says into my ear.

A sob escapes my chest. I've never been so relieved. Tears stream down my cheeks. I love this man more than anything and I nearly lost him forever.

Logan rips my chains from the ceiling and I'm free. I collapse into his strong arms. I can no longer hold on. Pain and emotions cloud my thoughts. My body aches. My brain hurts.

My vision dims until I black out.

***

I wake to screaming. I don't really wake. I'm somewhere between consciousness and unconsciousness. The blackness has a tight grip on me. I want to give in to it. Pain slices through me. I desperately want to go back to sleep.

"Casslyn, you've got to wake up," Logan says. I faintly feel him stroking my face, careful to avoid the gash on my cheek.

"What's wrong with her? Why isn't she healing? Why didn't she heal herself at the warehouse?" Xander. He made it. He got me out.

"Because there is something wrong with her powers. You would know that if you paid any attention to her or cared about her," Logan says, sniping at Xander.

"You know I care about her," Xander shoots back at him. "Besides, how could I have paid attention to her? It's not like our races are BFFs. Why are her powers not working? Didn't she age properly?"

I want to tell them to stop screaming at each other. I want to tell them I'm out, I made it, they don't have to yell. But I can't find my voice. I can't seem to escape the black abyss that would strangle me.

"She did. But she also regenerated twice before she aged and that's never happened before. Add to that the blood transfusion she had last year. It's not normal and I don't know what's wrong with her," Logan says. Fear laces his voice. I've never heard Logan so desperate before. Not even when the griffins attacked me on New Year's Eve.

"Who's blood was given to her?" Xander asks.

"Mine," the voice of my father fills the room. "Why are you even here, griffin? Give me one good reason I haven't killed you?"

"Your daughter is alive because of me," Xander says.

"Stop it. Both of you," Logan says. "We need to save her."

"Why can't you just do another blood transfusion?" Xander asks.

I try to listen to them. I try to wake up. I try many things in vain. My body is failing. I've lost too much blood. Even if Logan and Xander got me out in time, there is no coming back from this.

"It could mess with her powers even more. I'm not willing to risk it," my father says.

Logan takes a deep breath, then leans farther over me. I don't move at all. Not that I could. My chest hardly moves with my struggled breathing.

The room is silent. They are all waiting for something. Then I feel it. A wetness in my stomach, not my blood. Logan is using his tears to heal me.

The tears pool and mix with my blood. I smell smoke. My skin tightens, then begins to knit itself back together. It is uncomfortable and I want to cry out, but my body doesn't respond to my commands. Tears land on my wounds sizzling and cracking. This is the second time Logan has healed me with his tears. The countless time he's saved me. I will never be able to repay him.

But.

I'm going to be okay.

For now.

I relax into knowing I'll survive, letting the blackness grip me and pull me under.

Four

I wake up slowly. Everything hurts. I don't want to open my eyes. They hurt too.

My body feels heavy as it sinks into the mattress. My limbs stiff, as though I've been hit by a plane then run over by a train. I don't recommend being captured and beaten by your enemy as entertainment for the evening.

I can hear Logan breathing somewhere near me. I've only been a phoenix for a week, but it's weird to feel so different. Logan takes a breath and instead of hearing it in my ears, I feel it vibrate through my body. I wonder if he feels like this all the time. I am amazed by it now, but I can imagine as the years pass how irritating it could get.

I lie there for a while longer. I know Logan knows I'm awake, I'm just not ready to face the world, or him.

At least this time I'm not naked. Of course that leads to the question of how I got cleaned and changed into different clothes, unless I'm still wearing the blood stained outfit I was captured in. I seriously hope Logan didn't sponge bathe me.

"Why didn't I heal, Logan?" I ask without opening my eyes.

My chest rattles as he takes a deep breath, holds it a moment longer than he should, then releases it. There is weight to that breath. He doesn't know. He doesn't know and it's crippling him.

Finally, I open my eyes and turn my head to see him sitting in his desk chair, arms crossed, hair mussed, clothes crumpled. There are dark circles under his eyes that could rival a nasty black eye. I'm not sure how long I've been out, but I am sure he didn't sleep a second of it, even if he was told to.

I can tell, without him having to say anything, that he blames himself for me being taken. It's not his fault. It's not anyone's fault. I could tell him that, but it would fall on deaf ears. This is the second time since he moved to town that I've been attacked by the griffins without him being there to protect me. I won't get a moments privacy from now on I guarantee it.

We stare at each other until time stops. I've never known Logan to not know what to say. He's always got answers. Always something to say. His silence is uncomfortable.

I don't care that he hasn't answered my question. What

I care about is that he hasn't said anything.

We continue to stare at each other. Emotions neither one wants to deal with pass between our glances.

A jolt runs down my spine when Logan's voice shatters the silence.

"I've failed you," he says, his body still.

My heart squeezes until it becomes uncomfortable to breathe. I know he is hurting. I hurt for him. But he can't feel that way.

I throw my legs off the side of the bed, take a moment to recover when vertigo threatens to undo me, then walk to Logan, adjusting myself on his lap. I take his chin in my hand and say, "Don't start this shit. I don't have enough energy to argue with you."

"That is my fault," he says, trying to pull his chin from my hold. "You could have died. If it weren't for Xander, *of all people*, I'd have lost you."

"Logan, stop it. This isn't your fault. Don't take the blame for what *they* did. This is *their* fault. Xander's been my best friend forever, of course he wasn't going to let them kill me. Even if we are enemies."

"And if Xander wasn't your best friend I'd be too late."

I lurch to my feet tired of Logan's bullshit. "This is pitiful. This isn't you," I say moving toward the door.

"Where are you going?" he asks, pure terror in his eyes.

"I'm going home. I haven't seen my mom in days and you need to pull yourself together. Come see me when you do," I say, then walk out the door.

I listen for his following footsteps as I walk down the stairs but they don't come. I listen for them as I walk out the door. Still nothing. I know he'll be listening for me, to make sure I make it home, but I'd have thought he'd follow me. I don't like this Logan. I don't like sulking Logan. I want my warrior back.

I walk the mile it takes to get to my house. Running would be faster, but my body would have protested at me the whole way home. Logan may have healed the incisions on my body, but his tears couldn't heal the finger shaped bruises around my neck. My shoulder may be back in place but it still hurts every time my arm moves. I'm glad I was out for it being put back into place. I'm still sore from the beating I took the other night. I'm still not sure how long ago that was. The hits I took from their leader and the members responsible for capturing me didn't hurt so much as the ones from Xander. He was so angry, betrayed almost, when he thought I was a monster and had burned those people. I still can't believe he could lose faith in me so easily, that he could turn his back on a lifetime of friendship for some lie he was told by his people. Like when he stabbed me and found out I was a phoenix, and thought I had been deceiving him our entire lives. In reality I should be the angry one, he's known his whole life he is a griffin. I've known for months.

But, because of Xander, Logan was able to save my life. No matter what happens between our races from now on, I won't ever forget that. He's got amnesty as far as I'm concerned.

I walk into my house and push my hearing around trying to locate my mom. When that doesn't work I call out for her. When I come to the realization that she isn't home, I turn in the direction of Logan's house and yell, "You could have told me she wasn't here."

It's probably for the best she isn't here. I have no clue what I would have said to her about where I was for however long I was gone. I'm sure Logan or my father gave her some sort of excuse, but I'm not sure what that could be, so corroborating that lie would have been difficult.

I'm not too sure what to do with myself now. Watching TV doesn't sound too appealing at the moment. I'm sure I've got homework, but who actually wants to do homework? I make for the stairs leading to my bedroom when the phone rings. I run to the kitchen to answer it, my body complaining the whole while.

"Hello?" I asnwer.

"Casslyn, what the Hell?" Tucker yells into the phone.

"Hey, Tucker," I say to him.

"Where the Hell have you been?"

"Um," I start to say but have no idea what to tell him. "Hey, what day is it?"

"It's Wednesday. Why? Why haven't you answered any of my calls or texts? Answer the question," he says, frustration clouding his tone. "All of them."

"I've been sick, Tucker. Sorry. And I lost my phone."

"Oh, you've been sick, huh?" I can hear him pacing through the phone. I can even tell that he's in his bedroom,

One Direction playing in the background. "Xander too? That's what he told me. You two sick together? It's bullshit and you know it. I don't know what's going on with the two of you but I'm going to find out. I promise you."

"Tucker, I," I say but he's already hung up the phone.

I've got to fix my relationship with him. I've already lost Nash. I've all but lost Xander. I can't lose Tucker too. I won't be able to handle that.

I think it's about time I told Tucker the truth about what is going on. I don't care what Logan or my father have to say about it. Tucker is my best friend and the only musketeer left in my life. I'm not about to lose him because I couldn't trust him with my biggest life's secret. And I know I can trust him. I won't tell him about Xander, that's not my secret to tell, but it's about time I was honest with him.

I'm in my bedroom for a full minute before a deep seated need to shower comes over me. I grab fresh clothes and head for the bathroom. I turn the water on as hot as it will go then start to strip off the bloody clothes I just realized I was wearing. Yet another reason it's a good thing my mom wasn't here to greet me. I guess Logan didn't strip and dress me like I'd thought he had. Before stepping into the shower I stare at my body in the full length mirror. I was only semi-conscious Sunday night, but I was aware enough to know the reason I healed was because Logan used his tears. And even though my skin has healed, I can still feel every inch of my body affected that night. The split lip Xander gave me when he punched me in the face. The cut on my cheek from where Raphe sliced me with the ice knife. I've never known pain like that before. The same goes for my arm. My ribs are still bruised from being punched and kicked. My wrist still smarts from where it was stepped on when the griffins captured me.

My skin is unmarred. There is not a single scar on my body. All in thanks to regenerating when I fully aged into the phoenix. But staring into the mirror, I can see them. I can see them all. The scars from the night of my sixteenth birthday. The scars from the night I crashed Xander's car. The scars from New Year's Eve when I was attacked in the park. And now the new scars from Sunday nights assault. They may be removed by magical tears and the fire that burns inside me. But they are still there. Once etched into my skin, forever remembered.

It is Wednesday. I was attacked Sunday. I've been out nearly three days. I've been out of school for three days. Logan didn't sleep for three days.

I've missed three days of my life. Three days taken away from me merely because the griffins hate my race, hate my father, hate me.

Logan was sent here to protect me. My father showed up to look after me.

And what do the griffins do? Attack me, attack us, capture me, torture me.

I think it's about time we phoenixes get on the offensive, this defense crap isn't working out so well in my favor. It's about time the griffins start paying for what they're doing to me.

I stand in the shower, letting the scalding water beat at my skin. I have always loved taking showers. For the longest time they were always my escape. I could get in and stand there and let the waters rhythmic pulse erase everything that plagued me.

After the accident, after my parents split, after moving into this crappy house in the middle of nowhere, I wasn't in the greatest of places, but as long as the water was hot and streaming over me I could forget for a little while how much I hated my life.

But recently, my showers have taken on a lot of responsibility, so much that I'm not sure they are up for the task. I passed out at Logan's in the shower. I took a bloody shower after being attacked in the park. Now, standing in the shower after my most recent attack, the water can't keep up with my raiding thoughts.

I understand that we are the griffins' natural enemy. I understand that they have it out to get us. I also understand that they want us wiped off the planet. But I am getting sick and tired of being attacked. I try to put up a tough front for Logan, but under the surface my body is worn out and my emotions nearly crippled. A girl could take this abuse personally. Especially a girl who's already been through so much. I'm not one to throw myself a pity party, but there are moments when I'd like to curl up in a ball and cry.

But, one doesn't defend themselves in the fetal position with tears leaking down their face. So soldier on I must.

I towel off out of the shower, dress myself without looking in the pity mirror, and head downstairs. I'm hungry and in need of distracting TV.

When I get to the kitchen a sandwich, a bag of chips, and a grape soda sit on the counter accompanied by Logan and my father.

I have to stop myself in the doorway and take a deep cleansing breath to center myself. When I feel calm enough to talk to both of them at the same time I walk forward.

"Casslyn, we think we have any idea as to why you did not heal," my father says.

"You *think* you have an *idea*? That sounds promising," I say. I grab the sandwich off of the plate

Logan is really off his game, he doesn't even bat an eye at my snide comment to my father.

"We believe," my father says, more conviction in his voice, "the blood transfusion, my blood, that was given to you the night of your sixteenth birthday could have affected your transformation. Being given the blood of a full grown phoenix could have had adverse effects on your juvenile blood."

"This is just your theory? You don't actually know?" I ask, no longer snide. I'd actually like to know what is wrong with me.

"We could run some tests," my father says as though he's grasping at straws.

"Tests? What, like cutting me open until I heal myself?"

I turn to Logan for confirmation, help, his opinion, something. But he is silent. There is something going on with him. I just don't have time this second to figure out what it is.

"Casslyn. We must find out what is wrong with your powers?"

"Wrong?" I ask, crossing my arms. Tears threaten to break the plain of my eyelids. I can't crumple now. I won't fracture in front of my father. I never asked for this life, but I'll be damned it I let it break me. "So there's something *wrong* with me? I'm defective?"

Logan finally speaks. "Don't you dare think that for a minute. You are perfect in every way."

My father flinches at Logan's affectionate words.

"He said it, Logan," I say throwing up my arms in frustration. "Something is not right with me."

"We will figure this out, Casslyn," my father says. It almost sounds as if he actually cares. Must be a figment of my imagination.

"Right," I say, exhausted from the sort conversation.

I close my eyes and wish it was over. When I open them, my father is gone and Logan and I stand alone in my kitchen. Logan stares at the countertop as if he is trying to memorize the pattern.

I watch him, study him, trying to figure out what is going on with him. This distance between us isn't normal. Even when my father is around. I feel as though there is more than just the kitchen island separating us. I know he feels as though he failed me, but this feels like more than that.

When I can no longer bear the distance between us I

walk around the island and into Logan's arms. Suddenly I feel home. I haven't felt safer anywhere in the past few months than I have wrapped in Logan's arms.

I pull slightly away from him, enough to look up into his eyes. When he looks down at me I can see his love for me in his eyes, but there is something else there. Something deeper and darker. I would take that darkness away if I could. If only I knew how.

"You know," I say to him, "I haven't gotten any kisses from you in three days."

Logan smiles, one that reaches his eyes and crinkles his crow's feet. When he chuckles I can feel it in his chest but it doesn't quite reach the surface. "Is that so? You never know, I could have spent those three days covering your body in kisses."

That's more like the Logan I know.

"Haha," I laugh. "Somehow I don't believe you. Though I'm not sure how I would feel if you did. Creeped out or touched? I just don't know."

"Then maybe it's a good thing I didn't."

"Ha. I knew it," I tease.

I inch my face towards him hoping he will get the hint and lay his lips on mine.

When he doesn't, I raise an eyebrow at him and say, "Kiss me, Logan."

He hesitates for the slightest of moments then hits me by force, his lips crushing mine. I'm taken by surprise for an instant before I'm kissing him back with everything I've got.

This is a kiss that's passionate and all-consuming and I'm struggling for breath but I can tell Logan is struggling for something more so I don't break from him. For a split second I lose control of myself and can feel the flames between our skin where my hands hold him. I pull them away and clutch my fists hard at my sides to keep from lighting Logan on fire again. His arms grip mine and pull me closer to him, though there is no space between us. This kiss feels exactly like the one from months ago when Logan said we couldn't be together and I asked for one last kiss before I would leave him alone. It frightens me but I choose to ignore it. Logan loves me and I love him. Nothing is going to come between that. I know that. I have to know that.

When he pulls away we are both panting hard. Logan's eyes blaze. My hands are still on fire.

"Wow," I say. "Now that was a kiss."

I smile at him but he doesn't smile back.

I try to remain calm. He's still just upset about me getting captured. That's got to be what this is about.

I move one of my hands up to my face to watch as the flames dance upon my skin. It's really something to watch. My skin is literally on fire and yet there is no heat, no burns to my flesh.

"How can the flame work now and not when I actually need it to?" I ask Logan.

I know he doesn't know, but I feel like I needed to ask it.

"What is wrong with me?" I ask him. "Why am I never enough the way I am?"

"Don't," Logan says, gripping my arms hard.

I close my eyes and let his voice flow through me. A shiver follows. He could make the Statue of Liberty quake.

"There is nothing wrong with you. Do you hear me? You are just enough the way you are."

"I wish I could believe you," I tell him.

"Casslyn, your father was right. We are going to figure this out. We just need to make sure you are safe and to keep our priorities straight."

"What is that supposed to mean?" I ask, suddenly on edge.

Logan swallows, his Adam's apple throbs in this throat. "You remember when I said I was just supposed to protect you. That I wasn't supposed to fall in love with you?"

"Yes."

"That's what I'm going to do," he says, stepping off the island stool and facing me.

"What are you saying?" I ask, taking a step into him.

Logan closes his eyes, takes a deep breath, and rolls his shoulders back. "We can no longer be together?"

"What?" I ask, not sure he actually said what I perceived he said. "Why are you saying this?" But then I know. "This is because of him isn't it?"

"No. This was my decision. Your father merely opened my eyes to my faults. My love for you got in the way of protecting you."

"Are you kidding me? You loving me was the reason I was better protected," I reach for him but he pulls away.

His eyes turn savage when he says, "Did it? My loving you kept you from getting captured and tortured by those monsters?"

"Logan, that wasn't your fault."

"Maybe so. But I've made up my mind. I am terminating our relationship."

"You mean my father made up your mind," I spat at him. We both know my father told him to break up with me. My head is full of anger, my heart hurts. My breathing has become erratic. I'm not sure which emotion to fight with first.

"I have to go," he says, walking to the front door.

I feel my heart breaking with every step he walks away from me.

"Logan," I say as one last ditch effort to keep him from leaving me.

He turns back to me, sadness reddening his beautiful blue eyes. I know this isn't his decision and it is tearing him apart.

"I love you," I tell him, hoping he can hear in my voice just how much.

But it doesn't keep him from stepping out the door and closing it behind him.

I listen to him pause outside the door. I can hear him put his hands to his face, his choked breaths. I hang on to his footsteps as they crunch the gravel of the drive until he walks down the road toward his house.

I've stopped breathing to listen to him better. When he

is gone my breaths strangle me for oxygen.

Anger courses through me. He left. He actually left me.

I am aware as fire courses through my veins and erupts on my hands. I don't know what I'm doing as I call more of it into my hands then throw it towards the door. It stays together until it strikes the door, scorching it then flaming out. I repeatedly throw fire at the door until I'm afraid I'll set the house on fire.

I pace my kitchen floor breathing in through my nose and out through my mouth trying to diffuse the anger and heart ache. Maybe if I stop breathing I could pass out and see Nash.

No.

I'm not a coward.

Though maybe I am.

I sure want to be.

No.

Maybe I could talk to Logan. With enough persistence I got him to be my boyfriend. Maybe if I just don't give up on him he will change his mind.

Maybe I need to get my father out of town then Logan will change his mind.

Tears well up in my eyes. I don't want them to fall. For once I don't want to cry. But there are too many and they spill over, coursing down my cheeks.

I pace faster. Maybe if I can just be angry I won't be so sad.

But that doesn't work. The faster I pace, the faster my

heart beats, the faster it's clenched with pain and sorrow.

Logan was the only thing that made me feel safe. And now he's been ripped away from me. Didn't he know that? Couldn't he sense that in his arms was the safest I've felt since Nash died? Why would he take that away from me?

I want to curl up in a ball and wait out the swirling storm of emotions. I need to find high ground before the dam of anger and sorrow bursts. The longer I'm alone, the worse it all gets. I'm actually alone now.

I'm really alone.

Nash is gone.

Xander is gone.

Logan is gone.

Tucker is nearly gone.

My mother is never here.

My dad doesn't know where he stands so he stays away.

I don't want my father here.

I want to punch something but the punching bag is at Logan's and I'm not about to go there right now. I want to punch my father. How dare he come into my life and disrupt it so badly.

I don't know what to do with myself. I could go to my room and cry my eyes out. I could sit in front of the TV with a pint of ice cream. I could go for a run.

I really just want to talk to Tucker but I'm not sure he'd be willing to talk to me right now. Besides, if I went to him with my problems and didn't bother with his that would make me a horrible friend. More horrible than I've been lately.

When indecision leaves me with nothing I lie down on the living room floor and stare at the ceiling. Tears stream down the sides of my face and land on the rug. Rage takes over my mind until it is cloudy and lacks focus. The beat of my heart is sporadic and at an altered pace.

Logan left me. Because my father told him to. Apparently his love for me was less than his loyalty towards my father. Good to know. I won't make that mistake again.

***

I wake up on the floor. I don't remember falling asleep. Tears crust the corners of my eyes. I wipe them away and let out a deep breath. I'm alone.

I almost wish my mom didn't work so many hours at the hospital. My need for her is new but impatient. My mom and I have never had the closest relationship. We've never talked about boys. She tried once and I yelled at her effectively ending that conversation. We've never really talked about anything important. I always had Nash for that. Then when I didn't I turned to Tucker and Xander. Even if I would have turned to my mom during that time, she wasn't around. And my dad had left.

There really must be something wrong with me if I can't get anyone to stick around.

This may as well be the longest day of my life. When I look outside it's not even dark.

I contemplate staying on the floor and going back to

sleep but think better of it.

I still want to cry but not as badly. Though my anger is still there and raging.

I could really go for a cheeseburger and fries right now. Fries with nacho cheese and bacon. Anything with bacon would go over really well right now. I wonder if my car ever got back to me. Last I knew it was in the parking lot of the grocery store.

I'm too distracted by my thoughts to hear the door open when suddenly there is a figure standing in my kitchen. I turn fast ready to attack if I need to when I see my father. My body deflates the adrenaline that had begun to pump.

I stare at him in contempt. I'm too heartbroken to say anything, but too angry not to.

"Are you happy? You got your wish. He broke up with me. That's what you wanted right? So there you go, father of the year award." I glare at him then, before turning away from him I say, "Get out of my house."

"I'm not leaving," he says, holding his stance.

"Then I am," I tell him, walking away from him.

He is in front of me before I can get anywhere.

"Stop acting like a child," he tells me.

"What do you want?" I ask him, crossing my arms over my chest.

I can feel anger and fire building in me. I might lose it if he isn't careful.

"Casslyn, I came to town not just to protect you or to get recon on the griffins, but to be a part of your life."

I scoff at him.

"I know you lost Nash and that I haven't been a part of your life, but I want that to change."

"If you think you can come here and try to replace Nash or be my dad, you are mistaken. No one can replace Nash, and I've already got a dad."

He takes a step towards me, his hand held out. I take a step back. He says, "I'm not here to replace anyone, I just want to be a part of it."

"If you wanted to be a part of it, you should have never abandoned us in the first place. You come here after sixteen years, after you left us, and now you want us - me - to fight for you? To be part of your race? To be part of your life? I don't think so. It doesn't work like that."

"I didn't abandon you. I didn't even know you existed until Nash died. If I knew about you I never would have left you."

"I don't believe you. My mom told me about your romance, your love. If you loved her so much, wouldn't you have come back in the past sixteen years to check up on her?"

"I was near the end of my life cycle when I was with your mom. We'd had a fight about your dad. She clearly loved him and was conflicted about the situation, about choosing between us. I knew that I would regenerate and she wouldn't even know who I was, so what was the point of staying? So I left. Then, sixteen years later, I find out I have two children, that one of them is dead, and the other is near it. How do you think that made me feel? Casslyn, I loved your mother. And despite what you think, I love you."

"How could you not have known about us?" I ask, desperate for some argument.

My father stares at me, looking for his words. Finally he says, "I was afraid to return and find your mother with your dad. I was afraid to see that she'd forgotten about me and was now happy with another man."

My heart clenches for him. It's sad. It reminds me of how sad my mom was when she told me about their affair. They really did love each other.

"That's a sad story. I feel for you. I really do. But that doesn't excuse what you've done. I love Logan and you made him leave me, when I have no one else. Please get out of my house, I can't deal with this right now."

My father holds his gaze on me. He opens his mouth once, twice, as if to say something, but doesn't. He soldier pivots in front of me then walks out of my house.

My shoulders slump relieving me of weight too heavy to bear. This has seriously got to be the longest day of my life. Twenty four hours. It's always twenty four hours. Some days nothing of merit occurs. And others so many things accost you and batter you and threaten to break you and you think there couldn't be anything else to heap on to the stinking shit pile of your day and then there is and you sink a little farther into the mud and you wish it would just end, that a new day would start and reset itself so you could climb a little bit, broken nail by broken nail out of the whole that has consumed your life.

Needing this current twenty four hour period to be over, I make my way up the stairs to my bedroom, throw myself upon my bed, and pass out.

Five

My feet pound the pavement harder and faster. Logan may have dumped me but I still need to stay focused on my training. I'm even more determined to learn everything I can after being captured by the griffins.

Too bad I don't have a gym in my basement and a sparring partner. There is no way I can face Logan every day. I'd either kill him or beg him to be my boyfriend again. And that's not about to happen. I could use the weight room at school but I still wouldn't have anyone to spar with.

I run past the park, past Tucker's house. I can't hit the ground hard enough. I can't get enough speed. I can't do anything right. Logan knew something bad would happen if I went to the grocery store by myself and I didn't listen. I got the shit beaten out of me and ended up boyfriendless. Good plan, Cass.

I need to work harder. I need to get better, stronger, faster. That need. That desperation, leads me to the door I stand in front of.

I knock twice and wait for an answer.

When Xander opens his door he slams it in my face. Then opens it.

"What are you doing here?" he asks me. "Are you insane? They will kill you. They'll kill me. You can't be here."

"I need to talk to you," I say in a way I know he will do anything I ask.

"You can't be seen here,"

"Can you meet me somewhere?" I ask.

I know he wants to say no. I know he should say no. For the sake of both of us. But I also know he wants to talk to me. You don't both survive something like we did and not need an outlet for your feelings.

There is a long pause before he answers.

"Is your house safe? Could I meet you there, in an hour?"

"Yeah, okay. I'll see you in an hour, Xander," my tone is firm, meaning, if I don't see him in an hour I'm coming back.

"I'll be there," he tells me.

I feel the urge to believe him. I need to believe him.

So I leave. I run the ten miles back to my house, shower, then pace my living room waiting for him to knock at my door.

I hear him pull up in front of my house. I really hope

Logan and my father aren't paying close enough attention to me to see Xander show up here. I'm really surprised Logan wasn't following me on my run. Certainly if the griffins cornered me at the grocery store they could get me easier on a secluded run.

Xander does a full search of the property. He looks around, circles the house twice, listens for anything out of the ordinary. I almost chuckle at him, but we are no longer kids in a safe environment. We are enemies in danger of each other and outside forces.

I open the door before he knocks and usher him in.

I grip him in a hard hug. To my surprise he hugs me back. I've missed him and I think he's missed me too. Despite what we may be now, Xander and I have been best friends our whole lives. Trying to comprehend losing one another, like we could have the other night, is beyond imaging. The fact that he went to Logan to help me escape. The fact that he faced my father, his true enemy, is more than I could ever ask for in a best friend. I would have done the same for him. But I'm glad to know regardless of what is going on in our lives, we've got each other's back.

I pull back and inspect him. He's got a broken lip, black eyes, and bruises showing where his clothes don't hide. I know Logan landed a few punches to him so he wouldn't be a suspect in my escape, but this looks far worse.

"What happened to you?"

He shrugs, and nonchalantly says, "They suspect I helped you escape."

"Oh my God, Xander, are you okay?" There is true concern in my voice. I knew there was a chance of this happening, it was a concern. But I didn't think they would beat him. He is one of them.

"I'm fine. I'll heal. What about you?" he asks. "Are you okay?"

"I'm fine. Sore. But I'm fine." I can still feel the finger shaped bruises around my neck.

There is a silence between us we are all too aware of. The thread that connected us so easily for so long has been severed and we're not sure how to tie it back together.

"What did you want to talk about?" he asks me. He is trying to fill the void. He also looks at his watch to see how long he's been here. We are putting each other in danger by being together.

"I was wondering if you wanted to train together," I say looking to my feet, suddenly nervous.

"I thought you were training with Logan."

I swallow before I answer. "He broke up with me," I say, still not looking at him.

"Oh," he says. "Are you okay?"

I finally look up at him and say, "Not really. But what am I supposed to do about it? Anyway. I still need to train. Especially since I got my ass so easily handed to me the other night. I thought if we trained together I could still train and I would be training with a griffin so I could learn how you guys fight. Since you've been trained your whole life with them."

When he doesn't immediately answer, I say, "I know it's a lot to ask and I know we haven't been the best of friends lately but I just had to ask."

He stares at me for a long moment trying to figure out what to say. I know he wants to help me, it's clearly written on his face, but he also wants to keep his ass in the clear. Neither of us wants to be beaten again.

"I . . . can't," he tells me. "I'm sorry. If they caught us together they would kill us both. I can't put either of us in that kind of danger."

My shoulders slump, my face falls, but I shake it off and say, "I understand. I had to ask." I had to know that was coming. It's not like it would have actually worked.

"I am sorry, Cass," he tells me.

"It's okay. I'll figure it out," I say. I walk to the kitchen, to the fridge, then pull out two bottles of water. I throw one to him then say, "There is something else I wanted to talk to you about."

"What's up?" he asks me.

"I'm going to tell Tucker what I am," I back up as I say this, making sure the island is between us, like he might come after me. I quickly say, "I'm not going to tell him about you, just me. I just need to tell him. I need him in my life and the only way is to tell him the truth."

"Okay."

"Okay?"

"Okay."

"Hm. That's not quite the reaction I was expecting."

Honestly I expected him to jump over the island and throttle me.

"Yeah. I wasn't expecting to give it."

I place my hands on the island counter, palms down. "Do you want to come?"

"Yeah." Again. I didn't expect him to say that. But I'm really glad we are doing it together. I'm sure my father and Logan are going to be pissed, but I honestly don't care at the moment. This is my life and I'm going to decide how I live it.

Xander and I drive separately to Tucker's in the chance that literally anything could happen.

"We're really doing this aren't we," he says, before he's about to knock on Tucker's door.

"We are. Well I am, you don't have to," I say, giving him an out. I'm positive I want to do this. It's time Tucker knew the truth about us. But I'm not positive it's the best idea I've ever had.

"Nope," he says, knocking on the door. "We're doing this."

When Tucker opens the door he steps back and gapes at the two of us. For a long time. Longer than is necessary.

"Tucker, let us in," Xander tells him.

He snaps out of his daze and steps aside.

"You're both together," he says, still in awe.

"Don't get used to it," Xander tells him, though he's not trying to be mean, just frank.

"Are your parents home?" I ask him.

"No," Tucker says. He's got that suspicious tone in his voice. "What's going on? Why are you together after so long?"

"We need to tell you something," I say, walking into the living room.

"You mean you're actually going to tell me why you two hate each other suddenly?"

"Yeah," Xander tells him.

"Have at it," Tucker says, throwing his hands up.

"Maybe you should sit down," I warn. I didn't take it too well when I learned Logan was a phoenix. I didn't take it too well when I learned I was a phoenix. And Xander was a whole other story. I think warning Tucker he may need a seat is prudent.

"You're being weird, Cass. Just tell me," Tucker says, though he sits down in the chair opposite me.

Xander remains standing, I'm sure in case he needs to make a hasty exit.

My gut is twisted in knots. Sweat is about to sprout on my skin any second now. I've never been more scared to tell anyone anything. The look on Xander's face tells me he feels the same way.

I look calm on the outside. I know Xander thinks I'm fine. He's so wrong. My insides are trying to claw out through my belly button. But I have to do this. I owe Tucker this much.

"Okay," I say. "A few months ago I was stabbed in the chest."

Tucker gasps and bolts off the chair to come to me.

"It's okay. I'm fine. Obviously. Anyway. I didn't bleed. Instead, my chest burst into flames and those flames healed me."

"I'm confused," Tucker says.

"I was too. But then I was told that I'm a phoenix."

"A phoenix?" Tucker asks. "Like Dumbledore's bird that bursts into flames and is reborn from the ashes?"

"That's where I went with that," I say. Some minds do think alike.

"You're joking right?" Tucker says. "This is some elaborate joke you are playing on me right?"

Tucker turns to Xander and says, "What are you supposed to be? A werewolf? A vampire? A wizard?"

"I'm a griffin," Xander tells him, and we both watch as his face falls.

"Okay, I've got to think on this one," Tucker says, still trying to find the joke in it. "Griffin, half lion, half eagle right?"

"That's the one," Xander tells him. There are fine beads of sweat on Xander's forehead but he is getting through this. I knew it would be a struggle for him. I'm proud of him for being here let alone spilling his entire life's secret.

Tucker looks between me and Xander waiting for us to pull the rug out from under him. To start laughing and tell him it really is just a joke. When we don't he sits back in his chair and curls into himself. He pulls his knees into his chest. I watch as my best friend's eyes go blank.

Xander looks to me. I desperately want to say something, to soothe him somehow, to figure out how he's dealing with this. I know better. He needs to come out of this himself or he'll never get there. Xander shakes his head at me to let me know to leave him be for the time being. It's a hard thing to swallow.

Xander's posture becomes rigid in the time we wait. I can see that his body is still uncomfortable. But I think he's afraid if he moves from his position he'll frighten Tucker, like a deer in the headlights.

I curl up on the couch mimicking Tucker's position. Whether it is intentional or not, I'm not sure.

Finally, life returns to Tucker's eyes and he says, "So why do you hate each other?"

Out of all we told him, that's what he wants to know? I almost laugh. Xander does.

"I'm the one who stabbed her," Xander tells him.

Tucker gapes at Xander, wondering how he could betray him and me both.

"It's not really his fault," I say, surprising him by coming to his defense. "You see, apparently thousands of years ago Apollo chose the phoenixes over the griffins and the griffins got mad about it and have had it out for us this whole time."

Xander crosses his arms over his chest and says, "That's not how it happened."

"Regardless. Neither of us was there. We have no way of knowing what truly happened. But for as long as any of us knows, we've been mortal enemies, out to get each other."

Some form of realization comes over Tucker, sorrow filling his features. He looks at me and says, "They killed Nash didn't they?"

Tears well up in my eyes. Finally, someone else who knows. It's almost more than I can bear. "Yeah," I say, swallowing hard.

"And they tried to kill you that night you drove Xander's car home."

"They attacked me on New Year's Eve. I didn't actually slip on the ice," I say. I'm sure if I didn't Tucker would have figured it out.

"How does Logan play into all this?" Tucker asks, but before I can answer he already has it figured out. "Logan is a phoenix too, isn't he?"

"Yeah. He was sent here to protect me."

"By who?" Tucker asks.

"My father."

"But your dad lives here."

"My biological father does not."

"Oh," Tucker says.

He is handling this surprisingly well.

He turns to Xander and says, "So why weren't you in school this week. Clearly something didn't go well."

Finally Xander takes a seat next to me on the couch. He's tired of standing. I think he's aware that this is going better than we expected and feels comfortable enough to sit.

Xander tells him, "I found out Sunday afternoon that Casslyn had been taken by my people. Now, I was lead to believe that Casslyn and Logan had been going to the bordering states and killing people. Burning them alive with their powers. I went and confronted Cass."

"How could you have believed that?" Tucker asks.

"I don't know. It's what I've believed my whole life. It's hard to turn your back on that."

"Not too hard to turn your back on the best friend you've had your whole life?"

I can see by the look on Xander's face he knew Tucker would take my side. We've always known Tucker loved me more. I've always known I was the baby of the group, the only girl, the one they cared for the most. I never tried to lord it over any of them. I've always tried to treat them the same. But I've still always known. I always thought the boys knew and were okay with it, because sometimes I needed more love than the boys did. But I can see now that it grates on Xander, now that there are only the three of us. There will always be an odd man out. Xander made a mistake. I am aware of that. But I've made my peace with it and I don't think it needs to be shoved in his face.

So I jump in for him. "Once he realized it was a mistake, he went to Logan. Xander is the reason I'm alive today."

"So you were both beaten up and that's why you weren't at school?"

"Yes," Xander and I say together.

"So let me get this straight," Tucker says. "You're both mythical creatures who just happen to be mortal enemies. That's the gist? Did I miss anything?"

"No," we say together.

"Awesome," Tucker says. There is a mixture of fear, shock, worry, and sarcasm in his tone.

"Are you okay, Tucker? Do you hate me?" I ask. So far he is taking it well. But knowing what we are and still loving us after everything are two very different things. He could accept us for who and what we are but he may never accept us in his life again.

"That night at the bowling alley and I was knocked out. We were attacked by griffins weren't we?"

"Yes," I say carefully. I'm afraid Tucker is going to hate me for this.

"Huh," Tucker says.

"I'm so sorry, Tucker. I . . . I'm so sorry. I don't know what else to say."

"It wasn't her fault, Tucker," Xander tells him, his voice firm.

"Oh, I know. I'm actually glad to know I was part of it."

Xander turns his head in confusion. I mimic his pose. That's not what we were expecting.

"Tucker, are you okay?" I ask again.

"I've just learned my two best friends are not even human. And that they are mortal enemies. And that one of them has been nearly murdered several times. I'm going to need a minute. A lot of them."

"I understand," I say, my head falling. I've always been one to wear my emotions, all of them, on my face. I think that's part of why the boys were always careful of me. Why they felt like I needed more love. Logan breaking up with me is a lot of the weight bearing down on me, but Tucker means the world to me and I'm so afraid I'm going to lose him.

Xander and I will never be able to be friends again. My race would never allow it. I'm sure his wouldn't either if they were aware of it. I'll never be able to be seen with him without my people expecting me to turn him over to them. He'll never be safe in my presence. And I can't believe his people would tell him Logan and I are parading about killing innocent people. If that is the reason the griffins kill my people it needs to stop. We are being slaughtered because of false information. I'm going to be telling Logan and my father about this, just as soon as I can face them again.

"We'll leave," I say to Tucker. I understand he needs time to process this. I know I would. And doing so alone is sometimes easier when the thing you need to process isn't staring you down.

"No, don't," Tucker nearly screams. "You've both been AWOL for too long. You're not going anywhere."

"Oh, Tucker," I say, bum rushing him to hug him.

Thankfully, he hugs me back.

And just like that, though we are broken, frayed at the edges, and missing several pieces of ourselves, the musketeers are somewhat back together. If only for the moment.

Six

I scream as the griffin slides the knife across my rib cage opening my flesh. They've been at it for ages. I've lost track of time. I've lost track of myself. I'm not sure I can keep going. Too bad they don't care how I feel.

"Where is your father?" the one asks.

I spit blood and saliva on his face when he gets close enough. "Go to Hell," I tell him.

"You'll be there far sooner than I will," he says before stabbing the knife into my stomach.

I scream and scream and try to keep consciousness. The pain is too much. I wish he'd just end it. I'm not going to tell him anything. I may not want a relationship with my father, but I'm not about to sell him out, especially if it could put Logan in danger.

Blood spurts from my wound as he pulls the knife out. It runs hot and sticky down my leg and onto the floor. My head swims. Stars dance across my vision. I've lost a lot of blood. At least if I die now I can be with Nash.

"Where is your father? Where are the other phoenixes?"

My eyelids grow heavy. I could close them and wait for the end.

"I don't know," I tell him.

"Wrong answer," he says pulling back before he strikes my face with his large fist.

My head swings and hangs limp on my chest.

"Casslyn," a new voice calls.

I know that voice.

With all the strength I can muster I pull my head up only to be backhanded. Blood flies across the room spraying the closest wall like bad modern art.

"Casslyn."

I search for Nash, turn towards his voice.

He's here. He's going to save me.

Or maybe I've finally died.

"Casslyn!" he screams and suddenly he's in my face. "Wake up."

"What?" I ask. Or at least I try to.

"Wake up, Cassie. It's just a nightmare."

"I can't," I say as the griffin shoves past Nash to run me through with his knife again.

I gasp from the pain and writhe in agony. They've got me. I'll never again see Tucker or Logan or my parents or

Xander.

Nash is in front of me again. He grasps my shoulders, violently shakes me, and says, "Wake up!"

I jolt awake, choking on my breath.

I wrench the sheet that's strangling me from my neck. Breathing heavy, my heart slamming into my chest, it takes me long moments to gather my bearings.

I'm in my bedroom. I'm safe.

I'm alone.

Besides my battered body, I didn't think my capture by the griffins had affected me that badly. Apparently I was mistaken. I haven't had a nightmare that bad since I used to dream about the crash with Nash. I'm not prepared for re- curring nightmares if that's what is going to happen. I know being captured and tortured by an enemy is a lot to process and nightmares are my minds way of me dealing with it. But nightmares always leave me drained and more tired than when I went to sleep.

My heart still hammers in my chest as I lie back onto my pillow trying to push the nightmare and the memory of being tortured out of my head.

Then Logan bursts through my bedroom door.

I bolt upright expecting an actual attack. But no, it's just Logan. Even in the dark I know Logan's frame. I could tell Logan apart from anyone at any time. And yes I would take that bet.

He takes stock of the room, the situation, then rushes to my side.

"Are you alright?" he asks, concern in his voice.

"I'm fine," I tell him, pushing myself into a sitting position.

"I heard you screaming," he says, leaning forward.

"Bad dream. Go home."

"Casslyn, you can tell me. I'm still here for you."

"No. You're not, Logan. You effectively ended the being here for me when you broke up with me," I tell him. A frustrated sigh escapes my chest.

It's only been a few days, but I desperately miss him. My stomach does a little flip when Logan's gaze penetrates mine. We were only together a few months, but those months were passionate and intense and have lingered in my mind. My heart beats, then skips, then beats. Skips. My own body betrays me. Logan's presence is doing unwanted things to me. I certainly won't be able to get over him if he is so near.

"Cass, I," Logan says.

"Don't. I'm fine. I promise. You can go home," I tell him. I turn over in my bed and cover myself to end the conversation.

I wish he wouldn't leave. I wish he'd tell me he made a mistake listening to my father. I wish he'd tell me he loves me and wants to be my boyfriend again. But I know Logan. I know he stands by his convictions. I know he is loyal and stubborn. I know I have no chance of him coming back to me.

A small piece of my heart breaks off and joins its cohorts when Logan's weight lifts off the bed. Another when

I hear my front door close. Too bad the fire that burns under my skin can't heal a broken heart. Not that it can heal broken skin at the moment.

I slam my head into my pillow and try to clear my mind. I'm still shaken from the nightmare and from Logan's presence. It's been a long time since I've had a nightmare. Really, since Logan came into my life. I've never given it much thought, but now that I am, I realize my nightmares stopped once Logan was a steady figure in my life. And now that he's not, now that he's left me, my nightmares are back, with a vengeance.

This makes me wonder what else in my life is easier or better with Logan. Well, that's stupid, everything was better with Logan. But I wouldn't even go anywhere near my car before Logan forced me to drive it. Nightmares of the crash with Nash plagued me night and day until Logan showed up. I was an angry, miserable, scared mess before Logan showed up. I was wandering through my life with half of myself missing until Logan came and gave me direction.

Without my knowledge I have become dependent on Logan. I need him for strength and courage. For guidance and assurance. Logan has kept me from completely falling apart. I hope I can hold myself together without him.

***

After lying in my bed for a while longer and being unable to fall back to sleep, I got up, took a shower, and headed to Tucker's house. I really needed some best friend time.

"Not that I don't love getting to spend the whole day alone with you," Tucker says, while we walk down the center of the mall. "But why isn't Logan with us?"

"That would be because he would rather obey my father than be with me," I tell him, feeling the need to cross my arms.

"I thought protecting you was obeying him."

"Yeah, I guess," I say, curious as to why Logan hasn't been near me at all times lately.

"And he can't do that while shopping *with* us?" Tucker asks.

"What do you mean *with* us?"

"He's been following us all day. Why can't he just join us?"

I stop dead in my tracks and search for Logan in the crowd around us. When I can't spot him I turn to Tucker and say, "What do you mean he's been following us all day?"

"You didn't know?"

"No, I didn't know. Where is he?" Again I search for him in the crowd.

Tucker looks at the spot where I'm guessing is the last place he saw Logan. He's not there.

"You're telling me you don't know when your own boyfriend is following you around the mall all day?" Tucker asks, confused.

"That's what I would be telling you, if he was still my boyfriend," I say then start again in the direction we were headed.

"What?" Tucker practically yells. He rushes up to me then pulls on my sleeve to stop me. The people around us are bound to get annoyed.

"Please don't make a thing of it," I say, trying to contort my face in a pleading manner.

"When did you break up? Who broke up with whom? *Why?*"

"The day before Xander and I told you about us. Logan broke up with me. My father told him to," I say. I walk away from him knowing he will stand there in dramatic fashion for moments longer.

When he's caught up to me he asks, "Are you okay?"

I take a deep breath and release it while dropping my shoulders and say, "Not really. But there's not a lot I can do about it. Let's keep shopping."

"Fine. But when we're finished we're getting you ice cream and a sappy movie and we're crying it out at my house."

"We?" I ask.

"Oh, honey, if you didn't think I was going to mourn the end of your relationship you don't know me at all."

I laugh, a genuine laugh, for the first time in days. I can always count on Tucker to make me feel better about just about anything.

"Also," he says, "I can't believe you didn't tell me this before."

I furrow my eyebrows at him and say, "I kind of thought

you knowing about *me* was more important than my relationship status."

Tucker moves his hands up and down like a scale, like he's weighing which topic was more important. I slap one of his hands down, laugh, and move down the center of the mall, stopping to enter Hot Topic.

"Wow, you two really did break up," Tucker says. "You haven't been into this store since he showed up in town."

"Shut up," I tell him, walking further into the store.

Before we leave the mall I try to find Logan but fail. I can't believe Tucker was able to spot him this whole time when I can't find him once. For all I know I could have a tail of griffins following me. No wonder I got taken at the grocery store. I really need to start paying better attention to my surroundings. I even try listening for him, but in a mall my ears are assaulted over and over again by people walking by talking on their phones or to their companions, smoothie machines whirring, people placing orders for food, a popcorn maker popping out kernels for movie goers, heeled boots clacking against porcelain tiles, cashiers swiping credit cards through card readers, no Logan.

I'd like to confront him. Tell him to leave me alone. Tell him if he doesn't want to be a part of my life in the way I want him to then he can't be a part of it at all. But I won't. I'd end up blowing up on him, burn the mall down, then get thrown in jail for arson. What I really need, more than to confront him, is to get over him, and the way to do that is to spend as little time with him as I can.

***

Tucker and I sit curled up on his living room couch with a bucket of chocolate and marshmallow ice cream between us watching *Easy A*. It's light enough of a movie to keep me from weeping, but enough of a romance to stifle Tucker's need for happily-ever-afters.

Of course before the movie started, we had to have a heart to heart about how I was feeling about the breakup and how I thought Logan was feeling and had I even considered Tucker's feelings in the matter.

"So," he says, "you said Logan broke up with you because your father told him to. Why would he do that?"

"Because I got captured without Logan knowing it. I'm sure he thought Logan's feelings for me were getting in the way of his job to protect me. Stupid thing is, Logan actually agreed with him."

"You know," Tucker says, "You could just ask him to get back together. That boy would give you the moon if he could. I'm sure if you asked hard enough he'd have to say yes."

"No," I say, adamant.

"Why? You know it would work."

"Because, Tucker, I begged him for us to be together. I'm not going to beg to get back together."

"But look how well it worked," he says, a wry smile on his face.

I laugh, a rueful laugh, but one that doesn't quite reach any depth. My begging did eventually pay off, but only because I stood before him, my body covered in lacerations from my enemy. I've wondered before if Logan was just so scared of losing me he finally gave in to his love for me, or if he gave in because in that moment he felt so bad for me he felt the need to give me what I wanted. Of course I knew I was being stupid, I knew Logan loved me, but now, I'm not so sure. If it was so easy for him to break up with me, maybe he didn't love me as much as I thought he did.

"No, Tucker," I tell him, pretending to pay attention to the movie, like I haven't seen it a thousand times.

"I'm so upset about this. I was rooting for you, you know I was. I really thought you and Logan were the Ross and Rachel of our time. The Lucas and Peyton. The Rory and Jess."

"You do know Rory and Jess don't end up together," I say, raising an eyebrow at him.

"But you know they should have," he says, matching my eyebrow.

"I know. You know, when Logan and I became a couple, and everything was so messed up, I truly believed that if we loved each other hard enough, everything would just work out. But I was wrong."

"You're not wrong," Tucker says, sitting up and making direct eye contact with me. He's got his I'm-serious look on. "How many times did Ross and Rachel break up before they got back together for good? Huh? How many times did Peyton nearly die before they drove off in the sunset with their beautiful baby? Maybe you just have to take a few relationship beatings before you get your happily-ever-after."

I'm nearly in tears before Tucker finishes his speech. I smile a sad smile at him and say, "Thanks, Tucker. I'm just not sure you're right about this one."

"We shall see. And when we do, you owe me. And I mean you owe me big. Like naming your first child after me big."

"Deal," I say.

I shake his hand with one hand while crossing the fingers of my other hand behind my back. He'll never know.

Tucker and I return our attention to the movie. We've missed a lot but we've seen it so many times we could recite the whole movie in our sleep, or perhaps an off broadway production. I, of course would be Olive, Xander was going to be Woodchuck Tod, and Tucker always wanted to be Rhiannon aka Big Tits. Tucker playing Brandon was just too obvious.

We get to the part where Olive and Brandon are pretending to have sex at a party to fool everyone into thinking Brandon is straight when Tucker bolts upright, nearly toppling the ice cream to the floor. "I've got a great idea," he says.

"Scaring me half to death? Because I don't agree on it being a great idea."

"No," he says, his eyes going wide. "We are going to a party tonight."

"Excuse me? Have you met us? We don't do . . . parties."

"Listen up sista friend. We are not going to sit around and sulk all night long. You've had a rough few weeks, that with you nearly dying and getting your heart stomped on. You need to get liquored up and find new man candy to use for the night."

"I don't think so, Tucker. I'm sorry."

"No. We are going. You don't get to think about it."

Tucker throws the blanket off his lap and stands up. He walks around the couch and moves in the direction of his bedroom.

"I don't have anything to wear. And how do you even know there is a party tonight?"

"Cass, oh sweet, young, naive Cass. It's Saturday night. There is always a party. We're just never invited. And I'm pretty sure the hooker outfit you bought to make Logan jealous will suffice. Get off the couch, get dressed, and lets' go."

***

I'm into my third beer before my cheeks get warm. My fifth when I can no longer feel the tips of my fingers. I've seen enough movies and TV shows about supernatural humans to know some of them can't get drunk. The Flash can't get drunk because of his superhuman metabolism. Elves can't get drunk for whatever reason. So I wondered if I would suffer the same fate. That is a resounding no. Boy do I feel it. What I can't feel is my face, or my hands. I can't hear everything around me or see properly. I may not be able to get drunk, but the alcohol has dulled my phoenix senses. At the moment I could care less.

Tucker and I find a spot in the middle of the living room where the beat of the music is loudest and dance. The rhythm thrums in my chest, vibrating my entire body. Goosebumps pucker my flesh as the music beats under my skin.

I smile as Tucker does his best impression of terrible dance moves, the lawn mower, the sprinkler, the shopping cart. He's had as much to drink, if not more, than I have. I join him in his dancing, not giving a rats ass who would judge us. This is the happiest I've seen Tucker in a long time. I'll give him his fun and revel in his joy. I've learned lately to live in the moment and appreciate what you have because you never know when it could be taken away from you.

I spot Xander across the room watching us. His face is pretty much stoic but I can see the faintest hint of humor. After we told Tucker about what we are Xander said we couldn't be seen together anymore. I know it's for the safety of us both, and those we love, but I still miss him. Sixteen years of seeing each other almost daily leaves one wanting when they never get to see each other. I'm actually worried one of us is going to be in danger tonight. But there are too many people at the party for the griffins to attack me. Right? I hope so. Plus I'm sure there is some exposure law for both races. Can't let the humans know we exist.

I'm sure Ashley and her boy toy are somewhere around

here. I've never heard of Ashley missing a party in all of our high school years. Hopefully Ashley, Colt, and Xander make up the extent of the griffin population at this party because I know I'm the only phoenix. Three to one is not the best odds in my favor.

I shake off the worry, take one last look at Xander, then return my attention to Tucker who has switched to doing the running man. I laugh at him then tell him I'm going for a drink and ask if he wants to join me. He waves me off and continues to dance.

I find the kitchen and look for the beer. There is a kid from the class above me pouring drinks.

"Here, take this," he says. "You'll love it."

I grab the cup from him and take a drink. It is a lot stronger than the beer I was drinking earlier but it is fruity and tastes good.

"You're going to throw up," says a laughing voice behind me.

I turn around too quickly. My head spins and I nearly throw my drink on the speaker.

"Excuse me?" I ask, my voice slurring. My tongue feels fuzzy and heavy.

"You've been drinking beer, and now you're drinking liquor. Have you never heard the phrase beer before liquor, never sicker?"

"So what do you care? This is a party. Doesn't everyone get so drunk they throw up then pass out?"

"It's your headache then," he says, crossing his arms.

He raises one side of his mouth in a cocky grin.

I defiantly bring the cup to my lips and take another drink, longer this time. I'll show him. I raise an eyebrow at him, daring him to make a move, to say something else.

"You looked good out there," he says, nodding his head toward the living room where Tucker is still dancing.

"You're going to use that line? Please," I scoff at him.

He steps closer to me, invading my personal space, and fills my nostrils with his rich Abercrombie and Fitch cologne scent. I breathe in deep, taking it in, and nearly lose my balance. I regain control of my body then look up at him. His dazzling hazel eyes stare back at me. I stare at them studying the different colors that make them up. Again, one side of his mouth turns up in a grin. It's as attractive as his eyes. As attractive as the rest of his face.

He leans in until he's whispering in my ear, "I could use other lines." He pulls back and raises an eyebrow at me suggestively.

"Calm down, pal. I'm not that drunk," I tell him. I place one hand on his chest and push him back a step.

He places his hands in his low hung jeans and innocently raises his shoulders.

I take another drink for the cup, my cheeks growing warmer. I study good looking stranger in front of me. He appears to be at least two if not three years older than me. He's got sandy blonde hair that ends right below his eyebrows. It's slightly shaggy but looks wonderfully soft, the kind you want to run your hands through. His build is a cross between a pole vaulter and a soccer player. His black tee shirt is as fitted as his jeans are.

When my gaze returns to his face he winks and says, "Checking out the merchandise are we?" His smirk is deadly and extremely kissable.

A rush of something akin to lust flows through my veins. I shiver but am quick to stamp it down. I may be drunk but my relationship with Logan just ended. Though it may be over for him, I still love Logan. I'm not ready to throw it away for some guy I meet at a party. Then again, Logan is the one that broke up with me, I should be allowed to get over him in any manner I see fit. This new stranger may just be my ticket to getting over Logan. Even if it is for one night.

"So what if I was?" I ask, smirking right back at him.

Again he invades my personal space, the smell of his cologne attacking my nostrils and running into my lady bits.

I turn away from him, needing to clear my head when I see Tucker in the living room hopping to the music. When he sees me and how close this guy is, he smiles and gives me two thumbs up.

When I return my attention to this guy our noses bump, his mouth mere centimeters from mine. I inhale deeply, surprised by his proximity. I step back, meeting the counter with my ass. I down what is left in my cup as this guy steps forward intent on one thing.

Our lips collide and move together. My hand releases the cup and joins the other in their move to touch him. He does the same. My skin tingles at his contact. His hands roaming, finding the hem of my shirt, the pads of his fingers skimming my stomach. His tongue invades my mouth and claims mine. His kiss is electric and hungry. I kiss him back just as ravenous, hoping that for just a moment I can escape my life and be a normal teenager.

As he continues to kiss me my alcohol addled brain registers something not quite right. Something not quite normal. His hands cup my face. I move mine to hold his. In that moment, my fingers pressed to his pressure point, I feel it.

Two heart beats.

I push him back with force, my stomach churning, nausea creeping over me. His smirk is back as I run for the nearest bathroom.

When I reach it I throw open the door and hurl into the toilet bowl. My stomach tightens and convulses, rejecting everything I've eaten and had to drink this evening. Once my stomach is empty I continue to dry heave until my abs hurt. Sweat slicks my skin. When I'm convinced I'm okay, I stand up from the toilet, turn on the water of the sink and wash my face. I gurgle water trying to rid my mouth of puke taste. I haven't been this grossed out in a long time.

"I'll try not to take that personally," the stranger says from the door frame.

I turn on him, giving him the best glare I can. "Please do," I tell him.

"Oh, come on, Casslyn, my kissing isn't that bad. In fact I'm pretty sure you enjoyed yourself," he says, still leaning on the doorframe.

I ignore the fact that I did enjoy myself and try to move past him. He blocks my path.

"How do you know my name?" I ask, focusing on the other thing he said.

He leans in. I back away. I know I should be nervous, scared for my life even, but I'm not getting a threatening vibe off him. Plus, I still don't think a griffin would dare attack me in a house full of this many people. Unless. An extremely frightening thought occurs to me. What if the whole house is filled with griffins? No. There can't be that many of them.

"Who doesn't know you, Casslyn? You're the phoenix with the dead brother, the boyfriend who's her father's trained lap dog, whose powers are messed up, and who just won't die." His eyes turn dark, causing me to swallow hard. Maybe I should be nervous. Then he laughs. "I'm kidding. It's a party. Let's drink and forget who we are."

"Like that's going to happen." Again I glare at him and try to move past him. To no avail.

"What if I promise not to kiss you again?" he asks, throwing up his arms.

"I'm pretty sure I'd rather you didn't kill me."

"Why would you think I'm going to kill you? I just made out with you," he cocks an eyebrow at me like he's really confused.

"You happen to be my enemy. You made out with me to trick me into trusting you or something so you could lure me into a trap. And you just threatened me."

"I did no such thing. And enemy? You don't really think

all griffins are out to get you do you?"

"I've been attacked by your people enough to say a big yes to that."

He crowds me into the bathroom and closes the door behind him. He turns the lock and stalks towards me.

I back away until I'm trapped in between the toilet and the tub. My pulse quickens. My head pounds. This guy wouldn't really kill me in a bathroom would he? Would I really let him attack me without first defending myself? Is Logan really not going to burst through the door and save me?

The guy looms over me, placing one hand on either side of my head, caging me in. My head swims with thoughts. I wonder if I screamed out if anyone would hear me. I try to remember the things Logan taught me about fighting back. I wonder if Tucker will come looking for me.

I shudder when his face is inches from mine.

"Casslyn," the guy whispers into my ear.

I close my eyes and flashes of the griffins attacking me assaults my mind. I don't want to be attacked again. I don't want to be defenseless.

I'm not defenseless.

I turn to this stranger, anger in my eyes, hate in my heart, and shove him off me. He flies across the room and slams into the mirror above the sink. I make for the door but he catches my wrist before I can unlock the door.

I scream out but he clamps his hand over my mouth.

I struggle against his hold but he's strong.

I won't go down like this. Not again.

"Casslyn," he whispers into my ear. "I'm not going to hurt you. I promise."

I'm shaking in his hold. He's lying. He's just like the rest of them.

"I. Am not. Going. To hurt you," he says, his hold on me loosening with every clipped word. "I'm going to let you go. I would really like it if you would let me explain and not run away. Okay?"

I nod my head sure that as soon as he lets go I'm bolting for the door.

But then he lets go.

And I stay in the bathroom with him.

"Explain," I tell him, putting as much distance between us as I can in the small bathroom.

"I am a griffin," he says. When I give him the no-duh look he continues, "I'm not like the rest of them. I don't hunt phoenixes. I don't attack innocent girls. I don't believe in the ancient feud between our races."

With my arms crossed I glare at him and say, "I don't believe you. Why would you trick me into kissing you when you knew I would find out what you are?"

"Is it too much to believe I just wanted to kiss you?" I cock an eyebrow at him and he says, "I knew you would run the other way as soon as you knew I was a griffin."

"If you don't believe in our feud and aren't out to get me, then how do you know who I am?"

"Please," he scoffs. "Just because I'm not a part of the mortal feud, doesn't mean I'm stupid. I like to keep informed. Ignorance is not always bliss."

My body jerks when there is a knock at the door.

"I don't suppose there's any chance you might want to go somewhere and talk?" he asks, tilting his head to one side.

Despite knowing he is a griffin there is a part of me that still finds him attractive. I also admire the fact that despite knowing I'm his mortal enemy and the fact that there are other griffins in this house, he had the gall to not only flirt with me but kiss me too.

"No. I don't trust you. I don't trust any of you. I've been attacked too many times to fall for anything any one of you could pull. And I don't know you. So, no. Have fun with the rest of the party," I tell him while unlocking the bathroom door.

"I'm Cohen," he tells me as I pull the door open.

I turn back to him before I leave. He smiles at me, a smile that nearly changes my mind, then he shrugs his shoulders.

"I'll see you around, Casslyn."

I don't respond to him as I walk out the door and close it behind me.

I traipse down the stairs, find a cup of liquor in the kitchen and down it. Moving around the house I'm careful to avoid Xander, who has a girl draped over him, Ashley, who is sucking face with Colt, and any other griffin I might run into. I find Tucker in the middle of the dance floor and inform him we need to go. He doesn't even question me, just follows me out of the house.

I can still feel Cohen's lips on mine. There's a trace of his skin on mine.

I wanted to start getting over Logan, but not like this.

Seven

I wake up dizzy and upside down, my head throbbing. My arms, which are above my head, are asleep and have no feeling when I pinch my fingers together.

I turn my head to the side. It spins, angry at the movement. Tucker is in the same position I woke up in, upside down. I try to look up without my head pounding. My legs hang over the top of my couch. My middle resting on the cushion. I'm not sure what the hell happened. I'm not sure how we got to my house after the party. And I'm not sure how to get out of this position.

Lifting my head up, I try to pull my top half back onto the couch. That doesn't work. My sleeping hands won't grab onto the cushion of the couch. And my alcohol addled brain sloshes in my head making me dizzy. I swing my feet to the side to at least get them on the cushions of the couch, but momentum makes them swing all the way back and my body tumbles over itself onto the floor. A whimper escapes me, my entire body protesting everything I've put it through. This might be worse than waking up from being captured by the griffins.

The commotion wakes Tucker, who's so surprised he ends up somersaulting over himself and lands beside me. He groans, his body folded up, holding his head.

"What happened?" he asks, his voice groggy and pained.

"No more parties," I tell him, trying to move off the floor. When my body protests, I continue to lie there.

"Agreed," he says, still curled up. "I need coffee."

"Agreed."

"Cass?" Tucker asks, his head popped out from his bubble.

"Yeah?"

"How did we get to your house?"

I laugh but stop instantly when my head throbs. "I don't know."

"Do you think Logan brought us here?"

"I don't think Logan knows we went to that party. There were a few griffins there. He would have dragged me out of there in a second."

"How do you know there were griffins there?"

"Xander, Ashely, and Colt were there. They were all also there when I was captured."

"Got it." Tucker sits up on the floor. He sways slightly.

"Coffee. Need. I."

I raise an eyebrow at his backwards sentence then head upstairs to take a shower. There is no coffee in my house and there is no way I'm going into town looking like the mess I woke up in.

When I'm freshly showered and in new clothes, the ones from the party went straight in the trash, I find Tucker still on the floor, his eyes still glassy. When I call his name the first time he doesn't respond. When I yell it, he jolts, coming to attention, and I realize he fell asleep sitting up, with his eyes open.

We walk out of my house and spot my car. It's then that I remember Tucker picked me up to go shopping yesterday.

"We walked here?" Tucker asks. His mouth hangs open, his eyes wide.

"It appears so."

"No wonder my legs hurt.," Tucker says, rubbing his head. "Did you carry me? I think I remember you carrying me."

A flash of last night hits me. Yes, I carried Tucker. For miles.

"How strong are you?" he asks, almost aghast at the thought.

"I need coffee, Tucker. Get in the car."

"But seriously," he says, walking to the car. "How strong are you?"

"I carried you over five miles. Does that answer it?"

"No need to get snippy. I'm merely curious. You tell a

guy you're a mythological creature and don't expect him to be mildly curious? Seriously?"

"Alright. Sorry. I'm not sure how strong I am. I've never really tested it. Logan is much stronger than I am. He kicks my ass every time we spar."

"And I bet he looks amazing doing it."

My heart lurches not only at the mention of Logan's name but at how good he looks. There's a pang in my chest where my feelings for Logan sit. I miss seeing his face every day. I miss hearing that deep baritone of his voice. I miss making him laugh and seeing his wide, beautiful smile knowing that I was responsible for it.

"Sorry," Tucker says, noting his mistake.

"It's okay. I'm going to have to get over it. It's just going to take some time."

"Now that I actually know everything you two have been through, holy crap, you guys had one epic romance."

"One that is now over," I remind him.

"Oh, please. That boy loves you. Once he comes to his senses he'll be crawling back to you."

"From your mouth to God's ears, Tucker."

We pull up to the coffee shop and head inside. A few months ago this wasn't here and I thank the stars every morning the owners decided to open it. Especially mornings like these.

Tucker and I place our orders then sit down at a table to unwind and caffeinate. I'm hoping the caffeine and sugar will help with my splitting headache.

"Are you going to tell me about that guy from last night?" Tucker asks, breaking the coffee silence.

"What guy?" I ask. Not sure what he's talking about.

"How drunk were you? You don't remember talking to that guy in the kitchen?"

"I talked to some guy last night?" Why do I not remember this so called guy?

"About six foot. Shaggy blonde hair. You ran to the bathroom after you kissed him," Tucker says, spouting off a list of things that might jog my memory.

I nearly spit out my coffee and end up swallowing it down the wrong hole when the images of last night hit me.

"Oh my God, how drunk was I? I made out with a griffin."

Tucker lets out a surprised laugh and opens his mouth like he can't decide whether to smile or be shocked.

"Wait, how do you know he was a griffin?"

"When I kissed him I could hear, practically feel his hearts beat."

"You meant heart beats."

"No. I mean hearts beat. He's got two of them. Just like Xander."

"Xander has two hearts?"

"Yes," I say slowly. "All griffins do."

"Man. I really need to read up on mythology."

I lean back in the chair and think about what I did last night. As long as I can remember after I'd done something bad my parents would send me to my room to think about what I'd done but I never did. I get it now. I willingly kissed an enemy and I liked it. What is wrong with me? How could I have kissed someone so soon after Logan broke up with me? I'm still not over him and yet I kissed another guy. I feel sick. My coffee no longer tastes so good.

"So that's why you threw up?"

"What do you mean?"

"When you kissed him and found out he was a griffin. That's why you threw up?"

"Oh. Yeah," I tell him. Just now remembering that re-markably attractive event. "And he followed me," I say, slamming my head down on the table.

"Were you in trouble last night? Could he have hurt you?" Tucker asks, now worried.

"He sure could have. But he told me he's not a part of all that."

"And you believed him?"

"Not for a second."

I tip up my coffee cup to take another drink and nearly spit it out again when Logan walks through the door. Tucker turns toward the door to see who I'm gawking at and nearly laughs again.

"Rough morning, Cass," Tucker says with a smile.

"Shut up," I tell him then turn to Logan. "What are you doing here?"

"Are you telling me I'm not allowed to get a cup of cof-fee in the town I live?" Logan asks me a smirk covering his face.

"Not when getting said coffee involves following me," I tell him.

"Who says I'm following you? But if I was, why don't you tell me how you got to your house last night when you were at Tuckers?"

"It's none of your business," I say as Tucker opens his big, fat mouth and says, "We went to a party."

I turn to Tucker with large eyes that say why-would-you-tell-him-that.

He shrugs and says, "Sorry. His hotness pulled it right out of me."

Logan smirks but turns on me with a look that promises trouble. "Mind telling me why you went to a party last night, when you know you are in danger, and didn't mention it to me?"

"I would mind. Thank you for asking."

"Casslyn," Logan says, using his I-mean-business tone.

"What? Is it my fault you couldn't keep track of me?" I ask, my voice sugar sweet.

"Don't start with me."

"Diddo, pal."

Logan's jaw is throbbing. He rolls his shoulders back. I grin knowing I've gotten to him. What he doesn't know is how much he's getting to me. Just being in his vicinity is enough to undo me. I love arguing with him. But what I really want to do is claim his mouth with mine, pull him body to mine, warmth spreading between us.

"Hey," Tucker says, breaking the tension. "Why don't

you get a cup of coffee and join us?"

I turn my glare on him trying to mentally burn him. Logan on the other hand says, "I will. Thank you for the invitation, Tucker."

"What were you thinking?" I ask him when Logan is at the counter.

"I was thinking," Tucker says, leaning into the table, "Logan would sit with us and remember he loves you and you two would get back together."

"I appreciate the gesture but I doubt that will happen."

"As I was saying," Logan says when he gets back to the table. He sets his cup on the table then sits his big frame onto the chair that now looks small. "What were you thinking? The griffins could come after you anywhere at any moment. And you think going to a party and getting drunk was the way to not put yourself in danger."

"I don't know, Logan. Maybe I needed one night of normalcy. One night to forget what I am. To forget that I have mortal enemies who would like nothing more than to murder me. To forget that my boyfriend, the guy I thought was in love with me, broke up with me. Is. That. Okay. With you?" I ask, using a yelling whisper.

I don't allow him to answer before I get up from the table and head for the bathroom at the back of the shop. I close the door behind me and lock it, knowing there is a chance Logan could come after me. It's not like he hasn't done it before. I don't need to pee but I do need to get away from him. I stare in the mirror. And stare. And stare. Thoughts protrude my brain. I hadn't had time to think about what I'd done with that griffin guy last night when Logan walked in and bombarded me with a whole new set of thoughts. Why couldn't he have watched me from outside? Doesn't he know that it hurts to see him, to be near him, when he is no longer mine? Plus, since when was it his business if Tucker and I hung out at a party? I lived perfectly fine for sixteen years before Logan came into my life. Just because the griffins now know I'm a phoenix doesn't mean they would attack me in public. And last night proves that, so he can just take a chill pill. I want to say all of that to him, but I know I won't. I may be able to be a smart mouth to him, but that doesn't mean I always say everything I want to.

After staring at myself for long enough, after arguing with myself for long enough, I decide to head back out to the table. The air in the shop has turned warm and still. I look toward the table where Tucker looks as though nothing is out of the ordinary. But Logan is rigid. His face is contorted. He's listening for every sound, every movement. I'm scared for a second, wondering if we're under attack. That's when I notice the guy at the counter. The griffin from last night. The griffin I kissed.

"For the love of all things holy," I say through a deep breath. "Could this morning get any worse?"

I move around the side of the shop hoping the guy won't see me. If I can make it to the table without him seeing me I should be fine and I can tell Logan he doesn't have to be so freaked out. I take quiet steps, trying to be lithe as a cat. I listen to the sounds in the shop, the movements.

I stub my toe on a chair when the guy says, "Hey, Cass-lyn"

Logan's chair scrapes back on the floor when the griffin announces he knows me.

Crap. I am going to pay for this.

I've got two options. I could go talk to him and hope he leaves. Or I could ignore him and hope he leaves. Neither one of them is the greatest option. Neither one of them is going to be pleasing to Logan. But I really don't want the guy to come to the table if I ignore him. I don't want a fight in the coffee shop I've come to love.

So, I bite the bullet, hoping Logan will let me handle this.

"Hey," I say to him, because I don't remember his name.

"It's Cohen," he says, a smile playing at his lips. Lips I kissed. They look just as appealing in this light as they did last night.

I shake off that thought, knowing the guy I love is a few feet away.

"Right," I say. "Sorry. I had a lot to drink. It was a crazy night."

"Yeah it was. Though if you recall I warned you not to drink liquor after beer."

"That you did," I say to him. Noncommittal. I know Logan is listening. Maybe if I'm not too friendly with this guy Logan won't be so pissed at me.

"You know," Cohen says, leaning into me. "That was

some kiss last night. I'll have to make it up to you."

I cringe and close my eyes. When I open them Cohen is smiling like a thief. He knows Logan's a phoenix. He knows Logan's my ex. He knows Logan is listening.

Logan is suddenly at my side.

"Who are you?" he asks, he's standing straight, making himself as tall as he can, his arms crossed over his chest. He's at least downgraded Cohen from a threat to a nuisance.

"Hi, I'm Cohen," Cohen says to Logan extending his arm for a handshake.

Logan raises an eyebrow but doesn't shake his hand.

This does not deter Cohen. He continues, "I'm a friend of Casslyn's. We met at the party last night."

"That doesn't make you friends."

I can see Cohen's mind churning. Deciding whether or not to mess with Logan. I guess he wants to, because he says, "I think making out make us friends." He smiles big and proud like he didn't just ruin me.

I place my head in my hands and wish to be buried alive right now. If I'd ever thought there was a chance of Logan and I getting back together Cohen just shot it in the foot. He didn't just shoot. He took aim, he anticipated the wind, he used a scope and then he shot it, with a smile on his face.

The barista watches us from behind the counter. I wish he would go to the back and ignore our conversation. He's got a look on his face like he's reaching for the telephone, like he might call the cops. I look at him and smile, trying to diffuse his tension. He nods at me like you-better-have-this-under-control. Again I smile at him until he walks to the back.

"What did you just say to me?" Logan asks, on the verge of having a breakdown.

"Oh, are you her boyfriend?" Cohen asks, so innocently. "She didn't mention a boyfriend last night. Not before she kissed me, or after."

Logan's body shakes. He's mad. More mad than I've ever seen him. Cohen may say he's not here to hurt me but that could merely be entirely physical. He's hurting me as he speaks.

"Ok. That's enough," I say, grabbing Logan's arm. He's solid as a rock, rooted into place. "Come on, Logan. Let's go back to Tucker."

"Speaking of me," Tucker says, now beside me.

His presence seems to thaw out Logan who glances in Tucker's direction, though not taking his eyes completely off Cohen.

"I saw you with Casslyn last night," Tucker says, his tone not unkind.

"Yeah. I'm Cohen," Cohen says, extending his hand.

Tucker takes it, shakes it, and says, "Tucker, Casslyn's best friend."

Tucker keeps hold of Cohen's hand, looking him up and down, sizing him up. Tucker may be the weakest of the three of us, but his heart is not.

"It's nice to meet you."

"Yeah," Tucker says, unsure of how to take Cohen. He

knows Cohen is a griffin and he can see Logan seething, but he has a right to make his own decision regarding him. "Are you new to town?"

"Yeah. I've been here a few days. I haven't met many people so it's nice to meet you and Casslyn."

I don't think Cohen is aware that Tucker knows about griffins and phoenixes so he's trying to decide how to play the situation.

"Are you going to be going to school?" Tucker asks him.

"Actually I attended a private school before coming here. I graduated last year."

"You're not in college?" Tucker asks, their conversation becoming an interrogation.

"I'm taking a bit of time off. I wasn't sure what I wanted to do with my life so I didn't want to waste time and money in school."

"What brought you to town?"

"I've got some family here."

"Anyone we'd know?"

"I doubt it," Cohen says, sliding right past that question. He knows how small this town is. He knows we will know his family.

"I really think we should get going," I say.

Logan is still shaking from anger beside me and Cohen is about two questions away from realizing Tucker is fishing for information if he hasn't already.

"I'll see you around," Cohen says to no one in particular but he is looking straight at me.

I pull Logan away without answering Cohen. Tucker follows after lingering behind for a beat.

"I don't know about that guy," Tucker says once we've returned to the table.

I take a sip of my coffee, nearly gagging on it because it's turned cold.

"Yeah, me either," I tell him. "He seems harmless enough."

"He's hot," Tucker says, raising one shoulder.

"I'm glad you measure everyone on a hotness scale."

"Beautiful people make the world go round," he says, smiling like he actually believes that.

Logan is silent. I'm not sure he can even hear us. I don't know how he feels that I kissed another guy. Probably how I would feel if he kissed another girl. I shouldn't feel as terrible as I do because he broke up with me, but I still love him, I shouldn't be kissing another guy. I feel like I betrayed him. I gaze at him wondering what he could be thinking. He refuses to look at me, instead choosing to stare at the table.

I glance at Tucker and nod my head toward the door, indicating that we should leave. He agrees and gets up from his chair. I take my cup off the table, throw it in the trash and make it to the door before Logan has his hand around my arm.

"I don't want you seeing that guy again," he tells me.

"It's not like I sought him out today. He showed up after I was here. What was I supposed to do, leave?"

"You could have."

"Look, he told me last night that he's not even a part of the griffins. He doesn't want anything to do with their crusade."

"And you believed him?"

"No. I was just telling you what he said."

"I know Xander had feelings for you before he knew you were a phoenix, but we *do not* have relationships with griffins, Casslyn."

"Excuse me, but I didn't know he was a griffin when I kissed him. And I threw up after the kiss, so back off."

Logan winces every time I say the word kiss. I'm tempted to say it five more times just to cause him pain. But I can't bring myself to do it.

"I forbid you to see him again"

"Look, Logan. I get that you have to protect me on order of my father. But you can lay off. I never asked you to protect me. And in case you forgot, you broke up with me. You don't get to tell me what to do."

I look at him with every ounce of defiance I can muster then turn away from him and walk out the door to meet Tucker.

I've never been good at being told what to do. Being told to stay away from Cohen makes me want to find him. Besides being a griffin, scaring the shit out of me last night, and getting under Logan's skin, I didn't see much wrong with Cohen. He's got attitude and an edge to him, but I find his sureness refreshing. Besides what he did to Logan, he doesn't seem vicious.

No. He is a griffin. He can't be good. There has to be a reason he is interested in me other than the fact that he is merely interested in me. I've been attacked by enough griffins to know they can't be trusted. This has to be a trap. One I cannot get caught in.

Tucker sits in the car with me and doesn't say a word. He's letting me work through everything that just happened. He knows when I'm ready I'll talk to him. That's how we work. He doesn't push me because he knows eventually I will come to him. The one exception being Xander and I lying to him about what we are and why we were fighting.

I start the car and pull away from the curb when I see Logan walk out of the coffee shop. I'm not about to get into it with him again. I want to get back together with Logan but until the time that he wants to get back together with me, it is hard to be in his presence. All of the feelings I've ever had for him are still inside me. All of the things I've ever wanted to do with him are still there. I still remember every tender moment we have shared. I'm not sure how Logan can be so okay with not being together when it is stealing the breath from my chest.

***

When I've dropped Tucker off at his house and returned to mine I notice my mom is home. I feel like I haven't seen her in years rather than days. I walk in the door wanting to ask her to have a girls night. Maybe watch a movie, order a pizza, do our nails. But what I walk into is my mom and my father. I stop dead in my tracks, one foot in front of the other.

"Your father is here to see you," she says.

The relationship with my mom and father has been weird since he returned to town. My mom and dad have been working on their relationship. I swear they could get back together. Then my father shows up and threatens to ruin all of their progress. So far he has only been interested in me and spends little time with my mom, but when they are together there is a tension between them I'm not so sure is bad.

"What do you want?" I ask him, though not as rude as I'd like. It's hard work being mean all the time.

"I'd like to discuss something with you," he says and gives me the bug eyes as though to say phoenix-related-top-ics-will-be-discussed-and-your-mom-needs-to-leave-the-room.

"Hey, mom," I say turning to her. "I was wondering if you wanted to have a girls night. We could watch our favorite old movies. Order pizza. Make air popper popcorn. What do you think?"

"Sure honey. That would be lovely. We haven't spent much time together lately. Though I don't have the things to make popcorn."

I make a disappointed sound and say, "I was really hoping for air popper popcorn. Is there any chance you could go to the store and get the stuff to make it?"

"Sure, Cass. I'll go now."

"Thanks, mom."

When my mom has left to get groceries I turn to my father and raise my eyebrows waiting for him to speak.

"A group of our people is on their way here. The griffin population is worse than I thought in this town and I'd like back up in case anything like your capturing happens again. The group is also eager to meet you, their future leader."

"Great."

"Casslyn, it is my wish that you could be at least cordial to me when they are here. I know you have hang ups about me and our relationship but I at least would like to work on them."

"I'll be cordial," I say, not relenting to working on our relationship. I'm not ready for that. Not even after the four months he's been here. Not after he forced Logan to break up with me.

"Thank you. Logan will inform you when they arrive. I trust your training with him is going well?"

"Not so much. I haven't trained since my capture."

He opens his mouth to yell at me, to tell me I need to be training, but he closes it. He knows I'll yell back.

Thing is, I know I need to be training. I had hope Xander would train with me, but he turned me down. I don't necessarily want to train with Logan, but he's the best and really he's my only option.

"I'll talk to Logan about it. Maybe start again Monday after school."

My father stares at me, actually stares at me, like he can't believe I agreed to something he told me.

"Thank you, Casslyn."

I nod, not willing to say anything further.

He nods and walks out the door.

It's not so bad to not fight with him, though I'll never admit that to him. I still have abandonment issues. I've still got a lot of issues with him. Now is not the time to get over them.

Eight

My elbow slams into Logan's rib cage. He's stunned enough to loosen his grip on me. I spin on him, curl a leg around one of his, and pull. He falls to his back with a heavy thud. I stare down at him for a heartbeat more than I should then walk away.

I feel his stare on my back as I take a drink from my water bottle. I swipe a stray drop of water from the corner of my mouth and walk back to him. Logan has stood back up by the time I get back into fighting stance.

"That was good, Casslyn. You were able to adapt to the fight and take charge."

I give no reply before I lunge for him. He knows which way I'm going to strike. I know he knows. He's ready for me to strike to his right, my dominant side, so I switch sides mid attack and aim for his left. It is a weaker assault but it gets the job done. He's not expecting me to switch sides. He's gotten lazy in his defense, exactly what he's been teaching me not to do. I hit his rib cage with my elbow, grab his arm with my other hand, pull it behind his back, then swing his legs out from under him with my foot. He recovers quickly. I'm getting quicker. I'm getting stronger. I'm getting smarter. But Logan has been at this for years and years more than I have. He's faster. He's smarter. And he's got brute strength I'll never be able to match.

"Don't be afraid to use your power," he tells me.

When Logan and I began training a few months ago I wasn't a full-fledged phoenix. But I've since aged and come into my power. My skin tingles as the power builds in me. My veins spark as fire courses through them. My body is alive with untapped energy.

A sinister smile creeps onto my lips as fire erupts from my hand. My eyes narrow as I place a single finger to Logan's chest. His shirt ignites, the fire spreading. Soon his shirt is ashes on the mat, his skin untouched by the flame.

He stands in front of me, his chest heaving from something other than our workout. The feeling hits home and it's too much to be near him.

Backing away from his shirtless form I crouch down into my stance, both of my hands alight and dare him to attack me. The flame feels good as it licks my skin. I don't dare let it move across or down my body, at least not until I invest in flame retardant underwear. Logan's hands ignite like mine. Only, unlike mine, his blaze is far more deadly, bigger, stronger, hotter. No phoenix can be burned by the fire of another. He is showing off. He is teaching me a lesson. What a good teacher he is. It's really too bad he didn't take being a boyfriend as seriously as teaching me to be a phoenix. He would have been perfect.

I take his attack head on, ducking in time to miss his outstretched hands. I move in time to place my flickering hands onto his chest, pushing him backward. His hands find purchase around my arms, knocking them from place. I spin around to take him on from the back. He'll know it's coming but I might be quick enough to catch him off guard. But there's no chance of that, Logan is never off his guard. He spins faster than I can see him and hits me square in the gut. I take the hit hard and fall back on my butt, the wind escaping my lungs. I pound the mat with my palm and jerk into a standing position.

I'm never going to get any better. I can't ever surprise Logan. I can't ever get the upper hand on him. I'm thankful he never lets me win, that would ruin every effort I've made, but just once I'd like to beat him.

"Don't get discouraged," he tells me. "You're making progress."

I stare into his eyes. His encouragement is uplifting, but it's not what I want to hear.

I let the flames dancing on my fingertips go out. Looking at Logan is both empowering and soul crushing. Especially when all I want to do is crush my lips to his.

There are so many things I'd like to say to him. So many things I want to yell at him for. But I can't find the words. I can't find the strength to open my mouth and tell him everything I'm feeling. He's not the person I can turn to anymore. He took that away from me and I'm angry with him for it.

I pull air into my lungs, hold it there until it becomes painful, then push it out through my mouth. Turning away from Logan I make my way to the treadmill and turn it up until I'm running.

Logan is still standing in the middle of the basement. Right where I left him. He places his hands on his hips and throws his head back to stare at the ceiling. I turn my head away from him, needing a reprieve from his glistening, chiseled, shirtless torso.

My ears, however, stay attuned to him. I hear when he moves from his spot. I hear as he gulps down a drink of water. I hear him lift a free weight from the bench.

But even that is too much. Slipping my ear buds into each of my ears, I turn the volume on my Ipod up to an ear splitting degree. I close my eyes and focus on my breaths. In. Out. I feel every muscle in the feet move and glide as they step onto the treadmill. The fire in my veins ebbs and flows with the pumping of my arms. I breathe. In. Out. I need to find my center. I need to find my focus. In. Out.

When I open my eyes Logan is standing directly in front of me. His silent but immense presence is enough to make my miss a step, sending my sprawling onto the rotating belt of the treadmill. My head bangs on the belt, my body moving with its continued momentum. When my body hits the floor and the belt continues to move it scrapes the skin off my cheek.

Logan is to me in a flash, lifting me to my feet, moving me to the bench. He hands me my water bottle and a towel. Before I can bring the towel to my stinging cheek, I know it has started and stopped bleeding. I feel the fire rise in me, feel it move to my face, feel it about to heal me. Then, nothing. No fire. No flames touch my skin. My cheek does not heal. Well great. I can call upon my power to use the fire, but I can't use it to heal. Healing is a phoenixes greatest strength. Without it I may as well invite the griffins to kill me.

"Are you okay?" Logan asks. He doesn't apologize. I know he won't, but I also know he's sorry.

I don't answer him. I don't even nod my head. That would be answering him. For some reason I can't. Some part of me, some large part, has shut its-self off from Logan. A vital part.

"Are you going to give me the silent treatment forever?" he asks.

When I don't answer him I expect his shoulders to roll back around. I'm surprised when they don't. Maybe he expected this. Maybe he was waiting for it. He probably thinks I'm acting like a child. And maybe I am, but that's not what this is.

Being this close to him is heart breaking. Touching him, without being able to feel him is agony. Seeing that he is so clearly okay with us not being together is earth shattering.

I'm afraid that if I spoke to him, in any way, the last piece of me would fall from place and I'd be nothing. So I remain silent.

"Talk to me, Casslyn. Yell at me. You love yelling at me." Logan's hands move between us. I turn away before he will touch me. He pulls away. "I'd rather we were arguing that this silence."

A small smile plays at my lips. I do love yelling at him. But not today. Today I'm spent.

I stand up from the bench and move away from him. Logan stands too. I'm not sure whether or not he will follow me. I'm not sure whether or not I want him to.

I told my father I'd get back to training with Logan. I thought I could buck up, get over the fact that he broke my heart, and focus solely on my training. I was wrong.

I run up the stairs before I lose all my will power and turn back to him.

I run all the way home. I run up my stairs and into my bedroom. I run into the shower. Only there do I let myself relax. I take deep, calming breaths as the water courses down and around me. I want to cry. I want to let the sobs choking me rack my body. But I don't break down. I won't break down.

Once I'm out of the shower I stare at myself in the mirror. The belt burn on my cheek might just ruin my day. Stupid phoenix healing powers that don't work. Logan would have healed it with his tears if I asked him. But I'm already the ex-girlfriend who spends too much time with him. I'm not going to be the desperate ex-girlfriend who claims to need him just to get him back. I'm not even sure it would work.

There is no way to hide the hideous mark on my cheek. Makeup would just irritate it. I'm going to have to live with it. I've been the freak of our school enough times in the last year not to let this bother me.

I dress for school in an outfit that may just be as hideous as my cheek then step out the door ready to get this day over with.

The very first thing out of Tucker's mouth is, "Should I ask."

"No," I tell him, leveling him with my best this-day-sucks-and-it-hasn't-even-started look.

He shrugs his shoulders apologetically, plants a delicate kiss on my wounded cheek, links his arm with mine, then moves us down the hall. I'm thankful for his touch, for his comfort. I'm not sure what I'd do without it.

With Tucker's help I make it through the day as best as I can. Logan is here. I'm aware of his presence as only some-one who loves him could be. He could pass these classes with his eyes closed. Besides the fact that he has his diploma. It makes me wonder how many diplomas he has. I know he is here for me. If my father didn't think I needed a babysitter in a school full of griffins, Logan wouldn't be here.

It's not until the last period of the day that disaster strikes as it only could if your name is Casslyn.

Logan and I sit at our Home Ec station. We're each making omelets so not talking to him is fairly easy. Logan tries to hide his unease but it's there. I can feel it. Though he hasn't tried talking to me again.

I wish he hadn't destroyed what we had. Logan pushed me and made me stronger. He made me drive my car when I refused. He helped me see what really happened with the accident the night Nash died. He helped me uncover the real reason my parents split up. And he didn't let me break apart after learning both of those things. He held me up. He held me straighter. I don't want to regress. I don't want to lose ground because I lost him.

I just hope I can hold myself together until I can find strength of my own.

I'm lost in my thoughts when I feel warmth spreading from my fingers down my hands. I look down to see my hands are on fire. I quickly shove them under the table and look around the room to see if anyone has noticed. When I'm assured no one has, I look to my skillet to see if it is on fire. Perhaps my skillet started on fire and my hands caught. No such luck. My wonky powers are at it again.

By now I've got Logan's attention. He's giving me the are-you-insane look. I jerk my head in his direction hopefully indicating that I'm not doing this on purpose.

I look under the table to see that my hands are still alight. I clap them together to try and put them out. Unsurprisingly it doesn't work. I can't pat them on my pants for fear they'd light up too and I'd have to go home in my underwear.

I close my eyes to try to tap into my power to maybe

shut it off. It's only when I smell the wood of my work station burning that I panic.

This cannot be happening. And *why's it always me* run through my head.

I jerk a hand out from under the table to grab the oven mitts sitting atop it. I shove them over my hands and pray to any one listening they won't go up in flames. I breathe out a giant sigh of relief when I feel the temperature of my hands come down. I pull one out just to test and see that my hand has returned to normal.

Too bad my injured cheek wasn't paying attention.

But the situation is over.

Crisis averted.

Though not without a little panic on behalf of Logan and myself.

Nine

I got the text about an hour ago and have been pacing my bedroom floor ever since. The phoenixes have landed. My father's people are here. My people.

I try, to no avail, to convince myself that I shouldn't be nervous, that I have nothing to worry about. I'm not swayed.

Logan says I'll be fine, that they will accept me with open arms. I think he's full of it. The second I walk into that house those phoenixes are going to smell weakness on me. They will sense my failing powers. They will recognize my lack of enthusiasm at being one of them. I'm doomed from the get go.

I've got to get it over with.

I'd really like to go to Logan's before they show up. I can find a corner to hide in while I scope out the situation.

But what to wear.

What does one wear to something like this? I've never had to meet a race of people before. I'm not about to wear a dress. But are jeans too casual? Is leather too poser? Is a t-shirt too pedestrian? I've never had a problem with clothes before now. Is this just a meet and greet? Will they test me? Will I have to perform for them?

I take a deep breath and shake my head. I've faced the griffins three times now and lived to tell the tale. Meeting my own people should be a walk in the park.

I grab a pair of skinny jeans and a nice long sleeve shirt, pull it on, throw my hair into a ponytail and slip on some combat boots. This will have to do.

I drive to Logan's house not knowing what I'm about to get into. I might not have the energy to run home after the night is over.

I carefully tread into Logan's front door trying not to alert anyone to my presence. It is a useless maneuver but it's worth a shot.

"You're nervous," Logan says from the kitchen doorway. His hands are crossed over his chest. His expression is one of concern mixed with bafflement.

My heart leaps at him. Damn him for still making me react to him so intensely. I curse my body. And damn him for knowing me too well. He's taken himself out of my personal life but he still sees me too well. I hate it. There is no hiding anything from him.

When I don't readily answer him he says, "There is no

need. You will be fine."

I noncommittally nod my head at him then search out the place I will await my people.

Logan and I had words after the incident in home ec. Words, more like Logan yelling at me for half an hour while I remained silent, then I retreated home and cried. Having my powers scare the shit out of me in class was one thing. Feeling broken and inadequate another. But to have Logan yell at me for it, to shove it in my face was too much. The ground we were treading on was unstable before, now a chasm divides us so far I'm not sure we'll be able to cross it. I can't bring myself to speak to him.

And he knows it. He also knows he made a mistake by yelling at me. We were both worked up and scared someone would find out about me. But he reacted the wrong way. He knows it. He's sorry. But he's not about to admit to it. We're both stubborn. So stubborn it gets in our way.

He opens his mouth to say something but when I stare him down, daring him to do so, he closes his lips and walks to the kitchen. I reach into the house listening for my father. I know he's not living here with Logan, though I have no idea where he is living, but I should think he'd be here. Maybe he is bringing the phoenixes here.

My heart leaps into my throat when I hear tires crunch on the gravel outside. They are really here. I can't escape this. I'm about to meet people who probably know more about me than I know about them. Though that's not hard, considering I know nothing about them.

I focus my hearing outside trying to discern how many vehicles pull up outside Logan's house. Neither my father nor Logan would tell me how many phoenixes were coming to Cedars. Five would be nice. Five I could handle. But when at least six SUVs stop in front of the house, my gut plummets. There are far more than five phoenixes about to greet me. Feet after feet step onto the gravel. I lose count after fifteen sets of them.

My head throbs, my skull vibrating. I'm not ready for this. How could Logan and my father think I was up for this? I'm still recovering from being captured, mentally and physically, how could they think it was okay to subject me to this?

Suck it up and put on your big girl panties, I mentally chide myself.

I *can* do this.

My heart pounds as the feet near the front door. I'm barely aware as Logan opens it.

But then small arms wrap themselves around Logan's neck in an embrace so powerful I'm smacked upside the head with jealousy. It may not be that long since Logan broke up with me but the amount in which I miss his touch is unfathomable. It aches deep inside me, so deep it keeps me up at night.

The girl wrapped up in Logan's arms is skinny, tall, with long ass curly blonde hair and she looks like she's about twelve years old.

My stomach clenches into knots. I stare at them, my

eyebrows drawn down bringing my mouth into a frown.

I hate this girl who so freely gets to touch Logan without worrying he'll pull away. Who has captured his attention so fully he looks happy for the first time in weeks. A black cloud of envy swirls above me. Who does this girl think she is? Doesn't she know Logan is mine?

Not anymore, a little voice in my head reminds me. Bitch.

Logan carries the girl in his arms across the living room so more bodies can file through the door. I stand around the corner of the kitchen's wall, watching them enter. I'm not ready to face this. Especially if it continues the way it started. These are Logan's people. He may have been mine for a few months, but he is reunited with them and I don't belong. I feel more out of place than I ever have.

Two women follow the girl. They bypass Logan and the girl, carrying bags with them. They set their things on the couch and sit next to each other. They can't be more than twenty five. They look so at ease with each other they could be twins, if it weren't for the fact that one is blonde with cream colored skin and pink cheeks, while the other has dark curls and tanned skin. They are beautiful and yet fierce. I'm immediately intimidated.

My head snaps back when the next person walks through the door. It's a guy, around Logan's age. He wears tight acid wash jeans, a black leather jacket covering a concert tee. I can't make out his face behind large aviator sunglasses but the white Mohawk on top of his head is glaringly obvious.

After him walks in maybe the most gorgeous woman I've seen in all my life, magazines and movies included. Her chestnut hair is flawless and hangs perfectly around her heart shaped face. Honestly who actually has a heart shaped face? Her eyes are blue and nearly as piercing as Logan's. She's lean but perfectly built. I glace down at my boobs and do a quick comparison. I've got nothing on her. Her skinny jeans put mine to shame they hug her thighs so tight. The cherry on top of an insanely jealousy inducing cake, the thing that rips my heart from my chest, is when she marches up to Logan, places her arms around his neck and plants her plump lips to his.

This is all too much. I cower around the corner and wait for the rest of them to file through the door. For Logan to realize I'm missing and come find me. I keep my ears peeled to the steps placed through the door. There has got to be at least thirty people here. How am I going to face all of them? How am I supposed to remember all their names? How am I supposed to remove from my brain the earth shattering image of another girl kissing Logan when not weeks ago it was my lips on his.

Did he love me at all? Has he been with this girl the entire time he's been in Cedars? Has he been using me because he misses her? Did he break up with me knowing she would be back in his life in a few weeks? He let her kiss him. He's never let me get away with any sneak attack, he's too quick. And it's not like he pushed her away.

I'm going to be sick.

I double over and clutch my stomach, nausea rolling like waves.

I gave Logan my heart and he pretty much ripped it from my chest, stomped on it, then kicked it into the mud. There it lays shriveled and cold and broken. The gaping hole in my chest oozes and festers, rank and mangled.

Pull yourself together, Cassie, Nash's voice runs through my head.

"Nash?" I can't help but call out.

I close my eyes and try to call him to me. He's not there. He's not here.

I wish so desperately that he could be here with me right now. Here to meet the phoenixes. Here to guide me through this. Just here with me. The wound from his absence has since rotted and infected my soul. I've been told time heals. Time also leads to decay.

"Hey," a new voice says.

When my eyes focus I have to jump back. The first girl to embrace Logan stands but an inch in front of me.

A large smile spreads across her child like face. She's even got a freaking button nose. This girl is twelve times cuter than I am. No wonder Logan is enthralled by her. I'm not sure how I convinced myself Logan might actually love me.

I stare at the girl. I still hate her for getting to be held in Logan's arms. But at the same time, I'm supposed to be making a good impression on these people. I can't screw that up with the first one of them I meet.

"Hello," I say slowly.

The girl lunges forward and pulls me into her with more force than her dainty body might indicate. She begins talking before she pulls away from the hug. "You're Casslyn, right? You must be Casslyn. I'm Aspen."

When my face gives her no indication I know who she is she says, "I'm Logan's sister."

My hatred for her runs clean out of my body. Of course she and Logan were embracing. They are siblings. And from the little Logan has told me about her, it sounds as if they are close. Really that's all I know about her. It's yet another reason to question my relationship with Logan. Question it in ways I never did before.

"Oh, hi," I say. I try to modify my voice to hide the wavering. I don't think it works. "It's nice to meet you."

"You have no idea," Aspen says. "Logan has told me so much about you. I feel like I know you already."

I want to say you too, even though it would be a huge lie, but what really catches my attention is, "Logan talks about me?"

"Oh, all the time," she says. She leans in even closer to me and whispers, "Don't tell him I told you so. He'd pummel me. I'm so looking forward to hanging out with you."

Without my permission my eyebrow cocks straight up into the air. I say, "Did he tell you. . . "

"That you broke up? Yeah. I think he's stupid. I told him so."

A small smile splits across my lips, chipping away at the scowl nearly permanently affixed there.

"Thanks," I tell her.

"No problem. So why are you hiding here?"

"I'm a bit nervous," I admit.

"Well, come on," Aspen says. She wraps her tiny arm around my shoulders and pulls me away from the wall and around the corner. "Look who I found," she says.

I pull my head up to see a room full of people staring me down. I have to turn away when I spot the beautiful bitch hanging off of Logan. There is history there. I can see it in the way she looks at him. How could I have been so blind?

There are men and women circling the room of varying ages. As varied as phoenixes with the life span of seventeen years can get. There is no one over the age of thirty five in the room. Well, body age. I know for a fact Logan is far older than thirty five and there's no telling how old my father truly is. Some of the people in this room could be older than my father. I wouldn't be able to tell by looking at their faces.

I spot the two women who found their way right to the couch. I spot the Mohawk guy. Besides Logan's ornament and Aspen I didn't see anyone else walk through the door. When I say they are staring at me, I mean their eyes bore deep into me searching my depths for my soul. My cheeks are immediately tomato red. Sweat beads down my spine. I'm well aware the entire room can hear my racing heartbeat. It's rather disconcerting to have an entire room full of people so aware that you are nervous. I bet they can even smell it on me.

Aspen keeps her arm around my shoulders. I couldn't

begin to express to her how comforting it is, how thankful I am that it is there. Her embrace calms me, steadies me, gives me strength. I've known her for mere minutes, but just like her big brother, Aspen pushes me into something she knows I can make it through. I've known her such a short time and already she cares about me. She doesn't know me and yet champions my relationship with Logan. I have a feeling Aspen and I are going to get along spectacularly.

I quickly begin to see, as the faces of the phoenixes surrounding me shift, their postures change. I swallow hard when I notice disdain, their response to me lackluster. These people do not like me, it is written in their furrowed eyebrows, their crossed arms, their stiff backs. Logan assured me they would accept me with open arms, I knew he was wrong. Just because I'm the daughter of their leader doesn't guarantee their adoration. If anything they should judge me more harshly because I'm the daughter of their superior.

And that they do.

"She's too skinny," one of them says, the first to break the silence.

"She looks weak," another voices their opinion.

"She doesn't want to be one of us. I can sense it," someone in the back pipes up.

My body jerks with every comment, like a blow from Logan's fist. They may all be right, but hearing and knowing are two entirely different things.

My father stays next to the examining group members. Logan, on the other hand, breaks away from the bimbo to stand by my side.

"You're doing fine," he tells me.

I look at him, incredulous, and raise both my eyebrows.

"You're an idiot," Aspen tells him.

He gazes down at his sister, a look of discomfort clouding his face.

"Why should we trust her? She knows nothing of our ways. She knows nothing of what it means to be one of us," another phoenix says.

The walls close in on me bringing the penetrating gaze of my peers right upon me. Their eyes probe and pry into me. They are intrusive, laying my every fault before me.

"Aris, we've all heard about her griffin friend. Who's to say she hasn't betrayed us already?" yet another jury member ready to execute without evidence.

I feel naked and laid bare.

My father stands by his people unwilling to defend his own daughter. Logan stands beside me but voices no objections. I'm not sure if this is how this race works, but it's not to my liking.

"Am I just supposed to take this?" I ask Logan.

His head jerks towards me, his eyes wide. I'm sure he's reacting more to the fact these are the first words I've spoken to him in weeks, rather than my question.

I ask again, "Am I just supposed to let them judge me when they know nothing about me?" I know they can all hear me. I don't care. If they can all spit out their disdain for me, to me, I can do the same.

"It is our way," he says.

"It's not my way," I snap at him, keeping my voice low. Ok, so I know they can hear me, but I don't want to antagonize them.

"Perhaps that is what they are picking up on, why they judge you so harshly," he says, crossing his arms to keep from rolling them back.

His allegiance lies with my father, with his people, before me. I should understand that, but it doesn't keep the sting from my eyes, from my heart.

"Can I at least explain myself? Have you and my father not explained to them that I've only known what I am for a few months?"

"Yeah, Logan, have you?" Aspen asks.

I would appreciate her coming to my aid more if this wasn't such a precarious situation.

"They are aware. But they don't think it matters." When my mouth falls open he says, "Not all of them feel this way."

"Let me fight. Let me challenge one of them," I say, pleading with me.

"You will lose," he says this so steadfastly I take immediate offense. His lack of faith in me is jarring and hurtful.

Anger wells up inside me. Thirty against one. I've never felt so isolated. As if the entire world were against me. "At least I will be defending myself. That's more than I can say for you, or for my father."

"They will come around. Eventually," Logan states.

"Kiss my ass, Logan. What happened to always being

here for me?"

His mouth falls open then snaps shut. Anger flashes over his face, then disappears.

"Was that a lie too? Just like your love for me?" I ask, venom pulsing through my heart.

He opens his mouth to defend himself when my father finally speaks up.

I'm ready for him to tell them they are right. I'm ready for him to throw me to the griffins. But instead he says, "Casslyn was raised as a human. She was unaware of what she was, what she would become. She was also unaware of the identity of her friend. This friend may be a griffin, but he also went against his own people to save the life of one of us. His loyalties lie closer to my daughter, his one true enemy, than with his own people. That has to count for something. Casslyn may be new, she may not know enough yet, but she has been training as much as she can. I have seen vast progress from her, extreme dedication and determination and a will as strong as any of yours. She has been beaten, captured, and nearly killed more times than most of us can attest to and yet she is still here. I have not heard her complain once. She grows stronger. She grows more powerful. She is my daughter and I will stand for her. Does anyone else have any questions?"

I stand with my mouth agape. I'm aware of it and I'm not about to fix it. There is no way all of that came out of the mouth of the man I've spent little to no time with. The man who abandoned me and my brother only to return when I became useful. The man who sent his lackey before coming himself.

I stare at him in wonder and slight awe. His little speech awarded him some brownie points with me, but only a few. I still blame him for so much wrong in my life.

The phoenixes turn in on each other and whispers ensue. I tone them out, not wanting to hear the verdict before it is given. Aspen's arm has moved from my shoulders but hovers near my hand. Logan stands beside her, his arms crossed over his chest. His ornament has returned to his side. I want to spit on her. I want to hit her. I need to vomit.

The group of phoenixes finish conferring and turn towards us.

"She must be tested," one of them speaks for the group.

***

The entire group has moved to the basement. I'm not sure how well I'll be able to fight in skinny jeans, but I'm going to give it my all.

They've paired me against Logan. They know I've been training with him, but they also know he's their best, and that he won't give me an inch. I'll have to earn this on my own.

I stand on the mat opposite him and take calming breaths. Nerves rattle my limbs. I'd almost rather be back in the hands of the griffins. At least there I knew what I was in for. This, proving myself to people who know nothing about me, is foreign and unnerving.

I've never beaten Logan before. I'm not sure anyone has. I know I can't beat him now, but can I do well enough to satisfy these people? They know I'm new. They know I haven't had a lifetime of training. They know so much more and yet they expect more out of me, or at least they don't care.

I have a feeling nothing will impress them.

Logan walks up to me before we begin. "Do your best. Remember everything I've taught you. Don't hold back. Use your speed. Use your size. Use your powers. I won't be able to guide you through this."

I stare up at him, thankful for his pep talk, but still wounded by disbelief in me and the image of his lips on that bitch's. "I hate you," I tell him. I know it's childish. I know I will regret it later. But right now, it's how I feel.

Logan eyes me. His eyebrows narrow as if I've wounded him. Good. Then he pulls back and prepares his stance. I look around the room, at the people who sanctioned this. Some look expectant. Some hopeful. Some wary. Aspen gives me two thumbs up. Logan's lap lady glares at me, a sinister smile on her lips. One day I'm going to wipe it off.

I turn back to Logan and launch myself at him, not giving myself time to set. It's not a smart move but it catches him off guard and is enough for me to get a hit to his side. In typical Logan fashion, he recovers quickly, spinning me around like a top. I catch myself then wait for his attack, rather than lead it. He is lithe, his movements smooth, never giving away what he might be about to do. My hands light on fire a moment before his. His flames burn brighter, hotter, but mine will do.

I know enough not to run at him with outstretched, flaming hands. Besides looking like an idiot it would only result in him grabbing my wrists and throwing me to the ground. Learned that the hard way. Instead, I wait for him to make his move. I've learned when to strike and when to wait. It's not always so simple, but it can be.

I do my best to tune out the bystanders in the room. It's easier said than done. I hear oohs and ahs. I hear whispered words against me. I hear snickering. It is nearly enough to make me lose my nerve. I've never had an audience for my training sessions, let alone thirty of them.

Logan moves for me. Stepping out of his way I grab for one of his arms and reach out my foot to knock him off balance. It's not enough. He's prepared for it. He counters my move, twists my arm behind my back and grabs me around the throat with his other flaming hand. His burning skin is warm against my already sweat slick skin. I breathe heavy knowing he's bested me. I'm trying to decide whether to give in or try to escape his hold when I hear his make out partner giggle in the crowd.

Before Logan can release me himself, I shake him off, turn toward his bitch and hurl a ball of fire in her direction. None of these people like me anyway, I might as well deserve their hatred.

The crowd watches as the flaming orb sails towards them. I smile as it hits it mark then goes out. Logan's body ornament gasps at me, rage filling her eyes. I smile so big it hurts my cheeks.

The surrounding phoenixes stare from the bitch back to me. Several of their mouths are agape. I'm about to apologize, beg for mercy, something when Logan's hand wraps around my arms and pulls me back to face him. I expect to see anger on his face, but what I see is awe mixed with confusion and surprise.

I'm about to say I'm sorry but snap my jaw closed. I'm not about to apologize for defending myself. I'm not about to apologize to someone who's repeatedly hurt me. I'm not about to apologize.

"What?" I ask instead, attitude lacing the word.

I can feel the gazes of thirty phoenixes behind me, boring into my back. Silence permeates the room. No one says a word.

Nerves turn to fear. I've done something I can't come back from.

Then Logan says, "You can throw fire?"

That? That is it?

"Uh, yeah," I tell him. "Can't you?"

Surely I've seen Logan throw flames. Right? I mean, he doesn't use his powers around me unless we are fighting, or in danger, and our proximity is usually too close for fire throwing. My father has never used his power in front of me. I've never been around any other phoenixes. I just assumed because I could throw fire, everyone else could.

"No," he says, astonishment hovering over that one

word.

"Great," I say. "Just another way I'm broken."

I am so sick and tired of being the broken toy. I split in half when Nash died. My world was knocked off its axis when I learned Logan and I were phoenixes and Xander my enemy. And again, I splintered when my powers didn't work properly, not healing me, lighting myself on fire in the middle of a crowded classroom. All I can think is, *not again*.

I sigh heavily and walk towards the basement steps, no longer giving a shit what these people think.

"Do it again," someone behind me says.

I turn around, stare blankly at the room, then throw a ball of flaming rage toward them all. I watch them, awe marring their faces, then leap up the stairs, done being their plaything for the evening.

Ten

I trudge through the living room towards the door when I hear footsteps behind me.

"Um, excuse me," Logan says, following after me. "You can't just drop a bomb on us like that and walk out," he says.

"Watch me," I tell him, not looking back.

I lay my hand on the door knob and twist. Logan is quick behind me, slamming the door shut before I can get out.

I turn on him and cross my arms. Narrowing my eyebrows, I glare up at him, still pissed on so many levels about so many things.

"You're not leaving," Logan says, matching my posture.

"When did you become such an asshole?" I ask him. "Was it the minute your girlfriend walked through the door?"

"Girlfriend? What are you? You mean Lydia?" His

questions come rapid fire.

"So she has a name," I say, biting back words I might come to regret one day.

Logan looks as if he is going to say something. I pray he's going to deny the fact that that bitch is his girlfriend. But instead he says, "We need to talk about your powers. The others are concerned and want to know more."

"Oh, you mean the people who hate me?"

"They don't hate you," he says.

"Are you blind? Or stupid?"

"Casslyn, enough," my father says from across the room.

I'm fuming mad but his words are enough to shut me up. For now.

My father takes a step closer to us, Logan and I take a step forward.

"You are somewhat of an anomaly, Casslyn. There has never been any known phoenix with the power to throw fire. We simply wish to know more. That is all we are asking. And then you are free to go for the evening."

Logan opens his mouth to protest but closes it with a look from my father. Logan will have babysitting duty. He must be so disappointed he will have to leave his lap lady after just reuniting with her.

"Fine," I say.

I follow Logan and my father back down the stairs to the group of phoenixes. They watch me with new eyes. Eyes no longer filled with such disgust. Serves them right for judging me before they knew me. Though I'm still pissed about it.

They are all quiet. Waiting for my father to talk. Waiting for me to wow them. Waiting for something.

"Over the past few months I have observed Casslyn through her life and training," my father says. I feel the need to chastise him, to debunk his statement. I'm sure he's had Logan observe me and report back to him. But I don't. "Casslyn is caring and loving and friendly. She puts others before herself. Her training is going well, as you might have noticed from her sparring with Logan. However, her powers have been a topic of concern. On Casslyn's sixteenth birthday she and her twin were the target of an attack from the griffins. My son Nash was killed, but Casslyn survived. Not without a blood transfusion from myself. That is subsequently when I learned of Casslyn's existence. She came of age last month. Her regeneration went smoothly, as expected. However, before she aged she was stabbed by a griffin and regenerated. Since aging she has been attacked by the griffins and her body has refused to heal itself. Her powers have activated without her control. Logan and I have exhausted hours trying to discover what might have caused this. Did the blood transfusion from an aged phoenix cause her powers to activate too soon? Is there a glitch in her powers? Did losing her twin cause an adverse effect on her powers? These are questions we are trying to answer. At the time we have no answers. We all need to work together for her wellbeing. Casslyn is now one of us and she will be treated as such."

Yet another speech from my father in my favor. Not

something I expected at all, let alone two in one evening.

Every time he mentioned Nash I flinched. Tears threaten to spill over. I never considered before that losing Nash would have affected my powers. Yet another thing Logan and my father failed to mention to me. I'll just add it to the list.

"Has she ever been able to heal herself?" someone from the crowd asks.

"Besides the time she was stabbed before aging, no," Logan says from beside me.

"Which she shouldn't have been able to do," someone says.

"We think the power in my blood, which lingered in her body, was what caused her to heal in that instance," my father states.

Great, yet another thing I wouldn't have thought of. I honestly thought I had healed myself. I thought my power had saved me at least once. I'm a complete failure as a human and as a phoenix.

"But she can throw fire," the phoenix with the mohawk states.

"It would appear so," my father says. "Casslyn, would you please indulge us once again and demonstrate your ability?"

"Sure," I say, suddenly more aware that I'm on the spot than before.

I close my eyes and feel my power course through my veins, pulse under my skin. I pull it toward me, push it into my hands. When I open my eyes, bright orange fire dances upon my skin. I stare at the flames and will them to form a ball. When they obey, I look for a target, choosing the standing punching bag across the room, pull my arm back, and let the fire ball sail from my hand to the bag. The flames hit the bag, burst like a firework, then lick up the bag, catching more of it on fire. A phoenix near the bag pats at it to put out the flames. A scorch mark is all that remains.

"How did you do that?" asks the dark haired lady from the couch before.

I really need to learn some names here.

"I don't really know," I say, choosing that instead of the smart ass remark that was on the tip of my tongue.

"Fascinating," a voice from the crowd says.

"We will continue to train Casslyn. We will try and help her get a handle on her powers and perhaps sort out whether or not there is something wrong with them. She will learn more about us, more about each one of you. And in turn you will learn about her. We are a people about the people. The griffins may be a threat to all of us, but they have targeted Casslyn especially. We will protect her and in turn she will protect us," my father says, ending what could have been another speech.

I really want to leave right now, but don't feel like I can after what he just said. The word mingle floats around in my head. I must mingle with these people, get to know them, even if I'm not looking forward to it.

Logan steps away from me to talk with my father and

a small group of the phoenixes. Aspen appears at my side.

"That's really cool you can throw fire," she says. "I'm jealous."

Sarcasm, being my only defense most of the time, beats at me, forcing snide comments on me. I swallow them back. Aspen has been nothing but nice to me. And so far I really like her. I want to be friends with her. I'm not going to let my big mouth ruin that now.

"Thanks," I say to her. "I didn't know I was that special."

She laughs and nudges my shoulder.

"Uhoh," she says. "Bitch queen is making a bee line this way."

I turn to see the girl who was earlier hanging off of Logan approach me with her claws out. I mentally prepare myself for what is about to go down. I've had enough run ins with pre griffin Ashley to deal with this.

"That was some stunt you pulled," Lydia says when she's within spitting distance.

"I thought so," I say with a big smile on my face, my voice candy sweet.

"I heard you tried to get with Logan. And he turned you down. That must be rough," she says, faking concern.

"Oh, I got with him. Didn't he tell you?"

This hurts. This really hurts. I bet he called her and they laughed at how pathetic I was. My heart is broken and bleeding out of my chest. I hope I can patch it and stanch the bleeding before it dies altogether.

"Nice try. You are just a stupid, weak, little girl who will never be good enough for Logan. He will never be with you. He will never love you like he loves me. We've always been together. We will always be together. We belong together. You need to put aside your pathetic puppy love for him and get over it. He will never be yours."

"Tell yourself whatever you need to help you sleep at night. But Logan was mine. And he will be again. He sees right through you to your rotten core."

"Listen you little bitch," Lydia says but is cut off by Aspen.

"Give it a rest, Lydia. You're in town for an unforeseen amount of time. You don't need to mark your territory the first night. Unless that is, you're threatened?" Aspen says, a smile in her voice.

"Puh-lease. Me? Threatened? You must be out of your damned mind," Lydia snaps at Aspen.

"Is that right? Because I'm pretty sure Logan would listen to me before he listened to you. And I'm pretty sure you forgot to tell him about hooking up with half the phoenixes in this room while he was away."

"We were broken up," Lydia retorts.

"Exactly. And you still are," Aspen says.

I love this girl.

"Not for long," Lydia says, then turns on her heel, flips her hair, and stalks off.

"Don't let her bother you," Aspen says, an air of casualness surrounding her.

I know I'm pathetic for asking it, but I can't help my-self. "Do you think Logan will get back together with her?"

"If he knows what's good for him, then no. But, he's done it before. Those two have played relationship tag for over fifty years."

"Oh, god, I think I'm going to be sick," I say, bending at the waist, taking deep breaths in.

"You really love him don't you?" Aspen asks.

"More than you know," I tell her honestly. I'm not look-ing for her to tell Logan that, to make him take me back. But if I'm going to be friends with her, I'd like our friendship to begin with honesty.

"He'll figure it out," Aspen says. "He has this twisted sense of loyalty toward your father. After our parents died he stopped living for himself and started to live as your father's soldier. I just hope he can pull himself out of that."

"Me too," I tell her.

The group of us remains in the basement, everyone breaking off into smaller groups. I study the formed groups trying to scope out cliques or ranks among them. So far I've got nothing. Not that I am any good at it. The only reason I know the cliques in school is because they all sit at the same tables at lunch every day. The football team at one table. The track team at one table. The popular kids at one table. Apparently the griffins at one table. Who knew. I didn't until recently.

The groups stand amongst the gym equipment. Some sit on the equipment or use it to lean on. The phoenixes don't seem to mind making conversation in a basement. For some reason I feel the need to start asking around if anyone needs a drink or to prepare food for them. This isn't my house and I'm not their host, and yet I feel like I am.

I look around the room trying to spot friendly faces. I come across more abhorrence than acceptance. But there are a few who appear to be warming up to me.

"Hello, Casslyn," the girls from the couch say, approaching Aspen and I.

I'm glad to have Aspen next to me. Logan is threatening to be around. My father is even worse. I'm sure there is no way Lydia would have said what she did to me, let alone approach me if Logan or my father were next to me. I'm glad to have someone with me, but someone who is easy to talk to and will make the others meeting me and vice versa comfortable.

"Hello," I say, looking at each of them.

"I'm Anna," the blonde says. She has hair. Like a lot of hair. Like her hair runs down to kiss her ass. She has it pulled into a braid but I can tell her hair puts mine to shame. Besides her hair, she's about the size of Aspen. Skinny, short, petite. She's got pretty mom jean colored eyes. Her facial features are sharp and defined.

"Hi, Anna," I tell her.

"I'm Kristina," the other girl says. Like Anna, Kristina appears to be about twenty two to twenty five years old. Her skin is tan and rich and beautiful, without a single blemish. Her eyes are the color of dark chocolate and open to her soul. She's slightly more built than Anna with defined muscle tone, but she's just as short as Anna.

They both smile at me warmly. I'm hoping they welcome me more than the other members of the group did.

"It's nice to meet you," Anna says.

"Yeah, some of us were actually excited to meet you," Kristina says.

"I told you they didn't all hate you," Logan says, into my ear, from behind me.

I jump about three feet in the air before Logan places his hands over my arms to steady me. I swallow over my sandpaper tongue and turn to him.

"Hey, Logan," Kristina says.

"Hey, Logan," Anna says, a bit more sultry than Kristina. I see I've got more competition than Lydia for Logan's affections.

"Ladies," Logan says, causing Anna's eyes to roll back into her head.

"Did you want something?" I ask.

"Yeah, we were having a nice chat," Aspen says.

"I was merely coming to see how it was going," Logan says, sounding chastised.

"We're fine. You can leave now," Aspen says.

"Rubbing off on her so quickly, Casslyn?" Logan says, eyeing me pointedly.

"She's a smart girl," I say, cocking an eyebrow at him.

"That she is," Logan says.

The four of us girls stare at him until he holds his hands

up in defense then walks away. I see Lydia sidle up to him before I turn away from them.

"He is so fine," Kristina says.

"Your brother is *so* hot, Aspen," Anna says.

"So I've been told," Aspen says.

Somehow the four of us have moved into the center of the basement. It feels isolating and exposing, but I am the center of attention tonight, might as well live it up.

"It was nice to meet you," Kristina says.

"You too," I tell her and indicate to Anna. "Maybe the four of us could hang out sometime. Girls night or something."

"We would love that," Anna says.

"Me too," I tell them before they walk off to join another small group deep in conversation.

I push my hearing around the room, trying to pick up on my name, on their conversations, on anything that might be useful. But my head starts to pulse with the beginning of a headache the further I push. There are too many voices, too much noise. I can't focus on any particular voices without picking up on all of them. I pull back immediately, before my brain shatters. Maybe Logan can teach me to control and focus my hearing as well as my fire power when we train.

My eyes rove around the room as Aspen points out certain people and puts names to faces. There are too many for me to remember tonight, but I do my best.

I stop when I spot the Mohawk guy. Upon further inspection I notice he's wearing eyeliner and purple colored contacts. His nails are painted black and the concert tee is for Ed Sheeran. Either this guy is really eccentric or he is gay. I watch him, studying his moves, his mannerisms. He talks with his hands just like Tucker does. It brings a smile to my face. His eyes light up when he smiles. I continue to watch him, to make sure he's gay. There is no way I'm going to offend him in assuming he's gay if he's not.

Before I can grasp it, he's standing right in front of me. Crap. He noticed me watching him.

"Honey," he says, his voice smooth like honey. "You're wasting your time checking me out. I'm gay."

I smile, knowing I've hit it on the mark. "I know."

"Don't tell me you came to that conclusion because you've seen a lot of *Will and Grace* reruns."

"Oh, no," I say, taken aback.

"My best friend is gay," I tell him.

"The griffin?" Mohawk guy asks.

"Be nice," Aspen warns, reminding me she's still near me.

"No, he's human."

"Really?" Mohawk guy asks.

"Yeah," I say, a smile growing on my face.

This is nearly too convenient. A new gay guy in town. A very hot gay guy. There is no way I can't not set him up with Tucker. This is going to be perfect, magical even.

"I'm Gray," Mohawk guy introduces himself.

"It's nice to meet you," I tell him.

"You too, Casslyn. I'm sorry we gave you a rough start

there. The griffins have been getting the better of us lately. They outnumber us and have been letting us have it."

"I get that," I tell him.

"It would appear so," Gray says. "Sounds like you can hold your own."

"Oh, no. I got my ass handed to me each time. I'm lucky to still be here."

"Guess that's what Logan is here for," Gray says.

"I'm learning as much and as quickly as I can. It's just hard."

"We are here now. We've all got your back, even if it doesn't seem like it."

"Thanks, Gray."

"Anytime, Fireball," he says then parts from us.

"He already gave you a nickname. Aw, he likes you," Aspen says from beside me.

"What's yours?" I ask her.

"Cottontail. When Gray met me I had this stuffed bunny rabbit I carried everywhere with me. It stuck, I guess."

"And Logan's"

"Cap. Like captain. You should feel good, he's never given Lydia a nickname."

I watch after Gray trying to decide what the best way would be to introduce him to Tucker. Should I tell Gray about Tucker and see if he wants to meet him? Should I tell Tucker about Gray? Should I tell neither of them and just happen to make them meet? This is tricky. I want to set them up without them feeling forced to be set up. I need to play this cautiously.

"Don't even think about it," Logan says from beside me.

Again, I jump. This time I turn on him and punch him in the arm.

"Ow, what was that for?" Logan says, rubbing at his arm.

"Stop sneaking up on me," I tell him through my teeth.

"Pay more attention," he tells me.

"Whatever," I tell him.

"I'm serious," Logan says. "Don't even think about setting him up with Tucker."

"And why not? You don't want to be happy so you don't want anyone to be happy? Is that it?"

"It is one thing to tell Tucker what you are. It's a whole other thing to bring him into this world. If he's got distance he's at least got plausible deniability if someone questions him, if the griffins go after him. But the second you bring him in, the second you introduce him to us and our world, he's got a target the size of Jupiter on his back. Do you want that?"

"I want him to be happy, Logan. I want him to find love. I want him to feel like he's number one in someone's life. I want him to feel needed. Is that so wrong?"

Before Logan can answer I hold up a hand in front of him and say, "You know what? Don't answer that. Obviously you don't care about anyone anymore." I turn to Aspen, who apparently doesn't care that I'm giving her brother such a hard time and say, "It was really nice to meet you. I'd love to see you soon, but I've had enough for one night. Good night."

Without saying goodbye to anyone I trudge up the stairs and this time make it out of the house. I get in my car, planning on driving back to my house, but decide to turn the other way. I need a little space. A little breathing room. I roll down the windows, crank the music, and drive. I'm not sure where I'm headed, I just know I have to go.

Eleven

I've spent the past few weeks doing my best to ignore the new phoenixes, Logan, and my father. I can't say that it has worked all that well, seeing as how I have to train and they are all fascinated by my new power and lack of healing skills, but I am at least trying.

The phoenixes have all been taking their turns at being my trainer. I have a new one every day. Even Lydia takes a stab at being my trainer. And I do mean that literally. She stabbed me. She claimed that it was an accident and that she expected me to move out of the way, but I know better, even if the rest of them don't. It didn't help matters when I couldn't heal myself and Logan had to swoop in with his healing tears. Honestly any one of them could have healed me with their tears, but Logan insisted it was him. I was on the receiving end of a lovely glare from Lydia after that, and a few not so friendly words. Aspen told me to shake it off and ignore her, but that is becoming increasingly more difficult. The more time I spend in Logan's house in the company of the phoenixes, the more I see Lydia hanging off Logan. I'm not sure which makes me more irritated, the fact that Lydia doesn't know Logan hates clingy girls, or the fact that he lets her do it, despite hating it. It leads me to wonder why he lets her do it. Is he truly in a relationship with her? Is he trying to make me jealous? Is he trying to get over me? I wish I could escape it. Or at least ignore it. But that's difficult when it is staring me in the face every day.

I have been spending a lot of time with Aspen. That is, when she's not with Logan. They are close. Not as close as Nash and I were, but then again, we were twins. It doesn't get much closer than that. Seeing Aspen and Logan together takes me back to the good times with Nash. I find myself smiling just thinking about stupid things we did together or times that made us laugh. However, more often than not, seeing Logan and Aspen laugh at a joke one of them told, or smiling together, or sharing a hug rips me from the inside out. I'm racked with jealousy, torn by guilt, and left hollow, miserable.

When she's not with Logan, Aspen and I hang out. I have shown her around town three times now. I expected an entourage but Logan must have more faith in Aspen keeping us safe than he has in me. Shocker there. Aspen has been to my house many times just to hang out, watch movies, have girl time. I get the impression from her that girl time isn't something she gets a lot of. Lydia isn't her favorite person and the other phoenixes have more on their agendas than painting their nails and talking about hot male celebrities. I didn't necessarily get a lot of girl time when spending all my free time with Nash, Tucker, and Xander either. Tucker may be gay but he's still a red blooded male. If I'm honest, I quite enjoy the company of another girl, even if I wonder when she leaves if she's off to tell Logan everything we talked about. I know she wouldn't, but I still wonder.

I really am enjoying her company. It's nice to have someone to talk to about all the phoenix stuff without it being my mortal enemy, or me feeling so much pressure I crack. Aspen is kind and funny and ever so slightly devious and I love her for it. She takes my side, though we haven't known each other that long. She tells me she ships Logan and I together forever. I've tried telling her I don't think Logan is going to budge on the relationship status as it is, but she remains optimistic. She tells me a lot about being a phoenix without it sounding like a job, more like a hobby. She makes me relax about coming into my powers and not butt clenching so hard I feel like shit is going to come out of the wrong end.

The other day we sat on my couch lighting various parts of our bodies on fire. Just playing with the flames. I learned to move the fire from finger to finger like a match, from the outside. It was the most fun I've had with my powers since I got them.

I will admit, however, that I have been enjoying training,

even if I say I'm not. Logan and I were mostly training hand to hand combat. Once I got my powers we started working with those. Something that the other phoenixes brought to the table when they showed up was fighting with and defending myself against knives, since they are the used weapons of the griffins. Once I learned to twirl a knife over my fingers I couldn't stop. It's thrilling, and addicting, just like watching flames dance on your skin without being burned.

To say I've come into being a phoenix would be an overstatement, but I am learning. When the phoenixes first showed up I was nervous, overwhelmed, out of my element. They didn't accept me. They didn't like me. I wasn't one of them. I'm still not one of them. I can see it on their faces. But they aren't my people either. We tolerate each other. We work with each other. But there is no love there. Maybe one day. But that day is not today.

Anna, Kristina, and Gray are the only phoenixes who are nice to me. Anna likes to spend time braiding my hair. I've assured her I can do my own hair, but I think she likes it and it gives her something to do, so I've stopped protesting. Kristina is more subdued than Anna. But Kristina has been the one to tell me more about the phoenixes. Where they live, who they live with, if they have jobs. Learning about their daily lives helps me to see that they really are just people, besides being phoenixes. On the other hand, Kristina has been teaching me about the history behind the phoenixes. Logan did what he could, but Kristina knows more than he did. What can I say, Logan is a soldier, not a historian. I've started getting attached to Anna and Kristina. I'm glad I like both of them because they appear to be a packaged deal. Gray has become my phoenix version of Tucker. Besides Aspen, Anna, and Kristina, Gray is the one I'm closest too. It probably has something to do with the fact that I've had three male best friends my entire life and find it easier to get along with them. He's even asked me about Tucker a few times. Despite what Logan says, I think it is time for the two of them to meet. I can't wait for Tucker to meet Gray. I think they are going to hit it off immediately, and that's not just because Gray is the only other gay male in this town. Anna, Kristina, and Gray don't do much in the way of my physical training. Not because they aren't strong like the others, because I've seen them fight each other and they terrify me. But because they would rather spend their time with me in other ways. And I appreciate them for it.

As soon as the training is finished every day I sneak out of Logan's house in an attempt at escaping my new life. Most often Tucker is my only refuge. I am too easily found at my house, so close to Logan's. Of course when I'm not at Logan's with the rest of the phoenixes, I'm being trailed by Logan. I feel like I'm two years old again, constantly in need of a babysitter.

Today, my sanctuary happens to be the coffee shop, and my dad. I am well aware Logan is loitering around somewhere keeping a close eye on me, but I try to focus on my dad, who I haven't seen in a while, and who I've severely missed.

Despite being in a room filled with the aroma of coffee, I can smell my dad's aftershave before he walks in the door. A huge smile is plastered to my face and I can't shake it. I've missed my dad like I miss Nash. I didn't just lose one person the night of my sixteenth birthday, I lost two. I'm only slowly getting one back.

I stand up to greet my dad as he walks to me. I hug him for longer than is necessary but I'm not about to let go.

"Hey, kiddo," he says when we part.

We move to the counter to order then find a table when we have our drinks.

"How's it going, Casslyn?" my dad asks taking a sip from his coffee.

My hot chocolate sits in my hands, meeting the warmth that flows under my skin. "Oh, you know," I say, not really knowing what to tell him. As much as I have wanted to talk to my dad recently, most of what goes on in my life must remain a secret to him. There is no way I'm about to lose him or my mom like I lost Nash. Nash was an equal target like myself, but my parents would still be targets if they knew about me. I may have brought Tucker into this life, but I'm not ready to let my parents into the fold.

"Listen, kiddo, if you want to talk about your father it's fine with me."

I nearly spit out the liquid I'm swallowing and scoff. "No, thank you."

"Does that mean you haven't been getting along with him?"

"Something like that," I say.

"Do you want to talk about it?"

"Not really. I don't know," I say. "He's not my dad. You are. He doesn't need to be here."

"Casslyn, it's not like you to keep people out," my dad says, tilting his head in a come-on gesture.

"He's never going to replace you," I tell him, bowing my head.

"I am not worried about that. I am your dad and I will remain your dad until the end of my days. But that doesn't mean that he isn't also your dad. You need to let him in."

"Why? It's not like he stuck around to find out if I existed."

"You're not being fair, young lady."

"I wasn't aware I had to be," I cock my head at him, challenging him to reprimand me.

"All I'm asking is for you to give the man a chance. He is clearly trying. Once he found out about you he came back. Isn't that worth something?"

"He waited a year."

My dad raises an eyebrow at me, but holds his tongue.

His silence is enough to have me say, "Fine. I'll give him a chance. But only because you asked me to."

"That's a good girl," he says, taking another sip from his cup.

I feel thoroughly chastised. I move the cup to my lips to hide my reddening cheeks.

"So, what else is new? How is Logan?"

"Are you trying to hit every hot button topic today? Are you trying to meet some piss off Casslyn quota?"

Now my dad looks chastised. He pulls his head back and raises his eyebrows.

"Sorry," I tell him.

I say, "Logan and I are no longer a going concern. He broke up with me."

"Well, I always knew he was an idiot," he says winking at me.

"You have to say that because you're my dad."

"No I don't. I say that because it is the truth. You are an amazing girl and every guy on the planet would be lucky to have you as his own. You are special, Casslyn. I've always thought that. You have to be to have put up with Nash, Xander, and Tucker for so long."

I laugh at him and smile.

That is, until I hear his voice.

"He's right you know. You are special."

I swallow hard and turn to see Cohen standing next to our table.

Pushing my hearing out, I listen for Logan. His heart is beating fast, his breaths coming faster. He doesn't want Cohen anywhere near me, but is not about to make a scene in front of my dad. It would raise too many questions. And now that my dad knows Logan broke up with me, he might be mad and get into it with Logan, leaving me wide open for Cohen. So outside he waits and paces and huffs. I nearly laugh at him. He deserves it.

My dad stares up at Cohen, deciding whether or not to address him, or how exactly to address him.

"Dad, this is Cohen. Cohen, my dad," I introduce them, indicating between them.

Cohen turns an innocent and docile smile on my dad. If I didn't already know Cohen is crafty, I would fall for that smile. My dad is about to when he shakes his head and says, "And how do you know my daughter is special?"

Go dad!

"I am new to town and she befriended me no questions asked," Cohen says.

It's not exactly the truth, but I'd rather my dad didn't know how I met Cohen.

"That was very nice of her," my dad says, finally reaching for Cohen's hand.

Damn, he won him over in less time that I was anticipating. Dad didn't warm up to Logan until we'd been dating for at least a month.

"I only wish there was a way I could repay her," Cohen says, feigning sincerity.

"I'm sure you'll think of something," my dad says. "Something worthy of her, I'd expect."

"Nothing less, sir," Cohen says, inclining his head, a gentleman's gesture.

I balk at him and roll my eyes back.

"Sir," my dad says, impressed. "What a gentleman you've found, Cass."

"Yeah. Right," I say.

"Would you like to join us?" my dad asks.

I cut in and say, "I'm sure Cohen has things to do."

"I've got a few minutes," Cohen says, taking a seat.

I glare at him before my dad can notice then turn away from him.

"We're no longer talking about how special I am, got it?" I say, turning to each in turn.

"Yes, sweetheart," my dad says.

I make a disgusted noise as my dad slyly smiles at me.

"So, Cohen, you are new to town? How are you finding Cedars?"

"I'm liking it. It's small, and there isn't a lot to do, but the people are nice and it's got a little something special about it."

I scowl at him, making sure he knows I'm scowling at him. He just smiles and raises his eye brows at me.

"I have to use the restroom, if you two will excuse me," my dad says.

When he is out of ear shot I lay into Cohen, "What are you doing here? What are you looking to get out of this? Are you stalking me? My dad has nothing to do with our world. If you bring him into it I will end you. Do you understand me?"

"I haven't seen you in weeks. I merely came for a cup of coffee and heard you talking. I'm not here for some nefarious reason. I am getting really tired of everyone in this town being suspicious of me. If I was a human, without any super powers, and not a creature of mythology, no one would question me. And yet you and your ex-lover, even that enemy best friend of yours are hounding me, watching me." Cohen leans closer to me, his eyes darkening. His lips turn down in a grimace. His voice drops low as he says, "I'm telling you I'm not going to hurt you, that I don't want anything to do with the tirade the griffins have going. Why won't you believe me?" He stays leaned close to me, his chest heaving. Gone is his light, playful, devil-may-care attitude. He's serious about this.

I feel thoroughly reprimanded. "Look. I'm sorry. So far you've done nothing to make me suspicious of you, other than the fact that you have two hearts. I've just been through too much to trust you. What do you want from me?" I ask this with wholehearted sincerity. Why would he go against his people to be near me?

Cohen leans back in his chair, only half of his care free attitude back in place. "I'm not all bad, Casslyn. I want you to know that. And, I want to get to know the girl I met at that party. Nothing more, nothing less."

"I don't know that girl," I answer.

A corner of his lips curl up when he says, "Why don't we find her together?"

"I don't think so," I say, feeling the need to cross my arms.

"Give me one night. If you decide after that you no longer want to have anything to do with me, fine. But at least you gave it a shot."

I hear the bathroom door open, my dad's footsteps moving towards us. Cohen hears it too. He raises an eyebrow waiting for an answer.

When my dad is nearly to the table I say, "One night."

Cohen's eyes close and his head falls in a thankful manner.

In the distance I can hear Logan swearing very loudly. I didn't think about him and the other phoenixes when I agreed to Cohen's terms. I'm well aware Logan is going to forbid me from seeing Cohen, but I'm too tired of the restrictions that come with being someone's enemy to focus on it right now. I didn't know living my life would come with a handbook.

When my dad sits down Cohen turns to him and says, extending a hand, "It was nice to meet you, sir, but there are some things I must attend to."

"You too, Cohen. Will you and Casslyn be seeing more of each other?" my dad asks, shaking his hand.

"Dad," I say, exasperated by his outrightness.

"I hope so," Cohen answers. He turns to me and smiles, the beautiful smile I saw at the party and says, "Goodbye, Casslyn. I will be seeing you."

"Bye," I tell him.

"He seemed like a nice young man," my dad says.

"Seemed," I say. "I'm not convinced yet."

"Should we order some food?" my dad asks. "I'm starved."

"Let's," I say, a smile returning to my face.

My dad and I start talking about this things going on

in our lives, minus my life as a mythological creature. He tells me about work stories and I tell him about school. He's happy I'm no longer getting in trouble at school. I'm happy he's no longer shutting me out. I even venture to ask him about his relationship with mom.

"How are things going between you and mom?"

"They are going," he says. "With your father in town, your mother is . . . confused."

"Don't let him get in your way. Mom loves you. I know she does."

"I know, sweetheart. I'm trying to give her space, but also be there so she doesn't forget about me."

"She won't, Dad. Just because my father is back in town doesn't mean anything. He's bound to leave again. Don't give up on her. Please. I need you to be back together."

"Casslyn, listen. I love your mother and I love you. And as much as I want us to be back together, I'm not sure it can be like it once was. I don't know that we can go back. I just want you to be prepared if things don't work out like you want them to."

"They never do," I say, self-pity coloring my tone. "It's fine, dad. It's fine."

"I'm sorry, sweetheart," dad says, concern written on his face.

"Dad, really, I'll be okay. I've come a long way in a year."

"You sure have. I'm so proud of you."

"Thanks."

This afternoon is something I have desperately needed. It's something I'll never get back. I've always thought it was healthy to have more than one best friend and my dad is one of mine. When I get to spend time outside of Logan's house, outside of the fable realm, I feel normal again. Only too soon will I have to return to it.

Twelve

"Have you talked to Xander lately?" I ask Tucker as we lounge on my couch watching *The Wedding Date*.

"Yeah," he says without turning away from the TV. "We played video games the other day."

"Good. That's good," I say, feeling I need to drop the subject.

Tucker side-eyes me and says, "He asked about you."

"Oh yeah?" I ask, trying to be nonchalant.

"Yup. He asked how you were doing. I told him you were good. I hope that's okay."

"Yeah, it's fine. And I am. How did he seem?"

"Good. A little worn out. Like he hasn't been sleeping."

I wonder how bad it has been for him since he helped me escape his own people. I saw how badly he was beaten after it happened. I just hope they could get passed it since they couldn't find any evidence he helped me and Logan. I don't know what it's like to be a griffin but it doesn't seem like a group of people I would want to be a part of. I feel bad for Xander. But besides that, I miss him. I miss hanging out with him, and laughing with him, and just being with him. Xander has a presence about him that is quiet and yet intense and it's intoxicating to be around him. Just like with Nash, I feel a part of me is missing.

"He wants to see you, you know. He just can't," Tucker says.

"I know. I do. It's the same with me. Could you just let him know I miss him?"

"Will do, kid," Tucker says, winking at me.

"So, Tucker, how's life going?" I ask, trying to lead him into a whole other conversation.

"Fine. School ends in two weeks. I'll have all summer to hit the beach and work on my tan. Plus I have two missions in life now."

"Do tell."

"One," Tucker says, holding up his index finger, "I'm going to find a man. It's about damn time. You have or had Logan but now you've got Cohen so you're covered. Xander is tangled in that Greer chick. It is my turn. Do you hear me?"

"Loud and clear," I tell him, nodding with fake enthusiasm.

"And two, I am going to fix the rift between you and

Xander. I'm not sure how I'm going to do it, but I'm going to do it."

"More power to you pal," I say.

My hearing attunes to footsteps outside. Right on time.

"Hey, Tucker. You know how a group of the phoenixes has come to town to train me and help with the griffin situation?"

"I'm aware. Though I'm not sure why I haven't met any of them yet. You bring me into this life but keep me at an arm's length. Are there just so many hot guys you can't share with your best friend? Because that's rude. And selfish. And I did not raise you to be selfish young lady."

I laugh at Tucker's statements. This is why I love him.

"You know I was going to tell you I have someone I'd like you to meet, but I guess if you are going to go and call me selfish you don't deserve to meet them. That's just too bad."

Tucker's eyebrows shoot up on his forehead. Then he takes a breath and smooths his face down. "Now, miss sassy Cassie, I'll play nice if you will."

"Fine, fine, fine. Since you asked so nicely," I mock him.

"Please, Cassie, with sugar on top?"

I smile at him then move from the couch at a knock at the door.

My smile grows as the beats from Tucker's and Gray's heartbeats ratchet up a few notches. I take a deep breath and hope that this works out. I want Tucker to be happy so badly I can taste it. I want Gray to not lose faith in me. I want my worlds to collide without friction.

I open the door to hear a collective gasp.

"Come in," I tell Gray.

He walks through the door with seeming coolness but I can hear his heartbeat. I can see the slight shake of his hands. I walk him to the living room where Tucker is twisted around staring at our arrival.

"Tucker, this is Gray. Gray, this is my best friend, Tucker."

Gray takes a tentative step towards the couch while Tucker leaps up and comes around to greet him. I'm holding my breath as their hands move closer to each other. It's like I'm watching it in slow motion, near suspended animation. My body instinctively moves forward as their hands connect.

I've never set any one up before. My heart hammers in my chest. I had no idea it could be so nerve wracking for the person doing the setting up. That seems like it would be the easy part.

I stand a few feet apart from the two guys. As I watch them it occurs to me that maybe I should leave and give them some time alone. Or should I stay so they don't feel uncomfortable?

Gray and Tucker move to the couch. They sit close to each other. I can see their hands move, like they want to touch each other, but they aren't sure if they should yet. They both have large smiles on their faces.

I decide it is best that I should leave them alone. I venture to the kitchen, so I'm not too far away from them if they need me, but they still have their space.

I can hear them talking about me, oddly enough. I'm sure they will get over that quickly, I'm not much of a conversation piece. I try to tune them out by playing a song in my head. But soon enough I'm thinking about the new mystery man in town. It's been four days since I told Cohen I'd give him one night. And while I was reluctant to even give him that, I'm wondering why he hasn't shown up yet. It's probably some game he's trying to play with me. It's probably a trap the griffins are setting up. Whatever it is, I'm getting impatient.

I can't figure Cohen out. He was playing me the night of the party. He knew I was a phoenix. He knew I would find out he was a griffin. Since then he has appeared just when I don't want him to. Showing up when I'm with Logan, just to piss him off. Showing up when I'm with my dad, for who knows what reason. He said he was just getting coffee, but I know better. He's trying to get under my skin, and for some reason, I am letting him.

But what if he is what he says he is? What if he really wants nothing to do with the griffins and what they stand for? I'm friends with Xander, would it be so crazy to think I could be friends with Cohen? Logan doesn't trust him, will never trust him. But Logan has removed himself from my personal life, I'm not about to let him make my decisions for me. I'm not about to let my feelings for him continue to dictate my life. Even if it kills me to see him every day. Even if it rips my chest wide open to see another girl touching him. Maybe I'm using Cohen as a way to distract myself from Logan. Maybe I don't care. If Cohen's going to play games with me, I'm going to get down to his level and play right back.

***

I'm sitting in my room, a rare reprieve from the phoenixes. Tucker texted me to tell me he and Gray were going on a date. His text was in all caps and had nearly a million exclamation points in between sentences. His excitement was contagious. Gray texted me and told me he was pretty excited. He wanted some tips on Tucker, things that would break the ice easier, but I told him he had to do it the hard way and actually get to know Tucker. Gray may have decades on Tucker, but he needs to remember Tucker is young and vulnerable. He needs to treat him delicately but with respect. I'm happy for Tucker. And for Gray. He may be a new friend, but a friend he is and I want him to be happy.

I head down the stairs when I hear my mom exit the bathroom. She's got to work tonight and I won't see her again for a while. As often as she is scheduled or called into the hospital and as much work as the phoenixes are having me do, it's a wonder we still remember each other exists.

"Hey, mom," I call to her as she walks down the steps.

"Honey," she says, that worried tone in her voice.

I immediately wonder what I could have done wrong

but can't think of anything so I feign innocence.

"Yeah?" I ask.

"Your dad told me you and Logan broke up. Why didn't you tell me?"

"Um, I don't know. I haven't seen you much," I tell her.

"I'm very sorry, Casslyn. Are you holding up alright? Do you need me to call in sick? I'm worried you're spending too much time alone."

If she only knew how alone I wasn't.

"I'm okay, mom. I promise. Some night you aren't working though we could hang out."

"Sure thing. You name it," she says to me.

I move through the kitchen, pulling a travel mug out of the cupboard and fill it with coffee. When I hand it to her she watches me very carefully. I back slowly away from her, wondering why she keeps looking at me funny.

"How are you doing, Cass? Are you alright? You've been acting differently recently."

"How so?"

"Well, I can't remember the last time we had an argument. Your dad and I haven't been called to school because you have gotten in trouble. And I got your report card in the mail. You have all As and Bs."

I stare at her, my mouth hanging open. I didn't realize being a good kid was grounds for concern.

"I realize I should be happy about this. It is the way you were before your brother died," she says, nearly choking on the words. But she continues on, "But I'm worried you're,

I don't know, not being true to yourself. I'm worried you're only trying to behave because you've realized you can't get the attention you need."

I nearly laugh at her. Before, when I was acting out, she shut me out more, but now that I'm being good, and don't need so much of her time and attention, she's worried. It's certainly something I would have yelled at her about six months ago, but I'm over that. I'm most certain we will find something to argue about in the future, but right now, I'm nearly content with how our lives are going. I don't want to mess that up by being a problem child.

"I'm fine, Mom. Really. I've been spending time with Tucker. And I've met some new friends. I'm doing okay. I promise. If I need something, I will let you know."

"Sounds good."

I'm not really the hugging type, so I don't embrace her or kiss her on her way out the door, but I no longer resent her for it. I no longer wish she would stay and talk to me, even if we ended up yelling at each other over nothing. My dad was right, our family may not go back to what it once was, but it is still somewhat intact and I must accept what I've got.

I'm about to return to my bedroom to the magazine I was rifling through when I hear footsteps in front of the door.

I don't remember making plans with Aspen, Anna, or Kristina but I wouldn't mind spending time with any or all of them. I open the door after a sharp rap on the frame truly announces the presence of a guest.

My guest is definitely not one of the three I had suspected it might be. A well-defined male stands on the other side of the door from me. But it's not Logan.

"I'm here to call upon my one night with you," Cohen says, bowing ridiculously low to me.

"Here I was thinking you'd forgotten about me," I tease.

"That's not possible," Cohen says, though his voice is guarded and I can't tell how he means it.

"I'm not exactly ready to go out," I tell him.

Cohen's eyes roam over me from head to toe. He shrugs one shoulder and says, "I'll wait."

"Come in, then," I tell him, stepping aside so he can walk through the doorway.

His eyes scan around my house, or at least what he can see. He says, "Nice place."

"Thanks," I say. Months ago I would have scoffed at that. Months ago I hadn't even unpacked my belongings.

But recently I've come to terms with the fact that I will be staying in this house for the unforeseeable future so I might as well make myself comfortable, and that went beyond my bedroom. Plus, recently I hadn't minded at all living so close to my boyfriend. Now, I'm not so sure.

"I'm going to go get ready. I'll try to hurry," I tell him as he sits down on the couch.

"Take your time," he says with a wave of his hand.

I run up the stairs two at a time and head for the bathroom. I should probably take a shower, but that could take some time. He said to take my time but he's a guy, and they usually mean take no more time than fifteen minutes to get ready. Whatever, I'll shower, but I won't dry my hair.

My nerves ratchet up when I'm in the shower, so much so that I'm sweating when I step out of it. A lot of good that did. Standing in front of my closet, I can't decide what to wear. I could go for the whorish look like I used to wear to school. I could go casual, since I'm not sure what Cohen is trying to get out of tonight. He did say he wanted to get to know the girl from the party. I could wear the dress I wore to the party. But he's already seen that.

Finally I pick the dress I wore on my first date with Logan, the gray and green pencil dress. It has long sleeves but a short skirt.

Memories flood me as I pull it over my head. Logan's hands on the back of my thighs. The warmth of his skin. The taste of him when he kissed me for the first time. The hunger in his eyes. The need for him pooling inside me. And then he dropped me on my ass.

Good times.

I shake off the memory, braid my hair down the side, step into a pair of flats, then walk down the stairs. My nerves must have clouded my senses because I didn't hear Logan come in. Nor did I hear him begin to lay into Cohen.

"Why are you here?" Logan demands, a finger jabbing into Cohen's chest. "What do you want with her? Haven't your people done enough to her?"

"Listen pal, as I've told Casslyn, I am not a part of them. I'm interested in her as a person not her species."

"You can't fool me," Logan snarls. "I see right through

you. I'm not going to let you hurt her. So stay away from her."

"Logan, stop," I tell him as I walk towards them.

Logan pulls away from Cohen and stands straighter. He looks at me, really looks at me. His face folds in on itself when he notices the dress.

"Casslyn, don't go out with him. Please," Logan says to me.

I'm torn. I don't know whether Logan is asking me not to go because he thinks I'm in danger or because he still loves me. My whole heart begs for it to be the latter. My whole heart is still in love with him. But then I remember he broke up with me. I picture Lydia on his lap, in his arms, at his side and my heart breaks again.

I look him deep in the eyes. Begging him to tell me he loves me. I wouldn't go with Cohen if he did. But his face doesn't change.

"Don't go," Logan says again.

He doesn't tell me he loves me.

"Oh, I get it," Cohen says. "You're afraid she might actually like me and that you will lose her. Too bad you've already lost her my friend."

Logan's face snarls and he lunges for Cohen. Cohen takes a step back and I position myself between them.

"Logan, stop."

Logan stands in front of me, his face still beastly, his chest heaving.

"Let's go, Casslyn," Cohen says, extending his hand.

I take one last glance at Logan then take Cohen's hand and follow him out of my house.

I stop short seeing his vehicle for the first time. It's a Jeep Wrangler. The most ridiculous waist of gas ever but it is so sexy. I'd comment on it but now isn't the time.

Once we're to his car Cohen stops us and turns to me. "Are you alright?" he asks.

"I'm fine," I tell him, trying to shake off the encounter with Logan.

"I'm serious. If you're not okay, we don't have to go."

I take a deep breath, let it out, then cool my expression. "I'm fine," I tell him. "Let's go."

We get in the car and Cohen says, "Buckle up," then starts the car.

As he is pulling out of the driveway I sense Logan. I turn to my house to see him standing on the porch watching us drive away. Something in me hurts, pulls to him. But he watches me go. I'm sure he'll go straight to the arms of Lydia.

"I'm sorry about Logan. He's a bit protective," I say to Cohen as we drive past Logan's, a house full of his enemies.

"It's alright. It's not like I didn't expect it," Cohen says. He sounds nonchalant, but I remember what he told me the other day in the coffee shop about being sick of people not believing his intentions. "I have to ask though, where does he get off? He dumped you and yet he's acting like you're still his."

"I think it's more that my dad is forcing him to be my

body guard so he's doing just that. You are the enemy after all," I say to him as a joke.

"I don't think you're right. I think there's still something there," Cohen says as he turns his head to me, gauging my reaction.

"Well it's not like he's doing something about it," I tell him.

"Do you want him to?"

I remain silent. He can take from that what he will. Yes, I want Logan to do something about it, but I'm on a date with Cohen, not Logan.

"Why did he look at the dress like that?" Cohen asks, forging on with the conversation.

"Can we stop talking about Logan? I thought you wanted to know me?"

"Right you are," Cohen says.

Cohen drives us through town and then makes a turn to drive out of town.

"Where are we going?" I ask him, suddenly nervous. Since my capture I've learned that the warehouse I was taken to was on the outskirts of town. I don't want to go back there. I won't go back there. I will fight Cohen tooth and nail not to go back there. My dreams are still haunted by that night.

My heart slams into my ribcage, beating harder, threatening to bust from my chest. I won't go back to that room. I won't go back to a sadistic man carving me with an ice knife.

"Casslyn, you're shaking. What is wrong?"

"I won't go back there," my voice comes out as a choked

whisper.

"You're frightened. Look at me."

When I don't turn to him he says more forcefully, "Look at me, Casslyn."

I turn to him but keep my face down.

"You do not need to be afraid of me. I told you I won't hurt you. I promise I won't hurt you," Cohen says. His voice is so smooth, so even, so assured.

My eyes flick up to him. He is looking at me with such pure conviction.

"I *won't* hurt you," he says, his voice deep, a promise. "I'm not taking you to them."

There is truth in his eyes. It runs through him to his hands gripping the steering wheel.

Cohen takes one of my fists in his. I flinch back but he holds firm. He uses his fingers to pry my clenched fingers apart. He holds my hand and uses his thumb to caress the puncture wounds my nails left in my palm.

"What did they do to you?" he asks, a fearful whisper.

I turn away from him but he keeps ahold of my hand, his thumb still rubbing smooth circles in my palm.

It takes me a long time to calm down. My other hand has unclenched but the crescent moon shapes still mar my skin. My knee still bounces uncontrollably on the floor but there is nothing I can do about that. My heartbeat has returned to a somewhat normal pace.

Way to start a first date, Casslyn, I chide myself. Whatever, he knew what he was getting into.

"Are you alright?" he asks after a while.

"I'm sorry," I tell him, not looking at him.

"There is nothing to be sorry about," he tells me. He sounds like he means it. "Anyway, I was going to take you to the city, there is more to do there. I thought about taking you to the bowling alley but that's been done."

"Aren't you new to town?"

"Tell me you haven't been to the bowling alley for every date you've ever had," he says raising an eyebrow at me.

I roll my eyes in answer. I like the bowling alley. It has a lot of good memories. But then again, that's where Logan, Tucker and I were attacked. Maybe it's best we don't go to the bowling alley.

"So where are you taking me?"

"And ruin the surprise? I don't think so."

"Not even a hint?" I ask.

"Nope. Now tell me about yourself."

"What's to tell? You know I'm a phoenix. You know my story."

"No, no," Cohen says, shaking his head wildly. "Tell me about you as a kid. Tell me why you seem to be three different people."

"I had a twin brother. He died a year ago. I'm sorry if I haven't exactly gotten over it," I say, anger lacing my voice.

"I didn't realize. I'm sorry."

He's lying. That's the first thing he said to me when we met at the party, that I'm Casslyn, the phoenix with the dead brother. I know he's lying. But why would he lie? Did he think I wouldn't remember what he said at the party because I was drunk? Is he trying to distance himself from the griffins? Is this all some trick?

"I thought you like to stay informed. It was your people who killed him," I say, pulling my hand away. I'm not going to call him out on the fact that he lied. But I want to see his reason behind the lie.

Cohen slams on the brake and pulls us off the road.

"Okay, listen," he says, turning his whole body towards me. "Either you get over the fact that I am a griffin right now or get out and walk home. You are a phoenix and do you see me using it against you?"

So he lied because he doesn't want to be associated with the griffins. I can accept that.

My cheeks burn red hot. I feel ashamed of myself. Cohen hasn't been anything but nice to me. He's played his games, but he hasn't attacked me in any way. I'm not being fair. Even if I don't want to be.

I sit in my seat and look down at my lap. I should get out and walk home for being a bitch to him.

I tilt my head halfway to him, so he can see one eye. "If I said I was sorry, would you believe me?"

He lets out an exasperated laugh, shakes his head, and says, "Yeah. I would."

"I'm sorry," I tell him, turning fully toward him. My face sullen and apologetic.

"From now on," he says, his eyebrows up and serious, "you are Casslyn and I am Cohen and there are no such things as phoenixes or griffins. Can you handle that?"

It's like he answered my prayer. This is what I've been looking for since I learned I was a phoenix. It's what I had with Tucker until he was forced into this world. If there is a way Cohen and I can make this work, whatever it is, then I can be friends with Xander again. Hope fills my heart for the first time in a long ass time.

"I can handle that," I tell him.

"Good. Now, if one more thing threatens to ruin tonight I'm going to be pissed."

"Then let's not let it."

"Let's go. For the third time."

I smile at him and wait for him to pull back onto the road.

We stop at a Wendy's to grab some food then drive off. Cohen finally pulls up outside of a mini golf course.

"Mini golf?" I ask.

He mistakes my tone for mockery and says, "Yeah, do you have a problem with that?"

A small laugh escapes me and I say, "No, I just haven't played mini golf in . . . I don't remember the last time I played mini golf."

"Then get ready to have your fine ass handed to you," Cohen says, a wicked grin on his face.

"Cocky much?"

"Self-assured."

We finish our burgers and fries in the front seat then get out of the car. When Cohen steps up to the booth to pay, his face jolts then he takes a step back. I look around him to find quite the scene. A girl, who has to be seventeen, sits behind the counter. Her hair is pitch black, died black, blacker than Logan's hair. A large ring of eyeliner surrounds her sky blue eyes. She's got more piercings in her face than I've seen on a single person. The bright yellow t-shirt she wears with the golf course logo does nothing to compliment her ghostly pale skin. I nearly snicker but hold myself back. Cohen hands her money for a round of mini golf then takes the clubs and balls from her and walks swiftly away.

It's early enough in the summer we've got the course to ourselves. Cohen, standing beside me, opens his palm to show me the two balls. Pink and blue. He closes his hand around the blue one then offers me the pink.

"Uh, no," I say, raising an eye brow at him.

Cohen concedes, handing me the blue ball.

I step up to the first hole, set my ball down, then step back for Cohen.

"Ladies first," he says.

I stand up to the line where I'm supposed to hit the ball. I can feel Cohen step up behind me. I turn around and put my hand up to stop him. He stands so close my palm rests on his chest. "There will be no need to stand behind me and place your hands on mine, my back pressed into you so you can show me how to swing a club. I'm fine on my own. Thank you."

Cohen steps back, his hands in the air in an innocent manner. "Keeping my hands to myself. Got it," he says, dramatically shoving his hands into the pocket of his cargo shorts.

Using my club to position the ball where I want it, I step to the side and line up my shot. The first hole is a straight shot down the center of the green. How hard can that be, right? I pull the club back, and take a soft swing. My swing is too soft, my ball rolling down the green only to stop about two feet away from the hole.

"Nice shot," Cohen says, stepping beside me to take his shot.

He pulls his club back, swings it forward and strikes the ball. It goes rolling down the green right into the first hole.

Cohen turns back to me and winks. The bastard winks then smiles like a cat who's caught a mouse. I'm in for a long night if he keeps this up.

I head down the green, club in hand, and take a swing at my ball. This time the ball actually goes in.

Cohen takes out the two score cards from his pocket and writes down our scores. First hole and I'm already behind.

We step through the gravel to the next hole. This one is on par with the last one, the hole straight forward. There is a small slope about halfway down the green, then a second a little further on.

I line up my shot, figuring I'll need a little more oomph to my swing to make it over both slopes and to the hole. My club strikes the ball and sends it rolling down the green. The ball rolls up the first hill and goes sailing into the air off of the platform. Cohen bursts out laughing from behind me.

I rotate around to face him only to find him bent over, his hand clutching his stomach, howling with laughter. When he looks up at me I'm glaring at him so hard my face may remain that way permanently.

"I'm sorry," he says, only to burst out in a new fit of laughter.

I continue to glare at him until I join him in the amusement.

"Your turn," I tell him.

He continues to laugh while he walks up to the putting line. I retrieve my ball while he takes his swing.

When his ball rolls nicely over the hills and lands inches away from the hole the words, "Are you kidding me," burst from my lips.

This elicits a new round of snickering from him.

I place my ball back on the putting line and take a second swing at it. The ball rolls over both hills and lands about a foot away from the hole. That will do. Cohen makes the ball in the hole with one more shot. Luckily I manage the same. I'm now two strokes behind.

We move on to the third hole. I move up to the line and stare down the green. And stare. And stare. I pull back to swing, stop, and stare. I pull back again, stop, and stare.

"Would you like-"

"No," I yell back at him.

Cohen chuckles as I strike the ball. It rolls down the green, up and around the loop and stops about two feet away from the hole. I'll take it. Of course, when Cohen's ball comes to a stop mere inches away I hang my head and shake it back and forth. This is ridiculous.

By hole six I'm a good fifteen points behind. Cohen has laughed so hard I'm surprised he hasn't wet himself.

"Aren't guys supposed to be nice and supportive on the first date?"

"I told you I was going to kick your ass," Cohen says, a giant grin on his face and a chuckle behind his words. "You're so bad."

I cock my head to the side, give him a hard ass smirk and say, "And you're an asshole."

"Thus the basis of my appeal," he says, giving me a look that says, well-duh. "Be honest, it's why you like me."

"Yes, because every time you say something remotely callous, I get this warm, tingly feeling all over my body. And I can't help but think *oh Cohen, I want you.*"

Cohen stares at me without saying a thing for several seconds then says, with this wild look in his eyes, "I knew it."

I laugh and take a step closer to him. My foot catches on the wood framing of the seventh hole and I fall forward. Cohen lurches forward, catches me, and spins me around so I'm facing him, cradled in his arms.

He leans in close, the look in his eyes intense. Nerves fire under my skin. My heartbeat quickens.

Cohen brings his lips close to my ear and whispers, "Walk much?"

A bark of laughter escapes me. I pull away, squinch my

nose at him and dramatically say, "You cut me deep. Please kiss me."

The smile on Cohen's face fades replaced by something darker. "Gladly," he says.

My body stills in his arms. The kiss we shared at the party was one thing, when I was drunk and didn't know he was a part of the race of people trying to kill me. But now, now that I know what he is, I'm not so sure I can give that to him. Plus there is the fact that I'm still in love with Logan. Besides the fact that I don't know anything about Cohen.

"How about you tell me more about yourself and then I'll decide whether or not I let you kiss me," I say, removing myself from his hold.

"Let me kiss you? Honey, there is no letting me kiss you. If I want to kiss you, I'll kiss you," Cohen says, an evil smirk on his face.

"So cocky," I say. "How do you live with yourself?"

Cohen laughs deep in his throat, winks at me, and says, "By getting pretty things like you to beg me to kiss them."

"Wow. Good luck with that," I say, placing my ball on the line for the next shot.

"What do you want to know? I'd love to get this conversation over with so I can claim those pretty lips for my own."

I cock an eyebrow at him before returning my focus on the ball and my swing. The objective of the hole is to get my ball into a clown's mouth three quarters of the way down the green. And it's a small hole. With one eye closed I peer down the lane, slowly pull the putter back, and swing it forward. The putter connects with the ball which goes rolling down the green only to hit the side of the clown's mouth and comes rolling back to me. It wouldn't be so bad but the clown's mouth begins to laugh at me. Which makes Cohen laugh at me.

"Okay, how did you get so good at mini golf?" I ask him, shoving at his shoulder as me moves toward the line.

"I told you, I like to get pretty girls to beg me to kiss them."

"You're saying you bring all your girls here?"

Cohen looks back at me over his shoulder and says, "Only the special ones."

My hand moves to cover my heart as I fake swoon at his words, as if being called special by an admitted ladies' man has affected me.

Cohen strikes his ball with the putter and of course the ball sails right through the clown's mouth and down toward the hole. Without a word or reaction I move back to the line and hit the ball down the lane only for it to collide with the clown's cheek.

"How can you be this bad?" Cohen asks. The sad thing is he's being totally serious, not joking involved. "You are a phoenix. You have enhanced senses."

"I thought we weren't talking about that?" I snap at him.

"Are you even using your abilities?"

No. I'm not. Why didn't I think to use my abilities? Not like a ball of fire is going to help in this situation. But my eye sight is crisp. My hearing sharp. My focus pointed.

With the ball back on the line I rein in my senses. My eyes focus in on the clown's mouth, pulling it to me, clearing the image. I focus on the ball, on its placement on the line, on my stance and position to the ball, the weight of the club in my hands, the burden it carries as I pull it back and push it forward, the impact as it smacks into the ball. I watch as the ball moves forward, down the center of the lane and enters the clown's mouth with not as much of a graze to the sides of the tunnel.

"*YES!*" I yell, dropping the club and throwing my hands in the air. I nearly drop to my knees and tear my shirt open in full on Brandi Chastain mode. "Ugh! Yes," I chant, rocking my shoulders back and forth in a victory dance.

"It's about time," Cohen says, a chuckle in his voice.

"That's how you've been beating me this whole time?"

Cohen's eyebrows shoot up on his forehead in dramatic *duh* fashion.

"Okay," I tell him. "We're starting over."

"Care to make it interesting?" Cohen says.

I am struck hard by a flashback of Logan and I playing pool in the bowling alley where I hustled him for a kiss. Our first kiss.

I nearly tell Cohen no. But that wouldn't be fair to him. It's not his fault I'm a demented fool.

"Alright. For every hole I beat you in you have to tell me two things about you. And if I win the whole thing, you have to . . . let me drive the Jeep back home."

"I knew you liked it."

"I'm sure you're just compensating for something," I say, indicating his crotchal region.

"Try, complimenting it," he says, raising his eyebrows suggestively.

A disgusted noise gets caught in my throat.

"I agree to your terms. But if I beat you in the hole you have to do a victory dance in my honor. And if I win the whole game you have to indulge me in a kiss."

I suddenly feel self-conscious about my victory dance. It was special, in the moment. Doing one for Cohen every time he wins a hole might be cheesy, or make me feel like a stripper. But whatever, I agreed to play along and he agreed to my terms.

"Agreed," I tell him. We shake on it then go back to the first hole.

Theatrically linking my hands and cracking my knuckles I say, "Let the games begin. Let the best woman not kiss the playboy." I shake my head at him and give him a suck-it look.

"You will be kissing me. Even if I lose,"

"In your dreams, pal."

"Oh, you are," Cohen says, smiling that smile that could knock a girl out.

Again a disgusted noise escapes me.

Ignoring him, I place my ball on the line, focus on my shot, and make a hole in one. Cohen does the same. He argues that because we tied he should get a victory dance as well as me getting my two truths, but I play dirty and tell him no, because my ball went in first.

"Fine," he says. "When I was younger and started learning what we were about I refused to be a part of it and was thrust into a boarding school. Don't feel bad. I don't. Okay. Two. I've never been in love."

A tightness pulls at my chest, squeezing my rib cage together. I feel bad for Cohen. But I also know what it's like to hate feeling pitied. So instead of telling him I'm sorry, I say, "I wanted facts to get to know you, not to be depressed."

"If I'm not depressed, you shouldn't be. Now, I'm winning the next hole and getting my victory dance."

And that he does.

By the time we hit hole nine, I've gotten eight facts out of him, he's gotten four victory dances, and it's down to the final hole to decide if I get to drive the Jeep home or if I have to kiss him.

The last shot is set up like plinko. It's the biggest chance shot on the course. No matter where you hit your ball it could fall anywhere. It's a matter of getting it close enough to the hole. As per usual I go first. I hit the ball closest to where the hole is. The ball pings and pangs against the pegs falling farther down the slope until it comes out the bottom and rolls within inches of the hole. Yes. I've got this. My ball is so close. Unless I royally screw up my second shot I've got this.

Cohen scratches his head while he staring from my ball, to his ball, to the plinko pegs and back. I smile inwardly, and outwardly. I get to drive the Jeep back. I may even do a victory dance for myself.

Cohen hits his ball down the lane then turns around and closes his eyes.

I'm internally singing *I've got this I've got this.*

His ball zigs and zags as it hits the pegs and falls farther down the slope. My fists clench tighter as the ball rolls closer to the hole. My leg is shaking as it inches forward so close, too close to the hole. My lungs stop taking in air as Cohen's ball rolls to a near stop on the lip of the hole and then falls in.

"No," I yell, falling to my knees on the turf. "No. There is no way. No. No. That can't be possible."

Cohen has turned around and began to chuckle in fits as he looks down the hole at his ball. The grin on his face is smug and unbearable, yet so cute. Ugh. Damn him.

"I'll take my victory dance please."

"No," I say sharply.

"You spoil sport. Sore loser."

I move my hands up toward my face, put both pointer fingers in the air and move them up and down.

"Wow. I feel like a champion," Cohen intones.

"You should," I say, succumbing to my defeat.

Cohen and I turn in our balls and clubs to the booth then head towards the Jeep. When we get near it I move towards the passenger side when Cohen says my name. I turn to him in time to catch keys sailing straight for my face. I look down at them in my palm and say, "Did you miss the part where I lost?"

"Oh, no. I'm well aware you owe me a kiss. However,

I've seen your car and I saw the look on your face when you saw the Heep. I know you want to drive it."

"Really?"

"It's just a car."

"This is not just a car," I reprimand him. I place my hand on the Jeep and say, "Don't listen to him, baby. He didn't mean it."

Cohen laughs then hauls himself into the passenger seat.

I climb into the driver's seat and sit still for a moment while the chills run through me. I close my eyes and take in the sensation of sitting this high, feeling the leather of the seat against my skin. My body thrums when I turn the key and the whole vehicle vibrates under me.

"If this is how you react to a car, I *cannot* wait to kiss you again."

"Shut up," I tell him and pull away from the mini golf course.

As we drive back to Cedars, Cohen pumps me for information on me.

"I thought you knew everything about me already."

"I know about you as a phoenix. Not as a person."

I think about the information he gave me every time I won a hole on the course. It didn't sound like he had the best childhood. Or that he is too close to his family. He told me he's got a sister but they aren't close. I can't imagine what that's like. I wonder if Nash and I weren't twins if we would still be as tight as we were. He told me about boarding school and all the guys he hangs out with. He told me about sneaking out of said boarding school and going to the nearest town to hook up with girls. What he didn't tell me about is having actual friends. He didn't tell me about any real relationships he's had.

So I tell him about Nash. I tell him about Tucker and Xander. I tell him about my mom and dad and how close we all were. And still are. We talk back and forth, Cohen sharing stories that may pertain to things I share with him.

In no time at all we're outside my house and I am about to kiss him, even if I'm not sure I want to. I lean in to him, preparing to give him what he won. I can feel his breath on my lips as my eyes are closed.

"Casslyn," he whispers.

My eyes pop open and narrow. I'm not sure what type of game he's playing but I'm not sure I like it.

"What?" I ask, my voice a strained whisper.

"I didn't say I was going to cash in my winnings right away."

"Why?" I ask, skeptical of him. He's talked all night about me kissing him, me begging to kiss him, me kissing him when he won the game. And now he's saving it?

"Because I can tell you don't want to. I like you. I've made that plainly obvious. But you're not there yet. And that's okay. If you just want to be friends, I can try that. I've never done it before, but I can try. Being with you tonight was the most fun I've had in a long time. If you never like me back I think I'll be okay with that. I want to spend time with you. In whatever way I can."

I nod, unable to speak. Words have escaped me for maybe the first time.

Cohen nods back then opens his door. I snap out of my stupor and open my door. I step out of the Jeep and meet Cohen by the door.

He's about to step around me when I grab onto his shoulders and pull him to me. Our lips touch ever so softly. Cohen's hands move to my waist. He tugs me to him, our bodies colliding. His tongue slides over the seam of my lips, a silent invitation. I let him in. A moan sounds at the back of my throat from the first taste of him. Mint and ice. My hands move to his face, stubble scratching the pads of my fingers. He hums in the kiss causing chills to erupt at the base of my skull and crawl down my spine.

He pulls away first, only to rest his head against mine. Our heavy breaths mingle and merge together.

"I told you you'd kiss me," Cohen whispers.

"You're an ass," I say, pulling fully away from him.

He laughs and I walk away from him.

"Goodnight, Casslyn," he calls after me.

I flip him off over my shoulder and continue to my house.

When I'm inside the door and he's driven off I let out a deep breath. Spending time with Cohen is a mental workout. I have to be on my game at all times. He's cocky, yet witty, and slightly funny, if you can get past the cocky. He knows how to have a good time, and how to make me laugh if I need it. But he also seems to know when I'm not okay. And that unnerves me.

My thoughts are interrupted by the ringing of my phone. I'm afraid it's Cohen, calling to rub our kiss in my face some more, but the face I see is not Cohen's.

"Hey, Tucker. How was the hot date?" I say into the phone.

"Amazing is just not a strong enough word to describe the night I just had."

"Good. I'm glad. Turns out I had a date of my own."

"Really?" Tucker asks, using his intrigued voice. "Was it with hot griffin guy? Why do you get all the hot guys?"

"Are you telling me you don't think Gray is hot?"

"Oh God no. He is perfect. Have I told you lately how much I love you?"

"Remind me," I tell him.

"Casslyn, seriously. I love you. Thank you. If this works out I don't know how I will ever repay you."

"You deserve it, Tucker. Just think of it as payment for your friendship for all these years."

"You're my girl, Cassie."

"You too, Tucker," I joke, but am serious.

"Hardy har," Tucker utters. "So, you wanna hear about my date?"

"Spill," I tell him.

Tucker launches into the story of his date with Gray and tells me all about how perfect it was and he is and so on. And for the next half hour as we swap date stories I feel like a normal teenager. I feel like a girl who is talking to her best friend about a date they both had and there really are no other worries. For half an hour I am lost in tales of hot guys and first kisses and budding romance and I don't have to worry about training, or the failing powers, or being a part of something that feels so huge it's going to swallow me whole, or fearing for my life, or any of the other things conflicting my thoughts these days.

As Tucker talks about Gray and asks me about Cohen I find that I may actually not hate spending time with Cohen. We got off to a rocky start, and the guy can be a dick, but he may just be what I need in my life right now. He's a distraction from Logan, and the phoenixes, and the griffins, and everything else. He's a very good looking distraction who seems to like me. But beyond being a distraction, he appears to be a decent guy who wants to spend time with me. And that may be just what I'm looking for.

Thirteen

We've taken a day off of training to have a get-to-know-you day. The phoenixes have converged at Logan's to spend some quality time together. Not with each other, but with me. And me with them. I began the day suspecting some weird vibes, and that's how it started off, but it has grown into something more.

In the weeks I've spent with the phoenixes I've spent most of my time with a handful of the thirty or so who arrived. That handful includes Aspen, Anna, Kristina, and Gray. Not even a handful, because, as we all know, I suck.

Only recently, mostly today, has my handful grown. Gray introduced me to his friend Thomas, who I adore. Gray has been spending a lot of time with Tucker so he thought Thomas might need someone to hang out with in his absence.

We share an interest in the same TV shows, music, books. He's like me, with a penis. Last week we spent an afternoon making a list of all the things we love in common that we needed to discuss at length. Once we marathoned the entire universe, we made plans next week to see the new Marvel movie together. Thomas and I have spent an hour today discussing our favorite demon hunting brothers TV show. We geeked out so bad Lydia gave us both the stink eye. Let's just say she and I haven't warmed up to each other at all.

The other day I took Aspen, Kristina, and Anna to Missa Sue's Everything Boutique. They were enthralled by the racks of clothes and dresses, styles ranging anywhere from the nineteen fifties to the two thousand fifteens. Anna and Kristina selected an outfit for the other, purchased it, then made them wear it for the rest of the day. I wasn't sure how this was going to go but they ended up picking out really nice pairings. Anna chose a pair of black leather pants I've seen in here for years and a shiny blue swoop neck tank for Kristina, while Kristina chose distressed skinny jeans and a floral crop top for Anna whose long blonde hair flowed seamlessly with. Aspen and I watched the two browse with amused grins on our faces. Then the four of us went to the coffee shop and indulged in chocolate shakes.

Gray and Tucker have spent most of their free time with each other, but there have been times I've had to put my foot down. Either to hang out with them each individually or for them to let me tag along. Tucker still hasn't been to Logan's house or to meet the rest of Gray's people, but I think they are working up to it. I've never seen a relationship blossom so fully so quickly. Tucker has Gray beat by a few, but the number of times they have thanked me for putting them together grows daily. I'm glad I could be a part of their union.

A union I'm not so glad to be anywhere near would be Logan and Lydia. I'm so not okay with it I'm not even going to talk about it.

Oddly enough, I've become somewhat friends, much to her disgust, with Lydia's brother, Nathan. It is a tentative friendship, because he is loyal to her, while I'd rather throw fire balls at her all day, but we have been spending some time together. Mostly playing board games. My parents haven't had much time to play Monopoly or Trivial Pursuit with me lately so Nathan has been filling that void. And, much to the irritation of Lydia, Logan has joined in a few games of Clue. Nathan is so unlike Lydia in personality you wouldn't believe they were related, until you put them side by side. Put a wig on Nathan and you've got Lydia.

There are other members of the group, the older members, who needed more coaxing to warm up to me. Mostly the members who openly hated me the first time they laid eyes on me. They still eye me warily, but not so blatantly.

This afternoon I convinced them all, well not all, to play a game of football. It took a lot of cajoling, but it worked. I snagged the football from my house and rounded everyone up in the backyard. My father split us up in teams and off we went. Logan, Gray, Thomas, Kristina, and I were all on the same team with a few others. Lydia opted not to play. Aspen,

Anna, Nathan, and my father were on a team. Logan was the quarter back for our team. Because I've been playing backyard football for years, I became a receiver. Thomas and Kristina were part of the line and Gray was a running back. The near thirty phoenixes even dressed up for the occasion, painted their faces and wore head bands. It was comical but I've never felt closer to them than I did then. My father was the quarter back for their team. It wasn't exactly fair having him on a team because my team was too timid at first to lay a hit on him. Once I yelled at them thoroughly and told them I'd throw fire balls at all of them if they didn't defend him we got back into the game. They were only two touchdowns ahead so we had a fighting chance.

When we had the ball the next time Gray and I were able to make it closer and closer with every down to our delegated end zone. On one of the passes Logan over threw me and nailed Lydia right in the face. I laughed so hard I fell to my knees clutching my stomach and nearly pissed my pants. I laughed even harder when Logan couldn't hide his smirk and she stomped off into the house. But we got the touch down and were that much closer to winning the game.

Which eventually we did. When I scored the winning touchdown Logan bum rushed me and lifted me into the air then pulled me down into a tight victory hug. The rest of my team joined in moments later, but those few seconds that passed between Logan and I made sparks pass through our skin and nerves come alive at the touch of each other. Logan may have Lydia back in his life, he may be over me, but I'm still in love with him, and the sensations between us prove that.

While still in the team victory hug Logan leaned into me and whispered in my ear, "This rugged sporty girl thing really does it for you."

My heart jerked in my chest at his words. I stared up into his eyes to see if he was messing with me, trying to provoke me in some way. He didn't seem to be, but it was not fair of him to say something like that, not in the situation we're in. So I punched him in the arm, told him good game, and walked back to my house to shower and decompress.

But the day o'fun is not over. I'm back at Logan's, we've ordered twenty pizzas and have set up a karaoke machine. This is not something I want to take part in. I love singing, but hate doing it in front of people. Part of the myth of phoenixes - something I learned when I first found out about Logan and was internet searching, as one does - is that they have beautiful voices. It is said their singing voices are majestic and beautiful, even more so when they sing a lament. As phoenix after phoenix goes before the mic, I find that myth to be true. My cohorts sing brand new pop songs, they sing classic rock songs, they sing country songs, of all things. It is really not fair to have a race full of beautiful singing voices. Luckily tonight's festivities are volunteer only so I'm not forced to go before my jury and perform. I'm allowed to sit back, scarf my face, and enjoy the show.

My phone vibrates in my pocket so I pull it out to see my mom's face on the screen. I haven't talked to her all day, haven't seen her in a couple days, so I should probably answer the call. I hop out of my chair and move up the stairs to Logan's room and some quiet.

"Hey, mom," I answer.

"Hey, Cass, what are you up to?" she asks. I can hear noise from the intercom of the hospital through the phone. She must be on a break.

"I'm at Logan's hanging out with some friends."

"Is it a good idea to be at your ex-boyfriends house?"

"It's complicated, mom. But it's okay. I'm okay."

I sit on Logan's bed not knowing how long this conversation could take. My mom is complicated. Sometimes she's super chatty, other times she gets right to the point and hangs up. Of course that usually depends on how she's feeling about me at the time being. It was touch and go there for the first few months after the accident, when I was angry and lashing out.

"If you're sure, honey. Listen, I've got a couple hours left in my shift then I thought maybe we could hang out tonight. Stay up late, pop some popcorn and watch a movie. I feel like I haven't seen you much lately. Unless you don't want to leave your friends."

While listening to my mom I absentmindedly pull out the door of Logan's bedside table. I jerk away from the table and nearly gasp at the contents in the drawer. There are two of them. A box of condoms, and the picture of Logan and I taken on Christmas. Heat floods my face causing my vision to narrow. The combination of the two things is startling and crushing. The condoms have got to be for Lydia. Logan and I hadn't gotten to that point in our relationship. But having that picture still there, where he could pull it out right before he goes to bed, when he's thinking of me. No. He broke up with me. He hasn't even indicated that he may still have feelings for me. He lets Lydia hang all over him.

"Um. No," I say, distracted by what I've found. Remembering I'm still on the phone, and my mom is waiting for an answer, I say, "It's okay. I've spent all day with them. They will have to understand that I need some quality time with you."

"One more thing," my mom says slowly.

"What is it?" I ask suspiciously.

I eye the picture in the nightstand, a throbbing building at the base of my skull, and contemplate stealing it. How dare he hold on to something so precious to me, when it no longer means anything to him.

"I've invited your dad," she says, and before I can get a word out she continues, "Is that okay? I can tell him not to come."

"Mom, stop. Of course it is okay. I would love it if the three of us could spend some time together."

"Oh, good."

With one last look I slam the drawer shut and refuse to give it any more thought.

A boom sounds from downstairs, like a body hitting something solid. I jolt and move my gaze towards the door. Members of the group have gotten in fights before, small scuffles caused by nothing, play fights really. But this sounded different.

I wait to hear it again. I'm sure if it's something serious my father will stop it before it turns into something bigger.

But then I hear it again. This time louder. This time more bodies.

"Mom, I have to go," I tell her and hang up before she can answer.

I open the door of Logan's room to the sound of grunts and screams and thuds.

Running down the stairs my eyes land on my worst nightmare.

Raphe, the leader of the griffins, stands in the doorway of Logan's house.

His people spread out, fighting my father's people.

There seem to be more phoenixes than griffins. The phoenixes appear to be holding their own. But then, we were taken by surprise, and that has to cost us.

Logan intercepts me in the middle of the stair case saying, "Go back upstairs, I'll come for you when this is over."

"No," I tell him, nudging past him.

He grabs me by the arm and spins me into him. "I can't lose you," he tells me.

I'm not about to think about that right now. I can't think about that right now. "I'm not running from this."

Fire erupts from the hands of my peers. Fists are flown. Flesh collides with flesh. Screams ring out and reverberate off the walls. Jumping the last four steps I run for the nearest phoenix to lend aid. Thomas, sweet Thomas, looks like a straight up Roman warrior taking on his opponent. I'd be afraid of him if I didn't already know how kind he can be.

The guy he's fighting takes a swing at him with a knife. An ice knife. There is no way the griffins came to attack us without the thing most lethal to us. They didn't come to scare us. They came to wipe us out.

The fire within me pulses under my skin and comes alive. I concentrate my power to my hands and will them to alight. Pooling the fire, I create a ball of it and throw it at the griffin attacking Thomas. It hits him in the shoulder but burns out. It's not enough to ignite his clothes, but it is enough to divert his attention so Thomas can lay a hit on him. With one blow to the face the griffin is rendered unconscious and is down for the count.

Moving on pure adrenaline I move through the living room to the next fighting pair.

One of the older phoenixes squares off with a younger griffin. He's a kid from my school. How can this be happening? How could I not have known about this? How could there be so many of my enemies in my own school? Where is Xander in all of this? I hope he's not here. And if he is, I hope he survives.

I hear a scream and look toward it. Aspen is held around the throat from behind and attacked from the front. The griffins are double teaming her. One of the griffins uses his ice knife to slice gashes into her legs and arms.

"Stop playing with her," the one holding her says, "Finish the job."

Terror clouds Aspen's face. She knows there's no getting out of this. She's using her flames on the arms of the guy holding her, but they must have learned from holding me and are wearing thick clothes, many layers. Layers the flames will have to cut through and not in time. Aspen reaches for her captors face, clawing at him, but his grip is firm and his buddy holds her down.

Hatred and fear mix in my heart and surge me forward just as the griffin with the knife plunges it towards Aspen's heart. Pain dulls my senses for a spilt second as I make contact with the griffin. Ice enters my veins, staunching the flow of my power. The two of us crash onto the floor and roll away from each other. Pain slices through my side. I make to stand up just as Aspen gains ground on her attackers. She knocks one out and sends the other out the door, flames surrounding his body.

"Are you okay?" Aspen and I ask at the same time.

"Yeah," she says.

"Yeah," I tell her.

"You're bleeding," she says.

My hand, which was already clutching my side, is sticky with blood. I pull it away to reveal a gash about four inches long over my ribs.

Instead of asking if I can heal it myself, Aspen says, "Do you want me to heal it?"

"No," I tell her. "It will take too much time. We've got to help the others."

She nods her head at me then heads in the opposite direction. I spot Logan in the kitchen holding a butcher knife to a griffin holding an ice knife. The griffin looks frightened but determined. I know Xander said he loves being a griffin, that from the time they were aware they were taught to hate us, taught to believe in the cause with their entire being. But some of the griffins fighting don't look any older than me. Are they forced to be here? Do they want to be here? Are they ready to die for their people?

Before I can find an answer to that, I'm knocked forward from behind. I take a few unbalanced steps but remain on my feet. I turn to face my attacker, but find Nathan at my feet. I pull him up, give him a once over to make sure he's alright, then move to make sure the rest of the phoenixes are holding their own.

I take a step towards the doorway to the living room and come face to face with Raphe, the leader and most powerful griffin.

My heart leaps into my throat. I try to swallow it down but it's stuck. I'm rooted in place, unable to breathe. Unable to call upon my power.

Images of a dark room assault me. Headlights barreling down on Nash and I. The feeling of chains chafes my wrists. The scrape of asphalt against my skin. The burn of ice carving my skin opens old wounds. The heat of flames licking my skin. The nightmare of being surrounded by my enemy, facing death head on, paralyzes me.

The man responsible for Nash's death stands before

me. White hot hatred corrodes my brain. This man killed my brother. He destroyed my family. He ruined my life. As much as I'd like to kill him, I am terrified of him. He is here again, he is going to kill me and everyone I love and there is nothing I can do about it.

"I've come for you girl," Raphe says.

His voice sends a chill down my spine.

I'd like to think I have a retort for him. I'd like to think in most cases I'd hold my own verbally. But trepidation runs through me. My voice is silent.

Raphe takes a step towards me. An ice knife spins in his hand. My heart stops beating. My breath stills. I've never been more terrified. He places the tip of the knife on my cheek and drags it down, opening my skin. A shriek of pain escapes me as the ice eats my flesh. Blood bubbles and runs down my face.

Chaos rages around me. The phoenixes wage battle against the griffins. But in this doorway, the fight has come to a standstill. Raphe has me. I have lost.

"You're not getting her," says a voice from behind me. My father.

My heart twitters in my chest. Relief courses through my veins, relieving the ice frosting my fire.

My father pushes me aside and lurches at his arch enemy. The two most powerful beings I know going head to head. This is not something I want to be a part of. I have complete faith in my father's ability to survive this fight, my friends on the other hand I'm not so sure. They've trained their entire lives, lives far longer than my own. But the griffins are dirty and underhanded and don't fight fair. I've got to make sure they are okay.

Making my way through the house with nearly sixty moving bodies is almost impossible. Some of those bodies have been thrown through the windows and walls and are now fighting bodies on the front lawn, but the house is still cramped.

The last time I saw Aspen seems like forever ago. And Thomas. I haven't even seen Anna or Kristina or Gray. They have to be okay.

Just as soon as I think about them I see Anna and Gray taking on three griffins in the dining room. Anna's hands are on fire as she reaches for her attacker. His shirt goes up in flames but he ignores it in order to make his attack. The closer his ice knife gets to the flames lighting his shirt it begins to melt. Gray's whole body is alight, his white Mohawk shining in the flames. When he lights his attacker on fire the man drops to the floor bellowing in pain and rolls himself around.

There is so much action and chaos my concentration slips. My mind slips. How can this be happening? Why is this happening?

I can't lose my cool. Not now. Not when these people need me.

But what can I do? I've had less training than any single person in this house.

Kristina runs through the living room after a griffin. I see him turn back to her, seeing if she's following him. He appears to be scared, but there is a sinister look in his eye. He wants her to follow him.

It's a trap.

My body unlocks, sending me after them. I can't let him get her. Not her. Not any of them.

As I reach the doorway a griffin comes charging at me from the porch. He's taken me by surprise and knocks me back several feet.

I have to get to Kristina. But this asshole is standing in my way. I grapple with him, holding both of his arms in my hands as he presses an ice knife down at me. How do these guys make so many ice knives? They must have an industrial sized ice knife machine.

He presses down on me, hard, with strength the griffins are known for. We may have fire on our side, but the griffins have strength we will never match. When they out number us their strength gives them a major leg up. I'm pushing back with everything I have and momentarily forget about using my power. But then I remember. My concentration is pulled from pushing him away to channeling my power. He gets the upper hand on me and presses the knife into my chest. The skin around the knife sizzles and crackles dying as the ice flash freezes it. I bite back a scream knowing every second I waste could be the one that saves Kristina.

My hands holding the griffin's arms ignite and spread to his clothes. This griffin has fewer layers on than his compatriots and he goes up quicker than the others. It's enough of a distraction for me to kick him off of me and onto the floor.

I clamber to my feet as quickly as I can and run after the direction Kristina fled. My festering wounds ache and bite at me, blood running fast down my skin. The loss makes me dizzy and heavy on my feet. But I have to push forward.

I run after Kristina and the griffin she was chasing, right into the corn field separating Logan's and my house. It's the middle of summer and the corn is about shoulder high so I can see where they run, but it is thick and difficult to move through.

I'm several feet away from them, but if I can catch up, I can help her.

But then the griffin turns around to face Kristina, and three others pop up from the corn. I spot Ashley among them. They smile at her and just before she can scream, the four of them plunge ice knives into her chest. Fire erupts from her ribcage trying to staunch the wounds, healing her. Ashley faces me, smirks, then turns back to the others. I hate her as I have never hated anyone before. The four griffins flee from Kristina, knowing their job is done.

I run to her and catch her falling body. We sink to the ground, her weight heavy in my arms.

Tears leak from my eyes down my face.

"Kristina, you're okay," I tell her.

Her fire works on her wounds, healing her. But the fire spreads. And I know that can only mean one thing.

"I'm glad I got to know you," she says.

I'm crying openly now, my tears leaking down my face and onto her body. I try to aim them over the punctures in my chest. Phoenix tears have healing powers. But mine are defective. I can't heal myself, how could I possibly heal someone else?

"You have to stay with us," I tell her, clutching her tighter, my arms a vice around her body.

The flames continue to spread down her legs and arms. The heat passes to me, fire catching my clothes.

"Kristina, please," I beg her.

"Say goodbye to the others for me," she says, a sad smile crossing her lips.

Flames converge and cover her face, her pretty, happy face.

"Please," I say, tears clogging my throat.

She closes her eyes, sparks dance across her eyelids and merge into a single blaze covering her entire body. Within those flames her body collapses in on itself, the flames burn out, and I am left sitting in the middle of a corn field covered in the ashes of my newest friend.

Rage and sorrow so fierce build inside me and crawl up my body. A scream so bloody forces itself past my lips and punctures the sound barrier around me. I scream and scream and scream until my voice is horse and my throat raw.

I continue to scream.

Until Logan and shaking me, gripping my shoulders, and shouting my name more desperately than I've ever heard him.

My body is pulled from the corn. Pulled from the ashes.

My clothes have burned off me.

Phoenix tears are dripped onto my wounds, stitching my skin back together. I am put into a bath and cleaned up. I am questioned, talked to, begged to speak.

I have nothing to say.

Kristina wasn't our only casualty. Two other phoenixes were slain in the attack. Two I didn't know very well but still feel a loss for.

Kristina was my friend. She was so warm and bright and friendly. Her sudden absence leaves me feeling hollow. I was crushed when I found out Nash died, but I wasn't aware when he died, didn't witness the horror of watching the life pulled from him. But I held Kristina in my arms as she died. I watched as her fire consumed her. I saw the life leave her eyes. I can still feel the thick coating of her ashes on my skin.

At some point my phone is placed into my hand and I remember I'm supposed to be at home, watching a movie with my parents.

Without a word to anyone I pass through the house. Most of the phoenixes are lying down on couches and spread out of the floor. Some speak to each other. Others are quiet. No one looks to me. I spot Tucker and Gray tucked into a dark corner, kissing and holding on to each other. Tonight was so bad they let an outsider into the fold. Or Tucker forced his way in. Either way, that says something.

I'm sure Logan is in a room with my father, their war room, discussing what happened and what to do about it. I can't be here right now. I need to see my parents.

Anna sits on the floor by the door. Her legs lie flat in

front of her, her arms dangle down by her sides. She stares in front of her, a vacant expression. I'm not even sure she sees me approach.

I should say something to her. But I can't. I don't even know what I'd say.

So I take the cowards way out and I twist the door knob. When I pull the door open and take one step out Anna says, "She was my best friend."

"I'm sorry," I tell her, my voice cracking.

"I never told you I was sorry about Nash," Anna says, tears glistening in her eyes.

I swallow hard, fresh tears burning the back of my eyes. I could be mad at her for only now feeling sorry I lost my other half, when she has lost someone too. But where would it get me? Nowhere. I stare at her for a second more, knowing what she is feeling right now, walk through the door, and shut it behind me. I can't deal with this right now. I don't have the strength.

I walk blindly back to my house, hollowed out, alone.

I sit on the couch between my parents, putting on a smile when I need to, answering their questions when I need to. I don't have any idea what movie we are watching but I stare at the bright colors and the actors portraying characters, living out fantasies, falling in love, defeating the bad guy. My parents are back together, something I've wanted for a year now. We're a family again, and I can't enjoy it. I can't revel in something in my life going right when everything else is so wrong.

A heavy weight presses down on me. Kristina was my friend. She and Anna welcomed me when the rest of her people held disdain for me. She befriended me when she didn't have to. She included me. To her, I was one of the phoenixes. To her I was already a part of her people. And she was mine.

Despite not knowing about being a phoenix. Despite coming into the mythological game late, these are my people, whether I want them to be or not. Raphe came for me. Granted he came to wipe out my people. But he came for me, and the people in that house fought for me, fought to defend me. And some of them lost their lives because of it. The people in that house are my people. And it's about time I started acting like it.

No griffins were killed tonight. Some suffered heinous burns, but none died. They picked up their wounded and went home. They know where we are. They know how to get to us. They left us wounded and three good people down. And none of them died. It's unfair. It's unjust. They accuse us of being monsters. They wish to wipe us out because they think we are dangerous. And yet we did not kill one of their people.

They are the monsters. They attacked us. They killed us. And we only defended ourselves. It's a noble purpose but it's not getting us anywhere, and it's got to stop.

Fourteen

Raphe stands over me, ice knife in hand. He's been playing with me for hours, cutting small slits into my skin.

Sweat slicks my skin, mingles with my flowing blood, and trails down my body. A fog has settled over my vision. Maniacal laugher plays in my mind, whether it's real or not, I'm no longer sure. I've long since stopped screaming.

Kristina lays next to me, her body carved up to match mine. Aspen hangs in chains in front of us, her clothes soaked in her blood. Gray's screams ring out from a room outside of where we are kept. I am not the only one who cannot heal in this hell.

Logan won't come for us this time. Xander won't tell him where we are. We are trapped, dying, with no way out.

Ashley enters the room, a knife in her hand and a smile

on her face. She is just like her father, just as sadistic. I want to drive a dagger through her two hearts.

"I see you've made new friends, Casslyn," Ashley says in that innocent, playful tone of hers. "Too bad I'm going to take them away from you, and make you watch every second of it. And then I'm going to take my time killing you."

My scream joins Aspen's as Ashley slides the knife down her shoulder and drives it into her back. Aspen kicks back trying to fight Ashley, but her feet are in manacles and only reach so far. Ashley leaves the knife planted in Aspen's back and moves on to Kristina.

I wince when I hear a scream from down the hall. I can only imagine what they are doing to him. Hot tears stream down the sides of my face. This is my fault. I brought them all here. I drove them like lambs to a slaughter.

Ashley laughs at Gray's pain, menace coloring her pretty face. I am going to kill her if it is the last thing I do.

Kristina lies on the table, her expression stoic in light of her pain. She is too fierce to show weakness. Still Ashley does her worst. Placing a knife at the top of Kristina's hip she plunges it in and drags it down, through her skin, to her ankle. Kristina bites down hard, refusing to scream. I scream for her. My throat is raw. I'm sure I've ruptured something.

"Your turn," Ashley says in a singsong voice.

I close my eyes, refusing to face her. Refusing to give her the satisfaction of seeing my pain.

"Open your eyes, Casslyn," she says.

"Open your eyes, Casslyn," says a new voice.

A voice I know well.

"Nash?" I ask, opening my eyes to a whole new setting. Aspen is gone. Kristina is gone. Gray's screams are gone.

I stand side by side with Nash facing the swing set at the park.

"Why do we always come here?"

"Why don't you ask yourself that question? You pick the location," Nash says, moving away from me to sit on a swing.

I join him, the both of us pushing back with our feet, letting go, and pumping ourselves higher.

"Thank you for saving me," I tell him, wind whipping my hair back.

"You saved yourself, Casslyn."

I want to ask him what he means but I'm sure I'll get some cryptic answer about me saving myself.

"Why are you still here? Why can I still see you?" I ask him.

Nash shrugs his shoulders and swings himself higher into the air. "You still need me," he says.

I don't know what that means. But I'm glad he hasn't left me.

"I'll always need you."

"You think so, but you won't."

"Why are you being so weird?"

"I'm not."

I'd argue with him, but I have a feeling it would get me

nowhere. So I change the subject.

"I found Tucker a boyfriend. You should see them together."

"They seem happy," Nash says.

I've long since given up wondering where he gets his information.

"So what happened between you and Logan?" he asks.

I pump my legs harder, wanting to ignore his question.

"He left me to be with his bitch of an ex-girlfriend."

"You don't really believe that do you?" Nash asks me, giving me the you're-smarter-than-that look.

"What else am I supposed to believe when it's staring me in the face every day?"

"You honestly believe he doesn't love you anymore?"

After a long pause, two back and forths worth, I say, "I don't know."

"And what about the griffin? You trust him?"

"I think so. He's nice. He makes me laugh. He makes me forget about the world around me, the war around me. When I'm with him, it's not a phoenix and a griffin, we are just people."

"Just be careful," Nash tells me, eyeing me sternly.

"I will. I promise."

Nash and I slow our swinging down and sway back and worth, our feet no longer leaving the ground. Nash has grown quiet, his face clouded. The sky above us becomes dark, rain clouds rolling in. Within seconds thunder rumbles around us, lightning races across the sky, and raindrops pelt us. We do not move from our swings.

"Why am I still here, Casslyn," Nash asks, his voice hollow. I've never seen him like this. This isn't the Nash I know.

"You said I still need you."

"I want to go home."

"We can walk home," I tell him, standing up from the swing so we can head towards our house.

"I want to go home," he says again. And repeats himself.

"I want to go home."

I open my eyes to darkness, tears streaming down my face, Nash's words echoing in my head. I'm alone again. I'm always alone. Sweat slicks my skin but goosebumps pimple my flesh. As still as I lay my body quivers from the subconscious torture I went through.

I paw at the nightstand reaching for my phone. The display reads two thirty in the morning. It's probably too late to call him. But I don't want to be alone.

So I dial his number and listen as it rings.

"Hello?" he says, his voice husky from sleep.

"Can you come over?" I ask sheepishly.

"On my way."

When he gets here he lets himself in and comes to my room. He doesn't say anything, just crawls in bed beside me. I bury myself into his strong arms and close my eyes. I breathe him in and for the moment I feel safe. Safe enough to drift back to sleep.

***

When my eyes open again it is still dark outside. I'm still wrapped up in the body beside me. But something is different about my room. Something is off. A presence fills up the room. One that wasn't here when I fell back to sleep.

I look towards the door and find a large silhouette darkening the doorway.

"Logan?"

"I came to check on you," he says, his voice deep but clipped.

Cohen doesn't stir beside me. He must be sleeping hard.

"Logan, I," I say, but I don't know what to say.

"Don't," he says, then leaves the room.

I rest my head back on Cohen's arm and find sleep no longer wants me. I lie there until my room slowly lightens. I lie there until my dad sneaks out of my mom's room like a teenager, all hushed voices and quick kisses. I lie there until my mom gets ready for work and leaves the house. I lie there until Cohen wakes up and faces me.

"Good morning," he says, his voice soft but not cheery.

"Morning," I tell him. There's nothing good about it.

"Care to tell me why I came to your house at three in the morning when it wasn't for a booty call?"

"No."

"Fair enough. Are you alright?"

"No."

He doesn't pull his arm out from under me. But he

doesn't pull me to him. We lie in silence for minutes, taking in the morning, taking in the fact that we are in my bed together with no romance between us.

Then he nudges the back of my head with his arm and tells me to get up.

"Why?"

"I'm making you breakfast. Get up."

I make a disgusted noise but haul myself out of my bed.

I head for the bathroom while he moves down the stairs. I brush my teeth and take a shower. The feel of Kristina's ashes still coats my skin. I can't get it off, as hard as I scrub. I wonder if I ever will. I find clean clothes in my room and head downstairs.

The smell of bacon and eggs greets me half way down the stairs. I turn into the kitchen and see Cohen standing in front of the stove flipping the bacon with a fork. I sit at the island and wait for him to finish. Neither of us says anything, though we are aware of the other's presence.

Cohen sets a plate in front of me. It's piled high with pancakes, bacon, and eggs. I wouldn't have thought I was hungry, but looking at it I've never been so hungry. Cohen sits beside me and digs into his own plate. Neither of us says a word until we're done eating. It's a comfortable silence. But it's a silence I need. Words are too hard right now.

When we're finished eating I help him with the dishes. There's an easy rhythm to it, like we've done it before. I don't want to think about what that means. And I don't want to get used to it. When we finish with the dishes we move to the living room. Almost immediately I start to think about what happened last night, the loss of Kristina and the others, the dreams I had, and it's too much and I need to get out.

"Let's go somewhere," I tell Cohen.

"Where do you want to go?"

"I don't know. Take me somewhere. Please."

Without questioning me, without missing a beat, he says, "Let's go."

We hop in his car and drive off. I avert my gaze when we drive past Logan's. I'm not ready to see the carnage in the light of day. I'm sure I should be over there right now, having a rally meeting or something. Grieving together maybe, but right now I just need to get away.

When we are past I turn to Cohen and ask, "Do you want to go to your place to shower and change?"

"Why? Do I stink?" Cohen makes a show of raising his arm and smelling his arm pit. He makes a face but says, "I think I'm good. Unless this is your way of trying to get me to take you home with me."

"Hardly," I tell him, but it lacks the teasing I was going for.

Cohen drives into town and park in front of the coffee shop.

"This is where you're taking me?" I ask.

"No. I need a second to decide where to take you. And I need caffeine."

I wait in the Jeep while he goes in for his coffee. He comes back out minutes later with two cups in hand. He hands me one and I immediately smell the rich aroma of the hot chocolate. I didn't know how much I wanted this until it is in my hand.

"Ok. I've got a plan," Cohen says, taking a sip from his coffee and backing away from the curb.

"Do tell," I say.

"And spoil the fun? No way," he says, shaking his head like I'm a goofy child.

I sit back in my seat and sip on my hot chocolate. My mind lingers on the fact that he knew I prefer hot chocolate to coffee, but I'm not about to get into that now. Instead of sitting in silence, because I'm not ready for normal conversation, I tune into my favorite rock station and turn it up. Cohen eyes me from his seat but doesn't say a word.

We exit town limits making me wonder where he is taking me. We're heading in the wrong direction to go mini golfing, but we are heading to the second largest city nearest Cedars. But Cohen didn't want me asking where he was taking me and ruining his surprise, so I remain quiet. It suits me.

But soon my thoughts turn to the dream I had, the dreams I had. I'm not sure which was worse, being tortured alongside my people by my true enemy, or watching my brother suffer in his stagnant existence. I've had torture dreams before. After I was captured by the griffins, nightmares plagued me for weeks. This is nothing new. It's my worst fear come to life, then repeated in my dreams. But the way Nash was acting was off. He's not really there. His presence is my mind needing my twin brother. My mind shouldn't have thoughts separate from *my* thoughts. And yet when I dream of Nash, it feels like he is truly with me, not just my imagination. He keeps changing. Growing darker. Tired. This new Nash scares me.

I want to go home, he said. What does that mean? What is his home?

Without me being aware, Cohen has driven us past the turn for the nearest city and continues on. Now I'm really curious as to where we are going. Before long he pulls off onto a side road and our destination is clear.

We drive down a narrow paved road, lined with trees on either side. After a few miles on the road it ends and we pull over.

I step out of the car and into sand.

Cohen has taken me to the beach. Or, as much of a beach as you can get in Nebraska. The Missouri River lies in front of us, small waves lapping on the wind.

Cedars is so close to the river most people who can afford to own boats and spend their entire summers here. While the river wasn't my family's favorite weekend destination, we did make the occasional trek up here. My parents would swim then lay on the hot sand while Nash and I would climb on the rocks along the sides of the cliffs. Once, we found a wounded bird and tried to nurse it back to health using what we had on us. We rummaged around us finding small rocks and sticks and weeds we could use to build it a nest to rest while it got better. I'm wise enough now to know there is no way we saved that bird, but when you are ten years old you feel like a hero.

A year after saving the bird, Nash saved me. We were climbing on the rocks when my sandal slipped and I fell into the water. I was more than lucky not to hit my head on a submerged boulder. I was barely in the water for more than a couple of seconds before Nash dove in behind me and pulled me out of the water. I'd sucked in a good amount of water when I fell in and Nash beat me on the back until I'd coughed it all back up.

Nash was always there for me. He's still here for me.

"I thought you could use some fresh air. Maybe get out of town," Cohen says from beside me.

I didn't hear him approach but his presence is comforting.

"Thank you," I tell him, willing my throat not to clench.

"You want to sit? Swim? Hike?" Cohen asks.

"I didn't have much warning. I don't just walk around with my suit on under my clothes."

"Swim in your underwear. There's really no difference. Or we could always go naked."

"Do you have to turn everything dirty?"

"It's my job. And I'm good at it," Cohen says, shrugging his shoulder like eh-what-can-you-do.

"Can we just sit?" I ask.

"Your wish is my command." There is no joking in his tone. It unnerves me.

"Tell me," I say. "If you're new to town, how did you know to take me here? How did you know where the mini golf course was?"

I'd never thought about it before, but now that I am, he seems to know his way around these parts really well, too well.

"I grew up in Cedars," he says slowly, gauging my reaction. I narrow my eyes at him, new found suspicion taking root. "I've just been away for a long time. I told you I didn't want any part of the griffin's hatred, so I was shipped off."

"I'm sorry," I tell him. Not having a clue what it would be like to be to disagree with your family so wholeheartedly they would send you away.

"It's over and done with. Not something we need to dwell on."

So I don't. I drop the subject like a hot potato. Cohen doesn't seem too keen on discussing it anyway.

We walk down the beach a ways until we're close to the water. I sit down close enough to put my feet in but the waves won't make my shorts wet. Taking my shoes off I dig my feet into the wet sand under the water. I wiggle my toes and wedge sand in between them.

I close my eyes and listen to the rhythm of the water, the birds flying overhead, Cohen's steady breathing beside me. It's soothing. The calming sounds relieve some of the tension brought on by my dreams. Once I've calmed myself a decent amount, I open my eyes and face the world around me.

The sun dances on the surface of the water and dives in. Beside me Cohen scoops sand into his hand then closes his fist and lets it funnel through. He's leaving me be until I'm ready. I don't know many guys who would be so patient. He doesn't know how much I appreciate it.

"Casslyn?" Cohen asks. "Are you okay? And don't answer yes, you're fine, because obviously you are not. But truly, are you okay?"

"Not really," I answer him.

"What happened last night?"

I contemplate not telling him. He is the one who invoked the no mythical talk while we're together, I would only be honoring it by not telling him. But some part of him must know what happened last night. As far removed as he is from the griffins, he must know some of what they are up to. By asking me what happened, he must know what I'm going to tell him.

"The griffins attacked us last night," I begin.

He immediately jumps in asking, "Are you alright? I mean. You look fine. But are you alright? Were you hurt?"

"I was cut pretty good a few times. But Logan healed me so I'm fine."

"What do you mean, Logan healed you? You're a phoenix. Don't you heal yourself?"

"Um, yeah, not so much. I wasn't endowed with that ability."

"You can't heal yourself? Holy shit."

"Yeah. I've gotten past it."

"So, what's really bothering you?"

"Your people," I start and then stop. "The griffins killed

some of my people. My friend Kristina," I stop again. I'm not sure I can tell him. I'm not sure I can verbalize it. Giving words to it, giving life to it, will only make her death that much more real. "I watched as four griffins stabbed her in the heart. I held her as she died. Kristina, an innocent person. And good person. My friend, turned to ashes in my hands."

Suddenly the beach is too nice a place to have this conversation. Too nice a place to be after such horror went down the night before.

I miss Logan and his strong arms. I miss his unwavering assurance that he will protect me at all costs. He would be able to talk me down from this. I would have never had nightmares had I shared a bed with him, been wrapped in his embrace. I miss Nash. I miss the four Musketeers. I miss my life before this shit storm I've got now took hold.

Cohen is new, and fun, and nice, and seems to really care about me. But he's not Logan. No one will ever be Logan. But Logan isn't here. And Cohen is. Cohen is actively trying to help me through this.

"I realize that saying I'm sorry is nowhere near adequate for what happened or what you are feeling, but I am. Sorry."

"I just don't understand. You know? Why? What have we done?"

"I'm not sure there's an answer to that. It's why I got out."

I turn away from him, glad I have someone to talk to about this, who isn't so close to the situation, but who isn't attached completely.

"You want to go for a walk?" Cohen asks, standing up beside me.

"Sure," I tell him, making it to my feet.

We walk off into the sand, both carrying our shoes, the water rushing ashore to wash over our sand covered feet.

We walk a distance in silence. I've said what I needed to. I'm not sure what else there is to say. We could talk about something else, I suppose. I wish we could talk about something else. Cohen is the king of the light hearted. I wish now he would cheer me up. But he is as silent as I am. And not only silent, but contemplative.

I walk on, giving him the space he gave me.

When we're at least thirty more feet down the shore he turns to me and grabs my arm, stopping me in place. I turn to him, nervous for the first time since I met him.

"Ok, look. There is something I need to tell you. But first I need to tell you that I really like you. I do. I enjoy every minute I get to spend with you. I wish I could kiss you every second of every day. When you called me last night I was so glad you needed me. I know I haven't known you that long, but I want to know you forever. I'm not playing you in any way. I would never lie to you. I would never hurt you."

He pauses, swallowing hard, his Adams apple bobbing up and down. I like everything he is saying, but I don't like where this is going. I can feel panic rising in me. My power surges under my skin, sensing danger of some kind. I pull at it, making sure it is ready. That I am ready.

"What are you trying to say?" I ask him. I can't guess at

what it is, but I know it can't be good.

"You're going to be mad. Just, please, hear me out, and don't light me on fire. Please."

"Spit it out, Cohen," I snap at him.

My fingers tingle, the tips igniting without my consent.

Cohen takes a deep breath and closes his eyes. When he opens them the words fall from his mouth. "Ashley is my sister."

Before the thought can travel from my brain to my muscles, my fist is connecting with Cohen's jaw. I hit him hard and fast. The impact sends him sprawling backward landing in the water. I stalk towards him, angrier than I've ever been. I feel betrayed. Massively betrayed. And in the worst way. Just when I thought I could like Cohen. Just when I thought I could trust him.

I stand over him, fire in my eyes, hate in my veins. He holds up his hands in front of his face, to guard himself maybe. He is a griffin, he could just as easily over power me, but he chooses not to.

I look down at him, my mind waging a war against my heart on how to deal with him.

"Casslyn," he says.

My name on his lips jolts something inside me.

I'm not going to kill him. Not today.

But there is one thing he needs to know.

"I'm going to kill your sister."

Fifteen

Logan and I spar in silence. He hasn't spoken a word to me since he found Cohen in my bed. I'm silent in reverence to his anger and because I haven't gotten over the fact that Cohen is Ashley's brother and he waited so long to tell me.

I haven't spoken to Cohen since he uttered those damning words. I let him drive me home but gave him the silent treatment the whole way. He apologized several times and has since texted me at least fifty times every day since asking, if I would give him a chance to explain. I haven't yet. But with Kristina gone Anna hasn't been that willing to hang out. Tucker has been busy with Gray. Logan won't speak to me. And Aspen has taken note of Logan's anger and is only marginally friendly to me. I can't blame her, I guess. I would never have taken sides against Nash. The rest of the phoenixes spend their time working out together and sparing or on the lookout for the griffins. Given all of that, I may wind up giving Cohen the benefit of the doubt only for someone to talk to.

I throw my fist forward in an attempt to punch Logan. He blocks my hand but takes hold of it to spin me around and pin me to the floor. I get back up and start over again. I lunge for him but he deftly picks me up and throws me violently to the floor. The wind rushes out of my chest. I gasp for air and come up short. Lydia snickers at my fail from across the room. Logan is so silent he doesn't even chastise me for what I'm doing wrong. Which I'm pretty sure is his favorite past time. He extends a hand to help me up but doesn't ask if I'm alright. What would be the point, he knows I'll survive.

This is odd for me, usually I'm the one shutting him out. I guess he's giving me a taste of my own medicine. Though I'm really not sure what he's so upset about. Sure he's mad Cohen was in my bed. But is he mad because Cohen is a griffin, he doesn't trust him and he poses a threat? Or is he mad because he still has feelings for me?

Logan walks to the weight bench and sits down, drinking from a water bottle.

Taking a deep breath I move a step towards him, and another, like moving toward a wounded animal, afraid he might run away. I sit next to him on the bench, take a sip from my water bottle, then say, "Logan, can we talk?"

As if he didn't hear me he stands from the bench and walks towards the stairs, and straight up them. I wasn't aware we were done training for the day. I'm not done training for the day. If I want to defeat the griffins, which I desperately do, I need to work harder. Logan and I have been putting in extra training sessions the past few days, but it's not enough. I need to get better, faster. And that's not happening.

Stepping on the treadmill, I crank up the speed and start running. It's not the same as running outside, but since it's farming season, the chance of someone spotting me running faster than anyone should, is higher than normal. The treadmill will have to do. I put my ear buds in my ears and push play on my iPod. Before I can get halfway through the first song the ear buds are ripped from my ears.

I jerk from being startled and nearly lose my footing on the treadmill. When I right myself I find Lydia standing in front of the treadmill, her manicured hands on her trim hips.

"May I help you?" I ask, lacing my voice with snark.

"Yeah. You can stay away from Logan," she says, crossing her arms like it might intimidate me.

"Are you being serious right now?" I ask, stopping the treadmill.

"It's obvious you still like him. Everyone can tell. It's pathetic really. I don't know why Logan puts up with it, but I'm not about to. Logan is mine. Get that through your head."

I swallow around the anger clogging my throat. How dare she come at me like this. Can't she see she's won? Logan is hers and it's clear I'm not about to win him back.

"Is the little girl going to cry now? You poor thing. Logan never loved you. He is never going to love you. How does that make you feel? Let me tell you a secret. I always get what I want and I always win."

"Lydia," Logan says, his deep voice booming through the basement. "Leave her alone."

"I was just," she says, stammering a bit.

"I know what you were doing. Go upstairs, you're distracting Casslyn from her training."

Lydia huffs out a breath of reprimanded anger and stamps her feet all the way to the stairs and up to the first floor. I watch after her with a raised eyebrow at how childish she is being. Though I can't say I haven't done the same.

I slide my ear buds back into my ears and resume the rotation of the treadmill. I stare straight ahead trying not to seek out Logan and trying not to let him see me struggle not to shed the tears burning at the back of my eyes. Luck would not be mine as Logan comes to stand right in front of me.

I continue to run, ignore him, and listen to the music blasting in my ears.

"You wanted to talk?" Logan says, his arms crossed over his chest.

I almost snap at him and say, "Now you want to talk." But I know that's not going to get us anywhere so I don't.

I stay running on the treadmill, needing to keep my mind on something other than just Logan, but remove the headphones from my ears.

"The other night," I begin, but he cuts me off.

"It's none of my business," he says, holding a hand in front of my face as if to say please-don't-say-anymore.

"I want to be friends again."

"Aren't you the one who said we were never friends?"

Indignant rage boils in my blood and threatens to spill over. Now I know what it's like to talk to me when I'm feeling sassy. Holy shit. It's no fun. My tight grip on the railings of the treadmill shakes the whole thing. But I hold in any retort I might yell at him.

"Look, Logan, I was sad and scared and alone and I needed someone. You no longer fit the bill. Cohen was there for me. Get over it. Unless you want to do something about it." I give him a few moments to speak up and when he doesn't I continue, "Right now all I care about is getting badass enough to take down those bastards that killed Kristina. Can you help me with that or not?"

Logan tilts his head to the side as if in assent and tells me to get off the treadmill. I face him in the center of the sparing mat and get into fighting position.

Before I can attack or prepare to defend myself he looks at me with a deep, wary expression. I pause, waiting for him to trick me, sneak attack. But instead he moves slowly toward me until he's inches from me. He moves his face close to mine, our breath mingles between us. He simply says, "We were together a long time ago. We are no longer together. Haven't been for a long time. I will never again be with her. And I will never love her more than I love you. You are it for me."

My heart seizes in my chest. I hold my breath and wait for him to kiss me. He doesn't. I release the pent up breath, my heart still in a vice. "Are you saying . . .?" I begin the question, hoping against hope he's finally ready to go against my father's wishes and be with me.

"No. We can't," he says, though his voice is strained.

"Okay," I say, my heart breaking into more pieces.

I take one look at him, and walk away.

I'll resume training with him tomorrow, but right now I can't. Not after what he just told me. How could I? What I really wonder is how he expected me to react after that.

Okay, I wonder a lot more things than that. He really hasn't been with Lydia this whole time? If he's not with her why does he let her climb all over him? Are they sleeping together but just not emotionally attached? Will we ever get back together? We're immortal after all. If we don't get back together does that mean he's going to be single for the rest of his life?

I jog back to my house, these questions ringing in my ears. My heart still hasn't recovered. How could Logan tell me that? Did he tell me just so I wouldn't spend any more time with Cohen?

When I'm back at my house I head upstairs to take a shower but stop when I feel my phone vibrate in my shorts pocket.

The caller id on the missed call stops me in my tracks.

I call back immediately and hang on the edge of my breath until he picks up.

After the first ring he picks up and yells, "Oh my god you're alive. I've been worried sick."

"Xander. Is it safe to be talking to me?"

"I don't care. When I heard they'd attacked you I couldn't deal. But you're alive. Holy shit I think my heart stopped. When you didn't pick up you don't know what went through my mind."

"How did you not know they were attacking us? Why weren't you with them?"

"They still suspect I was the one to help you escape. They've basically got me on lock down. They no longer tell me anything. I just heard a few hours ago about the attack."

"Xander, it happened days ago," I tell him.

"Cass, what happened?" he asks, his voice thick.

"They attacked. We were singing karaoke for shit's sake and they attacked us. They slaughtered three of us. I watched a friend of mine die."

"I'm so sorry, Casslyn. I'm sorry."

"If I have my way, I'm coming for them. Every one of them. Ashley and Colt, Raphe, and the rest of them. They've taken Kristina from me. They took Nash from me. They're not taking anyone else."

"Be careful."

"You too. I miss you, Xander."

I hear a noise on the other end of the phone then Xander says, "I've got to go. I miss you too."

Before I can say goodbye the line clicks dead. A weight clips onto vital organs in my chest and drags them to the bottom of my stomach. Or at least that's what it feels like. I miss Xander every day. But it's not until I see him or hear his voice that I realize how much.

I shower quickly, not wanting to stand in the water for too long and let my thoughts drown me. When I'm dried off, dressed, and have combed through my hair I head downstairs, my stomach arguing with me. With everything going on lately, I sometimes forget to eat. And my stomach gets mad at me for it. I pull a frozen pizza from the freezer and start the oven. When the oven is preheated and I've put the pizza in and set the timer a loud knock sounds at my front door.

I pray it's not Logan, because I'm not sure how I would react to him right now.

I open the door and come face to face with Cohen. I contemplate slamming the door in his face, but where would that get us? Beside the fact that I'm sure he wouldn't leave, even if I did try to keep him out.

So instead I step aside and let him in. Even if it is against my better judgement. His sister is, after all, dead set on ending me.

"Look," he says, facing me. "I know you're mad."

"I'm not mad," I say, and his head tilts in a cute, confused sort of way. I continue," Mad doesn't begin to describe what I'm feeling."

"Casslyn," he says, but I stop him.

"No. You listen to me. And then you can talk."

I wasn't sure how I felt up until this point, but I'm sure now.

"I know what you're going to say, that you didn't lie to

me. No. You didn't lie to me. But you withheld the truth. And no, I wouldn't have given you the light of day had I known she was your sister in the beginning. Yes, I enjoy spending time with you and yes I would have missed out on that had I not given you a chance. But I still needed to know."

I pause to take a breath. He looks as if he is about to say something but I hold up a hand, not finished with what I have to say.

"You say you like me. That you want to keep spending time with me. That's fine. I'll forgive you for this. I can even let it go. Forget it happened. We can go back to the way things were. I may even kiss you again. But let's get one thing straight. Your sister is responsible for the deaths of two people close to me. I wasn't lying when I said I was going to kill Ashley. I am going to kill your sister. If that is something you can't deal with then leave now."

Cohen's chest heaves. His eyes are large. I'm convinced he's about to bolt. But instead he takes a step closer to me, grabs the back of my head in his large hand and pulls me in for a kiss. My breath catches in my throat but I've got enough air to kiss him back. If only for a moment.

I pull away from him and say, "I didn't say you could kiss me."

"Shut up," Cohen says and pulls me back to him.

This time I kiss him back with gusto. Logan told me I'm it for him. It's what I've wanted to hear for the months since he broke up with me. But he also said we weren't going to get back together. Logan isn't an option right now, but Cohen is. Logan will always be my everything, my forever. But why can't Cohen be my right now?

So, yeah, I kiss him back. I taste him and touch him and explore him like I haven't before. He holds me firmly but delicately in his strong arms. He moves us so he's leaning against the back of the couch and I'm tucked between his legs. And we continue to kiss, hot and heavy, our breaths locked between us.

When we have to come up for air, Cohen leans his forehead against mine, he gasps for air but manages to say, "Casslyn, I know what I want because I have it in my hands right now. I want you. But is this what you want?"

"It is right now," I tell him, then lean back into him, sealing our swollen lips back together.

We continue to kiss. Our hands continue to rove. That is until we are both startled when the pizza timer goes off. I pull it from the oven and we sit at the island sharing it between the two of us.

Bite after bite I try to convince myself that I really do like Cohen, which I really do, and that I'm not settling for him because I can't have Logan, which I might be doing. When we're finished and back to making out on the couch I still haven't convinced myself, but I am closer. Cohen makes a good argument for himself every time his tongue dances against mine or his fingers glide over my skin causing goose bumps to erupt over my whole body.

"Get a room," Tucker says from somewhere close to us.

I jump causing Cohen to bite my bottom lip.

"Ever heard of knocking?" I ask, a bit harshly.

"Not in this house," Tucker says, because he's got a point. He comes around the couch and wiggles his ass until we move and he sits between us.

Tucker looks straight at Cohen and says, "Sorry to interrupt, but I need to steal my best friend now."

Cohen looks past Tucker at me, his expression asking if he's really being kicked out.

Without missing a beat I say, "He comes first."

"And don't forget that," Tucker says, practically shooing Cohen away.

Cohen stands and steps toward the door, then pauses, turns around and walks back to me. He grabs my chin with his large hand and pulls my face towards him. He kisses me hard and steals my breath from me. I grab for his shoulders to steady myself. He takes it as an invitation and places his other hand on the small of my back pulling me to him and sealing our bodies together. I sigh into him as our tongues collide causing my brain to short wave. My hand hovers over his chest under which two hearts beat a distinct rhythm. It's a sharp reminder of what he is and what I am and why this could be so dangerous.

Tucker dramatically clears his throat behind us.

Cohen pulls away from me but still holds me to him. His eyes bore into mine but I'm not sure what he's trying to convey. Tucker stamps his foot and Cohen says, "I'll call you later," before walking out the door.

I suck my bottom lip into my mouth and savor the taste

of him. My heart gallops in my chest causing me to wonder what I'm feeling for the guy who just left. Cohen is fun and exciting and I want to spend more time with him. But the fact that he forgot to mention that Ashley is his sister eats away at me. Everything he tells me, the way he acts around me, leads me to want to trust him, to know that he's on my side. But he kept that secret knowing it would drive us apart. Am I a bad person for letting it? Or am I justified to be wary of him and possible ulterior motives?

"I would really like to go back to a time when I didn't know I'm a mythical character," I say to Tucker and to no one in particular.

"Wouldn't we all," he says, the two of us plopping down on the couch together.

When I glance over at him with a raised eyebrow he holds up his hands defensively and says, "Hey, you said it."

"So," he says, stretching out the word. "You and hot griffin ass together now?"

"He has a name. And I don't have an answer to that," I say, realizing I don't. Are we together? Is that what that kiss signified? I told him he could leave if he didn't like what was going to go down with his sister and he stayed. Does that mean he wants to be with me? Why can't any one ever just have a concise conversation? No one ever says exactly what they mean. No one ever can just get to the point.

"Really? What I walked in on looked pretty together to me," Tucker says suggestively raising an eyebrow at me.

"I thought you needed me," I say to him, diverting his

attention from the topic at hand.

"Yes. I do. Not necessarily to talk. I just need you," he says. His words slow down. His voice becomes lower, sadder, more melancholy. The last time I saw him, his face compressed against Gray's, he seemed truly happy. I can't imagine what could have changed so quickly.

"Do you want to talk? Or shall we watch a chick flick and you can talk when you're ready?"

"Chick flick. And maybe some pizza," Tucker says.

"As long as we can watch *The Holiday*," I say, hopping up from the couch to head to the kitchen and pop a frozen pizza into the oven. I've already had one today, but if it is what Tucker wants, it's what Tucker will get.

"We've seen it a million times," Tucker whines.

"But it never gets old," I call to him.

"Yeah I know. Just stating a fact."

"Whatever," I say, putting the pizza into the oven.

"That better be meatlovers," Tucker yells to me.

"Is there any other kind?" I ask.

When I'm back in the living room I hop over the back of the couch and sit next to Tucker. We both lay back and put our feet up. In the Musketeer days Xander and Nash would be in the same position either on the floor or on another couch.

When we've successfully eaten the whole pizza plus chips and ice cream and are to the point in the movie where Kate Winslet's character is talking to her brother on the phone and ends up yelling at the lady staying at her house instead and my mom has returned home from work and gone to bed, Tucker turns to me and says, "I'm mad at you."

"Whoa, whoa, whoa," I say, my head snapping in his direction. "What on earth are you mad at me for?"

"I am in love with Gray, Cassie," Tucker says, his shoulders slumping further into the couch.

"And you're upset with me because?" I slowly ask, feeling like I'm dealing with a mad man.

"I'm mad because you introduced us."

My face scrunches questioningly. "I'm confused."

"You're immortal. Gray is immortal. Hell, Xander is practically going to live forever. And I am looking at another seventy years, tops."

"I don't know what to say, Tucker."

"There's nothing to say," he says, throwing his hands into the air then slamming them down on the couch. "I'm being stupid, but I think about it every day. The closer I get to Gray the more I realize I'm getting older and he's not getting older with me."

"He sort of is," I say.

"Not funny."

"Sorry."

"What happens when I get older? What happens when he's sick of me? So maybe he stays with me for a little while. But what happens when I get older than thirty-five years old and he reverts back to a seventeen-year-old? What are people going to think? What is Gray going to think? What happens when I'm fifty and he's an insanely good looking twenty-year-old?"

"Have you done the math?" I ask.

"Again. Not funny."

"Sorry."

"I love him."

"Have you talked to Gray about this? He's been around a lot longer than I have. Maybe he's got some insight I don't."

"No. I'm afraid if I bring his attention to the minor detail that I am in fact mortal he's going to realize his mistake and leave me."

"Gray would never do that," I say, feeling confident in my assertion of the guy, when I've only known him for a few months.

"I know. What do I do?"

The words that come from my mouth seed from my heart. They are words I needed months ago. "You love him while you have him. You forget about what tomorrow *could* bring and live today as best you can because that's all you are guaranteed. I'm sure Kristina thought she would have tomorrow."

"I guess you're right," Tucker says, though he doesn't sound so sure about it. Maybe a little chastised but he's still afraid of the day Gray will leave him. I don't wonder if Gray is worried about the day Tucker leaves him.

"Are you okay?" I ask him.

"I'll get there. Thanks. I'm not really mad at you. I just, I don't know, I'm jealous. Just promise me you'll be there for him if he needs you."

"I promise, Tucker. Though you may end up living longer than I do. What with the griffins gunning for me and everything."

"Thanks." Tucker says, disregarding the comment I made.

"You're welcome. Now rewind the movie. We missed the funniest part."

Before the movie is over, Tucker and I fall asleep side by side, holding hands. It's been a long freaking day. First with Logan and Lydia, then Xander, then Cohen, and ending with Tucker. I'm not sure it could have gotten more jam packed.

Tucker is right though. What happens? I'd planned on being friends with Tucker and Xander for the rest of our lives. That's slightly up in the air now. What happens when Tucker is too old for Gray? What happens if Logan never wants me again? What happens if I can't ever be friends with Xander again? What happens if Cohen isn't who he says he is? What happens when the griffins come for me and Logan isn't there to protect me?

Sixteen

My father stands in my doorway. My surprise at seeing him has delayed the reaction time from brain to mouth to ask him to come in. So I stand and stare at him.

"May I come in?" he asks, nodding towards the inside of my house.

"Oh, yeah," I answer, stepping aside to allow him entrance.

Besides me insisting that we need to go after the griffins and my father telling me we need a plan before we go busting down doors, I haven't spoken much to him in the last few weeks. I get that we need to be prepared, that we need to do some reconnaissance, that we need to know the weaknesses of the griffins before we attack them, but I am not about to let Kristina's death go unpunished. And that's exactly what it feels like we are doing. But I can't seem to get that across to the phoenixes. Again, I get that we suffered a low blow and must recover from it, but my patience is wearing thin.

Gray, Logan, and other members of the group of phoenixes staying in town have gone on scouting missions the last few weeks. The old factory building the griffins were using as a base has been abandoned. We expected that after Logan rescued me from there but we had to cover all of our bases. We know where Raphe and a lot of the other griffins live but staging an attack in town is a lot more obvious than the one they landed at Logan's house, which is in the middle of the country. So that's a no go. We need to find out where they are stationed and make an attack there. It is just taking longer than we expected. Longer than I was hoping. I need to get out there and kill them. I need to do something.

Kristina's death haunts my dreams every night. My dreams replay her death. I've seen her stabbed and killed more times now than I can remember to count. Every night it is a different form of torture but always it ends with her dying in my hands, her ashes covering my body. I wake up nightly screaming, covered in sweat, the feel of ash coating my skin.

I thought maybe having Cohen sleep with me, which he does, would help, but alas, it does not. He merely helps to hold my shaking form while I try to calm down.

"Casslyn, are you alright?" my father asks.

"Yeah, fine," I tell him, though I'm not sure I will ever again be fine.

"I'd like to talk to you," my father says.

"Okay," I say heading for the couch.

My father follows me and sits on the couch, but as far away as he can.

"I would like to say that I'm very proud of you and the way you have handled yourself since our people arrived and since everything else has happened. I realize a lot has happened and you could have reacted badly, and you chose not to. Thank you. And I'm proud of you."

"Thanks," I say slowly, wondering where he is going with this.

"I know we haven't gotten to spend a lot of time together. I know I told you I wanted to get to know you better and I have failed at holding up my part of that. I wish to change that. I would like to spend quality time together and get to know you as my daughter, not as a part of my people.

"Okay," I say.

"Really?" he asks, his head moving in surprise.

"Yeah. That's fine. If you plan on sticking around, then yes we can get to know each other. However, if you are just going to up and leave again, then no, I don't want to spend time with you."

"I will stay as long as you will have me," my father says.

My heart does a strange little flip in my chest. A dip and twirl. I wasn't expecting that. And that I am in charge of how long he stays is even more than I thought I'd get.

While I try and process actually having a relationship with my father, he turns to me, his face pulling together like he wants to tell me something but is not sure if I'll listen.

Finally, he decides to speak. "Do you remember your time in the hospital after the accident with Nash?"

"Not the first week, no."

"As far as I can tell, you regenerated during the accident. It saved your life, however, you still had internal injuries and you had lost a lot of blood. They gave you blood transfusions but your body was rejecting them. I'm sure you know why. They weren't sure you would survive so your mother tracked me down and asked if I would come and give you blood," my father pauses in his story. He looks up at me, silently asking if I would like to hear the rest of the story.

He's cautious, probably because I've spent months now accusing him of abandoning Nash and I. I nod to him and tell him to continue.

"Casslyn, I know you feel like I abandoned you and your brother. That I knew about you and chose to not be a part of your lives. But I don't think you can imagine how it feels to learn that you have two children, that one of them has just died and that the other might be headed that way. As soon as I found out about you I was here. I promise you."

He swallows hard and looks around the room. I can hear as his heart race quickens. Mine moves to join his. I'm not sure I want to hear this story but I need to hear it. I want desperately to know that he loves me. I know I said I didn't want to replace my dad, but to have two dads who love me is more than a girl can ask for.

He turns back to me and stares me down, pulsing the

story into me by his gaze.

"When I got to the hospital I gave blood and then walked into the tension caused by my presence and the fact that your mother told your dad about me. I am honestly sorry about ruining their marriage. I loved your mother when we conceived you and your brother, I love her still, but I also know she loves your dad and that your dad loves her. I'm not about to break that up. The doctor's asked me to stick around town for a few days just in case you would need more blood.

"Your dad was mad that I was there. He didn't want me to go in to see you. But now that I knew you existed, I couldn't leave without at least seeing you. So your mom permitted it. When I walked into your room and saw you, I couldn't breathe. I couldn't. You were lying in this huge bed and you were connected to all these wires and machines and you looked so fragile and broken. I've seen a lot of carnage in my lifetime, but I've never seen damage like I saw when I looked at you. I sat by your bed, took your hand in mine, and I wept. Like a little boy. From the first second I saw you, you were suddenly the most important thing in my life. And that still stands."

Again, he pauses, catching his breath and wiping away stray tears from his cheeks. Mine flow freely, unchecked, drenching the collar of my t-shirt.

"I know we have had a rough go of it. And I know you're still mad I had Logan come protect you instead of staying myself, but I thought I was doing what was best for you. You have to know that. I had no idea the griffins were targeting you and your brother, or that they would persist in their pursuit. All I can say is that I'm sorry and that I'm here now and I would like to have a relationship with you. Because I love you. I'm sorry you lost your brother. I can never bring him back. I'm sorry I didn't get to know him. But if he's anything like you, I know I would have loved him."

I try to swallow but find it difficult. My eyes sting from the tears cascading from them.

"Thanks," I say. What else is there to say?

My father leans towards me and awkwardly pats me on the back. Without thinking I lean closer to him and clutch him to me. We hold on to each other tight, finally embracing one another as family.

"We'll get there, Dad," I say as I pat him on the back.

He pulls away from me, tears in his eyes and says, "You called me dad."

"Let's not make a thing of it," I tell him, pulling fully away from him so we're separated on the couch once more.

He clears his throat and wipes at the tears falling from his eyes. "Right," he says, again clearing his throat.

Silence descends as our gazes travel away from each other and around the room. I'm not sure what to say to him. I'm sure he has more to say because he would have left otherwise. In the months I've gotten to know my father I've learned he isn't one to beat around the bush or linger after he's said his peace.

He slaps his knees with his hands then stands. "I'm glad we had this talk, Casslyn."

He moves towards the door, but slowly, and I know he has something more to say.

"Before I go," he says and I nearly jump in the air because I was right, "we are having a meeting this evening. Your presence is requested."

"Yeah, okay," I say, noting the oddness of his request.

"Good. Seven o'clock at Logan's."

"Alright."

He nods, takes one last look at me, then leaves.

I spend the afternoon wondering what the meeting is about. Praying we have the intel we need to go after Raphe and the rest of the griffins. I shower and dress in a pair of yoga pants and a hoodie, in case we are going after them. I need us to go after them. Even if we don't have enough information, I'm itching to get my hands on the griffins who stabbed Kristina. Logan stopped me from killing the man who killed Nash, but I'm not about to let him stop me again. The griffins have already taken four of our members without us even harming them. It's about time for pay back. And I'm ready to serve it up to them.

I walk to Logan's, needing to expel some extra energy coursing through my body. I walk in the door as soon as I get there. Knocking has become a waste of time. I enter expecting to be met by a barrage of sound and chaos. Any normal time I walk into Logan's lately. But I walk into silence. Like dead silence. It's eerie. Logan's house hasn't been this quiet in months.

I walk into the kitchen thinking I may find someone. No

one. I move into the dining room. No one. I move on to the living room. Logan stands in the middle of the floor, his arms crossed over his chest, like he's been waiting for me.

"Logan, where is everyone? I thought we were having a meeting," I say to him, taking steps toward him.

"We are. They are downstairs. We are waiting for you," Logan says, still positioned in the middle of the floor. He looks damn good in the dark jeans and black tank top he's wearing. His muscles bulge where his arms are crossed and it's all I can do to keep myself from walking to him to touch him.

"You're staring," Logan says, his voice teasing like it hasn't in months.

I snap my attention to his eyes and defiantly say, "Was not."

A corner of his mouth turns up in a small smile. "Whatever you say," he says.

"Are we having this meeting or not?" I ask.

Logan walks up to me and gets right in my face. He's so close his breaths falls over my face. The scent of rain overwhelms me. I've missed that scent almost as much as I've missed Logan. It's not fair of him to stand this close to me. It's not fair of him to tease me. It's not fair that I still miss him so much.

"Follow me," he says, his voice low, a hitch moving through it.

I stare after him as he walks to the basement, wondering why he's acting so weird, then follow behind him.

Logan said everyone was in the basement waiting for me to begin the meeting but when he opens the door it is still eerily quiet.

We walk down the stairs and I see everyone turned towards us. They form a half circle and have odd half smiles on their faces. I walk toward them the feeling of some sort of initiation washing over me. Or that they're going to give me some sort of bad news. Either way, my body isn't reacting well to it. It reminds me of caged animals in the zoo. I don't want to be a caged animal.

"What's going on?" I ask, nerves taking hold of my throat and squeezing tight.

When I'm nearest the center of the basement the half circle becomes a whole circle as they surround me. I'm no longer nervous but scared. I look around the basement for Logan. Surely he won't let anything bad happen to me. Right?

When my gaze connects with him his eyes lock on mine and try to convey something. That everything will be alright. That I'm where I'm supposed to be. I believe him but it doesn't do much to calm my nerves.

"Welcome, Casslyn," my father says from somewhere in the surrounding circle.

Did I mention that it's really dark down here? Because it is. There's only like two lights on in the whole basement. Like I said, initiation vibe.

"Is anyone going to tell me what's going on?" I ask, though my voice is shaky.

"Momentarily," my father says, finally stepping through the throng of phoenixes corralling me into this circle.

"How long have you known you are a phoenix?" my father asks.

My heart hitches to the base of my throat and becomes comfortable. It's hard to swallow around it. I'm nervous but I'm not about to start a fuss. They never get my anywhere anyway.

"About six months," I answer trying to do mental math.

"And how did you react to the news?" someone else from around the circle asks.

"I'm going to go with not too well," I say, because that memory is a bit fuzzy.

"And now, how do you feel about being a phoenix?" another phoenix asks.

"I've adjusted," I say. The need for sarcasm is strong but it will get me nowhere with these people. But how I really feel is too personal.

"In the time you have known about us, known what you are, you have accepted us, you have trained to be one of us," another member says.

Aspen steps out of the circle and says, "You have defended us. You have nearly lost your life for us."

Anna, whose hair in now shorn so close to her chin she could be an entirely different person, steps up and says, "You have fought with us. You have held one of us in death. You have grieved with us."

Logan steps through the circle and says, "Through your

struggles, more struggles than most of us here can imagine, you have loved us and become one of us."

My heart inches up my throat to lodge itself there. I can't swallow. I can't breathe through the emotional snot clogging my nose. I can't see through the tears in my eyes. I'm a mess.

"Casslyn," my father says, taking a step towards me. "You are my daughter. You are the future of us. You are one of us."

Logan steps toward me and says, "Are you prepared to lay down your life for any of us? Are you prepared to do what it takes to be one of us?"

I can't speak around the lump in my throat so I merely nod and try to smile.

Logan lays one of his large hands on my cheek. Warmth flows from his hand onto my skin. The heat grows until I see an orange glow peak out between our touching skin.

"Welcome home," my father says, placing a hand on my shoulder, the fire from his skin igniting my hoodie.

Aspen walks up to me, places her hand over my heart and says, "You were always one of us." Fire erupts from her hand and washes over me.

Lydia moves up next. "I still don't like you," she says and places her burning hand on my arm.

Other phoenixes move towards me, say kind words of welcome and acceptance and light me on fire.

Gray is the last phoenix to light me of fire saying, "About time, Fireball."

I can barely see him through the tears and intense blaze

that surrounds me. Each phoenix who has a hand on me lays a hand on the person next to them extending the fire into a raging inferno. Two things occur to me. I hope the smoke alarm doesn't go off. And I hope everyone brought clothes to change into or it's going to be awkward as Hell when the fire goes out.

Besides that, this may be the most amazing thing to ever happen to me. I've been accepted into a body of people, into a race of people. It isn't until now, as I watch hands connecting a people, a blaze bonding us together, that I realize what these people mean to each other. How truly deeply they care for each other.

And then the fire is out, everyone is naked, and no one is awkward about it. That's proof of love right there.

Logan sneakily went into my room at some point and stole a set of clothes because afterward he presents them to me without staring at my naked body. For too long. I smile at him accusingly but I wouldn't mind too much if he stared longer. I wouldn't mind if he took me into his arms and started making out with me. But instead the gentleman in him has him turning away from me while I dress. I have to remind myself for the thousandth time that we won't ever be getting back together, according to Logan. I also have to remind myself that I'm currently, in some fashion, in a sort of relationship with Cohen. And I like Cohen. I can see what I have for Cohen growing stronger. I can see what I have with Cohen growing stronger. If only I could stop the feelings I have for Logan. I just have to work harder on that. Put more focus on Cohen. Maybe after we've taken down the griffins I can spend less time with Logan and that will help lessen what I feel for him. Then I can spend more time with Cohen and see where it goes. I'd like to see where it goes.

Before Logan disappears though, I need to talk to him. There has been something I've been wanting to ask him. And only him. He's the only one I feel remotely comfortable asking.

"Hey, Logan," I say to his back. When he turns I see he's talking to a half dressed Lydia. I bet she would do anything to get Logan to look at her naked. But whatever. He's no longer mine. "Can I talk to you?"

He looks between Lydia and me and says, "Yeah, sure."

Lydia scoffs loudly and crosses her arms over her chest. The act presses her boobs up higher. She arches her back and points her boobs in Logan's face. "I thought we were going to go eat," she says.

"Yeah," Logan says, "all of us, in the kitchen. I'm sure Casslyn only needs me for a moment."

Lydia snarls at me and heads up the stairs stamping her feet on every step.

"Wow. That's a healthy thing you've got going."

"Don't start with me," he says, his tone somewhere between laughing and heavily sighing.

I laugh at him when he runs his hands over his face.

"What did you want to talk about?" he asks.

"Well, before I ask, I want you to know it's really personal and serious and if you don't want to answer me, I understand."

Logan's shoulders move back a bit like he is preparing them in case he needs to roll them back in frustration.

"Go ahead," he says slowly.

I lean in to him, not wanting the other phoenixes to eaves drop, even though any of them could be listening in in the close quarters. "Have you ever killed anyone?" I ask, my voice a low whisper.

Logan's face changes expressions at least three times in the matter of seconds. The first is shock, then surprise, then understanding.

"I have," he says. There is more for him to say, but he's not sure where I'm going with the question.

"How do you handle it?" I ask.

"I suspect differently than you would," he says, his voice stiff.

"Logan, I'm serious. You asked me if I would be willing to do what it took to be a phoenix. I'm willing. But I want to know how I'm going to feel when I finally kill a griffin."

"I understand that. But I'm hoping you never have to find out."

And now I understand his coyness.

"You can't protect me from everything," I say.

"I can try," he says.

"Logan," I growl.

"Hey, can I steal Cass for a moment?" Aspen's voice says from behind me.

"Yeah, sure," Logan says.

I keep my gaze locked on him, not willing to move until he answers me. He is well aware of this.

"When the time comes, I will answer your question," he says.

It's not the answer I was looking for, but it satisfies me enough until I can get him alone and pester him for the real answer. The twitch in his eye tells me he knows it's coming.

"Hey, Aspen," I say, more cheery than I feel.

"Hey, can I ask you a favor?" she says it like it's a big deal. I'm really hoping it's not.

"Yeah, sure," I say, parroting Logan's words.

"Logan's birthday is in a few weeks and I want to do something special for him or get him something special. But I'm not from around here so I was hoping you might have some suggestions."

"Oh, my God," I say, internally punching myself. "I forgot all about his birthday."

"That's okay. You've been kind of preoccupied."

"That is no excuse. He didn't forget my birthday."

"It was kind of important for the both of you," she says, using another excuse.

"I feel terrible," I tell her. "I'm a terrible person. I claim to love him and yet I've forgotten his birthday."

"Calm down, Cass. You know now. And anyway it's not for a few weeks. I'm sure you would have remembered at some point."

"Okay. Let me think. There's really not much to do around here. I'm not sure he has a favorite spot. Oh, I got it."

"What?" Aspen asks.

"We can have a party for him at my place," I tell her, planning everything in my head.

"Really? You would do that?"

"Yeah. Why not?"

"I don't know. I guess you two haven't been on the best of terms lately so I just didn't think you would go out of your way like this."

"He may not want to be my boyfriend," I tell her. "But he is still important to me. I want to do this."

"Great. This is amazing. Thank you so much. I'll think of a gift for him. But a party would be awesome. He's going to hate it."

We both laugh at that and then duck our heads together and begin to plan.

Seventeen

I use the next two weeks to plan Logan's birthday party. The food. The decorations. The cake. His present. That takes the longest. Aspen was right, shopping for Logan is hard. He has or buys everything he needs and doesn't seem to want for much.

I am no longer obligated as his girlfriend to get him a gift, but I want to and I want it to be special. So I racked my brain and came up with what I think is the perfect gift. I can't wait to see the look on his face when he opens it.

The party is tonight and I've spent all day getting ready for it. Aspen has been over helping me but we haven't actually told Logan about it so she can't be gone all day. He might get suspicious. The rest of our people have been invited. It's really a miracle Lydia hasn't spoiled the surprise for him. I wouldn't put it past her. But as far as I know, Logan is still in the dark about his party. I haven't even texted him to wish him a happy birthday. If he thinks I've forgotten, the surprise party will mean even more. At least I'm hoping.

Gray and Tucker show up sometime in the afternoon to help me decorate and start preparing the food. We blow up balloons and place them all over in different rooms. Some we fill with helium to hang and others we place on the floor, on couches, in chairs. I thought about getting streamers but felt like the balloons were pushing it as it was. Logan isn't really the balloon type, I'm sure streamers would send him over the edge.

I got a bunch of foam swords and spears to wage an epic battle. I set up Nash's old Nintendo so we could play Mario Kart or 007. I also pulled out all of Logan's favorite movies. Most of them included sword fights, fist fights, gun fights, really any type of action movie. I even brought down Monopoly, Battleship, and Life. This is going to be an epic party if I have anything to say about it.

For the food I decided standard party food was the best. I bought out the grocery store when it came to pizzas, nacho cheese, chips, and pop. I even got some burgers, brats, and french fries. I made a few dozen cupcakes of varying flavors. I even made and decorated a cake just for Logan. About an hour before people were to show up I started in on the food. It's not like baking a pizza or warming cheese for nachos expelled too much energy or took too much time.

The guest list was pretty simple. No one from school

was invited because Logan either doesn't know them or he scares them. Since I've recently learned more of them are my enemy than I originally thought that cuts down on their chances of getting an invite. Tucker is invited because he's my best friend, because he and Logan have gotten closer over the past few months and especially the last few weeks, and because he and Gray are practically attached at the hip. Logan doesn't have any friends outside of the phoenixes so that pretty much narrows it down. I wanted to invite Cohen. This happens to be an event in my life, and I want to start including him in my life. But tonight isn't about me and I know Cohen would feel awkward in a house full of people who hate him. Not to mention the fact that having Cohen here might make Logan a murderer on his birthday. So I didn't invite him. I will see him tomorrow. Hand picking the things I include him in might be the best thing for everyone for a while. At least until things settle down.

My father showed up with the first wave of people. We couldn't empty the whole house or Logan would get suspicious. Aspen was in charge of distracting him so we could get everyone here so we could properly surprise him. She said she was going to take him out for a game of bowling before she got a text message from me with a fake emergency to get him here.

When everyone is here, everyone expect for Lydia, because we all know she won't show up until the party is in full swing, just in time to ruin everything, I text Aspen and find a hiding spot. Knowing Logan and how protective of me he is, it won't be long before he is here to rescue me.

Rightly so, his car pulls up outside my house minutes after I text Aspen.

Like the hero he is, Logan comes charging into the house calling out for me. "Casslyn," he shouts in that deep voice of his. He sounds panicked which rips at my heart for a second between his call and me jumping from my hiding spot to yell, "Surprise!"

The rest of the house jumps up with me bombarding Logan with shouts of surprise and well wishes for his birthday.

The smile on my face falls as the look on Logan's face turns murderous. I swallow hard and prepare for a lecture. Logan stalks toward me, his steps full or rage and purpose. When he's to me he gets right in my face, snarls, and says, "You threw me a birthday party?"

I try to swallow around my heart beating in my throat, my breath skipping a beat, and say, "Yes."

Logan's lips turn up just the slightest, the smallest smile I've ever seen. He says, "Thank you."

The people around me cheer and clap and pat Logan on the back.

I look into his eyes, his gaze still locked on mine, and say, "Happy birthday, Logan."

His brows furrow and move down on his eyes. I wonder what could possibly affect his mood this way when he says, "I thought you'd forgotten."

"Never," I tell him.

His smile spreads to the other corner of his lips. He

opens his mouth to say something when Lydia positions herself between us and wraps her hands around Logan's neck, crooning a happy birthday into his ear.

I choke back the need to throat punch her and move into the kitchen to check on the next round of pizzas in the oven.

I find Anna absentmindedly stirring the nacho cheese, her look far away. I haven't had much of a chance to talk to her or spend much time with her since Kristina died. Not that I haven't had the chance, I just am not sure what I would say to her. The guilt of not being fast enough to save Kristina gnaws at me every day. Anna has told me she doesn't blame me. Has told me she's glad someone was with Kristina when she left this world. But I can't convince myself that there really was nothing I could have done.

"Anna, would you like to come play Mario Kart with me?" I ask her, making myself a plate of nachos.

Moments pass before she registers my words. More moments pass in which she appears as though she is going to turn me down, but decides against it and says yes. I wrangle two controllers away from people who sport frowns on their faces from losing to Tucker. Anna and I, Tucker and Gray wait on baited breath as the light flashes three, two, one, then press down as hard as we can on the controllers and race forward in the first round of the Mushroom Cup. Tucker has amped up the speed from 50cc to 150cc. I'm not intimidated. Tucker, Xander, Nash, and I have spent countless hours facing off against each other. We've played so many times we've each got nearly the same number of wins. Xander was always just a little bit better than the rest of us, but only by a hair, not enough to really count. Thinking about it makes me wish Xander were here. I know he can't be. I know he might not ever be again. But I still want for it. I'm not sure what kind of situation Xander is living in, but from how he sounded the last time I talked to him, and how Tucker talks about him, sulking, sullen, scared, I worry for him. I wish I could get him out of there and away from the griffins. I know he was raised his whole life believing in them, but I think that belief has turned sour.

Tucker and I come in first and second in the first race, followed by Gray and Anna. Gray and Anna both yell no at the TV as their avatars come in third and fourth. The second race is the Moo Moo Farm, a track I've lost in only a handful full of times. I race forward, around the leaping ground hogs, which trip up Gray and Anna almost every time. I come in first, Tucker second, Anna fourth, and Gray sixth. Koopa Troopa beach is a track that trips me up sometimes. I'd like to think I'm better at it than I actually am, but I get so frustrated when I can't hit the short cut and force everyone to play it until I can hit it. Not wanting to annoy anyone this evening, I bypass the short cut entirely and play the track normally. But by some hidden talent or sheer luck, Anna hits the short cut and wins the race. I'm so proud of her I hug her tightly and laugh at the chances. Gray beats us all on the last track when he skirts in front of the train and leaves us all in the dust. Tucker winds up getting first place. I get second. Anna and Gray are not on the podium with us.

I pass off my controller to my father, surprisingly. He says he wants to know what the kids are playing at these days. I don't tell him that this gaming system is already out dated by our standards. He's going down so hard, I'd love to watch, just to laugh at him. Gray and Anna I know will take it easy on him, just because he is their leader, but there is no way Tucker is going to let off the gas at all.

I do watch them play for a short time. I've watched my father with our people a lot lately. I hope it never comes to it, but if my father ever dies, I'm next in line to be the leader of the phoenixes. It's not something I want, but if there comes a day I'm forced into it, I would like to be prepared, in some fashion. So I learn how he treats his people. He is kind to them. He listens to them. He gives them time and attention. I'm not sure I would have the patience he appears to. He treats them like equals, but knows when to bring down the wrath. If an outsider were to peer in on our group I don't think they could spot our leader. We are a people of equals. We are kind to each other. We are supportive. We are there for each other. We make time for each other. They may have sworn me in as one of their own, but I only hope I'm worthy of them. I couldn't face it if they were left wanting.

"I'm having fun, thank you," Logan whispers into my ear from behind me.

I'm so focused on watching the group race around in circles, my thoughts racing in circles, he frightens me. I jump but regain control of myself fairly easily.

"Good. I'm glad. It is your day after all," I tell him, turning fully to face him. "Hey, I got something for you."

"You didn't have to. The party is enough."

"It's not a big deal. It's in my room whenever you want it."

Logan shrugs like it's no-big-thang but says, "I'm ready now."

"It's your party. Are you sure you can leave your guests."

"I'm ready now, Casslyn."

"Alrighty then," I say.

I head for the stairs, Logan trailing behind me, hoping not too many people are paying attention to us leaving and heading in the direction of my room. I know Lydia is glued to Logan like a barnacle on a ship, so she knows where we're going. And I guarantee she's pissed about it. At this point, I don't really care.

When we get to my room I go straight for my desk to get his gift. Logan enters my room and shuts the door behind him. I don't register it, not thinking much of it.

"Happy birthday, Logan," I tell him and hand him his gift.

He tears into the wrapping like he's five and can't wait to see what is inside. When he sees what it is he laughs, that deep, throaty laugh I love so much, that I've missed so much. Who knew he'd be so enthused about getting Sunday morning cartoons on DVD.

"Now you don't have to wait until Sunday mornings to watch them," I tell him, pushing down the memories of us watching them together. It was our Sunday morning routine.

But the last time we watched them was the last time we were together as a couple. It was also the day I was captured by the griffins. Not exactly a memory I'd like to be reliving.

Logan takes a step towards me until he's invading my space. It's not nearly as uncomfortable as it should be. "Would you be watching with me?" he asks.

My head bows down, my body instinctively pulling away from him. "Don't tease me, Logan. It may be your birthday, but it's not fair."

Again he steps forward and invades my space. "What if I weren't teasing?"

"What are you saying?" I ask. Because he's said the exact opposite so many times I've lost count. Lost faith in what I thought we had.

"I miss you, love," he says, bowing his head down closer to mine.

My heart slams into my chest. I can't breathe from his nearness. The need for him, the need I've so long suppressed, awakens, alive and on fire.

My eyes meet his, that same need shining from his flaming blue eyes.

"Don't look at me like that," I tell him.

"Like what?" he asks, his voice shallow and breathless.

"Like you're going to kiss me."

"So what if I am?" he asks, leaning closer to me until our lips meet and heat explodes on contact.

Pent up rage and passion and need and desire and want and love and anger well in my chest and crash into Logan, ricochet off and hit me again. I kiss him with all I've got, six months of wanting this, six months of missing this. His lips move against mine just as passionately. I can't breathe but I don't care. There is no way I'm breaking this kiss.

Something pulls at the back of my head but I can't pay attention to it. Surely it's not as important as this kiss. Nothing is as important as this kiss. Nothing is as good as this kiss. Cohen is a good kisser, but Logan takes the cake.

Shit.

Cohen.

I pull away from Logan, the both of us gasping for breath.

"What? What is it? What's wrong?" he asks, barely scanning the room for threats.

"I'm with Cohen," I tell him, trying to pry myself from his arms.

He growls and holds on tight, not letting go.

"Seeing you in his arms nearly killed me. Do you know that?" he says, his voice strained.

"You did that," I tell him.

"And I have been living with it. Every day. I love you more than you will ever know. Part of me died when I walked away from you. But you have to believe I did it because I thought it was the right thing to do." Logan pulls me closer, holds me tighter, as if he is willing me to believe him.

I break free from him and take a much needed step away from him. I need to think. I need to clear my head. I need the taste of him to not be filling my mouth. But I'm still mad.

"How can you just expect me to forget you broke my heart? How can we just go back to what we had when so much has happened? Where do we go from here?"

"I am in love with you, Casslyn," he says, reaching out for me. "I haven't stopped loving you. I want to be with you, from now until forever. I don't know how I'm going to do it, but I promise you I will spend every day of forever trying to make it up to you."

His eyes bore into me, pleading with me. My chest heaves and compacts. It's painful.

When I don't say anything Logan says, "I know you are with him. I know I messed up. If you want to stay with him, if there is absolutely no chance of you wanting to be with me, just say so. Tell me to leave. Just say the word and I'll go."

Logan's chest rises rapidly, waiting for me to tell him to leave. I should tell him to go. I'm with Cohen. Logan left me. Logan broke my heart. Cohen is trying to piece it back together.

When I don't say anything Logan says, "Time's up," and rushes me, his lips crashing into mine.

I fall into him when his strong arms enfold me in his body. I haven't stopped loving Logan. I couldn't move on. No matter how hard I tried.

Logan pulls away from me, breathing hard, his breath kissing my skin. "I love you, Casslyn," he whispers into my ear.

My heart slams and clangs into my rib cage. It expands

and grows and hurts so much, in pure ecstasy. I could search my memories forever and find that I've never been happier.

"I love you, Casslyn," Logan says, speaking against my lips, teasing me, begging me to kiss him.

Let him suffer.

"I love you, Casslyn," he says again, breaking my resolve.

"I love you, Logan," I say, lightly touching my lips to his, savoring in the taste of him.

My eyes close and take in the feel of Logan's body against mine. There is no way I've gotten him back and yet I can feel his skin under mine. I've wished for this for six months and it's come true. But that can't be right, I don't get things I wish for. And yet, here he is. I press down the negative thoughts. Logan is here. Logan wants me back. Logan is kissing me. Think about that, Casslyn. So I do.

Logan's hands slide under my shirt causing my skin to sizzle, crackle, and light on fire. Literal fire. There goes another outfit, and I can't seem to care. He grips my hips and lifts me from the floor. I wrap my legs around his waist gripping him to me. He moans in the back of his throat and rocks his hips into me. Heat spreads deep in my core.

Logan carefully lays me back on my bed and leans over me, never breaking the kiss. I wonder if the blankets and mattress will start on fire, but I don't care. I'll make Logan replace them. But then Logan moves his hands over my arms and down my legs and the flames extinguish. That's a nifty trick I'm going to have to learn.

"You think they've noticed we're missing yet?" Logan asks against my lips.

"Who cares?" I say, so deliriously happy I don't ever want to return to the party.

"Who cares," Logan says, trailing kisses down my neck and across the top of my boobs. My heart beats harder when his lips hover over it. His lips curl up in a wicked grin savoring in the way my body reacts to him. I slap the side of his head causing us both to laugh.

Logan moves his head up to meet my gaze.

"I love you," we both say in unison.

"Alright, we're probably missed downstairs by now," he says.

The urge to fake pout comes over me, but that's a total Lydia move and I'm not about to go there.

"Um, I need to maybe put some clothes on," I say, remembering I've burnt off half of my outfit.

Logan looks down at his chest and realizes he's no longer wearing a shirt. We both laugh again and he retrieves a shirt from my closet he left here when we were still together. Having extra clothes at each other's houses seemed prudent when either one of us could burst into flames at any given time.

When we're dressed and can keep our hands to ourselves for a respectable amount of time we descend the stairs and rejoin the party.

Only for the front door to slam open. Cohen sprints through the door, his chest dragging in breath as though it is difficult, like he's run all the way here. He doubles over, panting, clutching his knees. I haven't seen him this winded or disheveled before. He's usually so put together. This version of him is alarming.

Cohen's eyes scan the room and find mine. "They're coming," he says.

Eighteen

"What do you mean 'they're coming'?" I ask, stalking toward him, followed closely by Logan.

"The griffins," Cohen pants. "They're coming. They found out you would all be here and are on their way to attack."

"What?" Logan demands.

"You have to get out of here," Cohen says. He looks panicked, like he's the one they are after.

"How long do we have?" my father asks, charging towards Cohen.

"This could be a trap," Gray says, his hand firmly holding Tucker's.

"Why should we trust you?" another one of my people asks. "You're one of them."

"Casslyn, how do you know him?" Anna asks, a look of betrayal splashing her beautiful face.

"I met him at a party. I've spent time with him. He doesn't want anything to do with them. We can trust him."

"If he's so trustworthy and wants nothing to do with them, how does he know they are coming?"

"Raphe is my father," Cohen says.

The room erupts into shouting and arguing. Mostly aimed at me. I see where they are coming from. But I've spent enough time with him to know he's not going to hurt me. And the fact that Logan hasn't killed him yet is proof enough he isn't about to betray me.

Through all the yelling Cohen comes up to me, takes me face in his hands and pleads, "Please, Casslyn. You have to leave. They are coming for you. I can't lose you."

"There is no leaving now," Nathan says from the living room window. "They are here."

We all stare past Nathan out the window to see several dark shapes headed toward the house. They've got to be at least a mile down the road but are coming fast. I'm not sure why they wouldn't drive. It seems kind of odd for so many people to be running down a gravel road. But that's not what is important right now.

"Everyone prepare yourselves," my father says. "We protect each other. We fight together. We survive together."

Logan is suddenly at my side, pulling me to him. The room, the people, the chaos slips away as he locks his gaze with mine and says, "I love you. Don't you dare leave me."

"I love you," I tell him, despite the fact that Cohen is near enough to hear.

Logan nods at me, then walks away, giving commands to the rest of our people.

Fear grips me as I watch him take step after step away from me and holds tight. Swallowing becomes difficult. Breathing becomes difficult. I can't do this. I can't face them. Not after last time. Not so soon after they took another person I care about from me. I stand in the middle of the room, my vision a blur of my people moving around me. Blinding lights bear down on me. Nash's broken body lies next to me. I feel the ice knife penetrate my skin as it did Kristina's. Her burning body ignites me and scalds the skin of my body. Her ashes coat my skin. I breathe them in, choke them down, suffocate on them. I'm paralyzed by fear. The griffins are attacking and I can't move from fear that they are going to take everyone else I love away from me.

"Fireball, do you have somewhere to hide Tucker?" Gray asks. I faintly hear him and can't find words to answer him.

"I'm not hiding," Tucker says.

"Cass," Gray says.

"Casslyn, snap out of it," Cohen says, gripping my shoulders and shaking me.

Headlights. Ice knives. Fire and ash.

That is what I see. That is what grips me.

"Casslyn," Gray shouts before a fist connects with my jaw.

I reel back, my head spinning. But I'm back.

"What?" I ask.

"Where can we hide Tucker?" Gray asks.

"Oh my god," I say, realizing my best friend is in a house about to be overrun by my enemy, the enemy who so nearly destroyed us last time.

"Stop," Gray says. "Focus. Where can he go?"

Right. Focus. I can do this. My mind runs over every room in the house. The griffins will surely check all the bedrooms and any open area so the rooms, bathroom, kitchen, living room are out.

"The basement. There is a cellar down there that is tucked away and hidden. Take him there."

"Be safe, Cassie," Tucker says, hugging me hard.

"I love you, Tucker," I tell him, holding on hard.

Gray rips Tucker away from me, but it's too late.

All I can think as the griffins bombard the house, charging through the front door and large bay windows, is if the griffins don't kill me, my mother is going to.

Cohen grabs my hand and squeezes, reassuring me, holding me present.

I turn to him and ask, "Will you fight with us?"

"To the death," he says.

The first wave of griffins knocks into the first wave of phoenixes. One is armed with pure hatred and knives so cold it literally freezes our power. The other armed with fire and a will to survive.

I flinch at the sound of flesh marrying with flesh. The

dull thud of a landed punch. The grunt of being hit. The sizzle of fire connecting with flammable skin. The smell of blood leaving the body and permeating the air.

I don't have time to process before the enemy breaks through the first line and rushes us. Fire courses through my veins, wanting to be used, needing to live outside my body. I hold my hands away from my body and ignite my power, setting it free, just as a griffin charges at me. I dodge his knife, grab for his hand, and listen to him scream as his skin begins to melt. He whirls around nearly dislocating his own shoulder to reach at me with the other hand. I let go of his knife hand to block his other hand. It is a mistake. He fakes with his uninjured hand and moves the other to swing the knife at my face. I'm not quick enough to dodge it and have to bite back a scream as the blade slices open my cheek. Pain slices through my face hitting every nerve ending, screaming in agony.

There has got to be something special about those knives. The ice doesn't only shut down our power, it infects it, poisons it. The affect is more painful than anything I've ever felt before. Ten times worse than being sliced by any steel blade.

Cohen tackles the griffin from the side and wrangles the knife away from him. I stomp down on it, breaking the knife into small ice shards. They can still be used against us, but not as lethally.

I'm distracted by watching Cohen wrestle the griffin and am grabbed from behind. My power surges through me as I turn to face my opponent.

"Xander! What the Hell?" I yell.

"Are you okay?" he asks.

"What are you doing here?" I ask. Then remember. "I swear, if you hurt any of my people I will end you."

"Calm down. I'm here to make sure you don't get hurt. Just don't let my people know. They are testing me."

"What happens if you fail?"

"I think you know."

"Be careful," I tell him, and embrace him like I did Tucker. I'm sure it's not doing anything to help his case, but I really don't care. If there is a way I can get him away from Raphe, away from the rest of the griffins, I'm going to find it. Maybe I'll ask Cohen for help. He got out and he's the son of their leader.

"You too," Xander says, and heads away from me back into the fray.

"Are you alright?" Cohen asks. "You're hurt."

"I'm fine," I say, though my cheek stings really badly.

A battle cry sounds from behind me. I turn to face it and watch as Logan body slams the griffin right in front of me. I would swoon and say my hero if it weren't for the ice knife sticking out of Logan's back.

I advance towards them and rip the knife from Logan's back. He yelps in pain, his head and back surging up in agony. Without his knife, the griffin attacks with his fists, throwing punches at Logan while he's unfocussed. But Logan's never unfocussed. He catches the griffin's clenched fist and squeezes it. I hear as the bones crack and break. The griffin's cry is enough to split my eardrums. His hand is limp and useless when Logan lets go.

All around us my house falls apart. Glass breaks. Wood creaks and moans. Bodies are thrown or slammed into walls and book cases and the TV. Picture frames fly from or hang limply from their designated spots around the house. Smalls fires burn on the floor, on the couch, in the kitchen. It is mass chaos.

I catch a glimpse of Anna across the room fighting a griffin hand to hand. As in, Anna's not using her power. There is no fire in her eyes, no will to win, no desire to remain. Not without Kristina. I rush for the fighting pair, throwing fire balls at the griffin. The first two miss. The next two hit their mark but burn out on contact. I throw another. It catches the girl's shirt and spreads quickly. I throw another and another until she backs off her fight with Anna.

When I get to her I slap Anna across the face. She looks angry but surprised. "Get a grip, Anna. She's gone. I know it sucks. But you have to keep fighting. Do you hear me? If you give up I will never forgive you."

"But," she says, but I cut her off.

"Don't you dare but me. You heard my father. We fight together and we survive together. You may not be alive inside right now, but you bet your ass you are going to survive. Do you hear me?"

"Yeah," she says, and though her tone doesn't completely convince me, I will take what I can get.

Gray runs past me headed into some fray with some griffin. It's hard to separate the bodies moving through the house.

"Gray, is Tucker safe?" I yell at him.

"He's safe," Gray answers. "I'm going back down. Just had to help first."

And only because I know Gray loves Tucker as much as I do, I know he is safe.

We nod at each other and head in opposite directions. I find my father and Logan facing off with three griffins. I know enough to stay away from this fight, not about to be a distraction for Logan. If he can see that I'm in danger he'll lose it. The fact that he hasn't come looking for me yet is astounding, but it warms my heart to know Logan has enough faith in me to know that I can hold my own in a fight. He is my trainer after all.

Air escapes my lungs as I'm body slammed from behind. My teeth rattle as my body connects with the floor. It's a miracle my spine is still intact from the impact of the blow. I lift my head to gather my bearings only for it to be slammed into the floor. A sickening crunch sounds as my nose connects with the linoleum of the kitchen. Blood runs down my nostrils and fills my mouth. I can't breathe through my nose. When I lift my head up a second time the angle of my broken nose makes me woozy.

The body sitting on top of me weighs me down. A snicker I know all too well plays in my ear.

"You've got a lot of nerve corrupting my brother," Ashley says.

I push up with my hands trying to knock her off. She's stout and strong, I'll give her that. I can't lift off. She laughs at my wasted effort.

"Maybe if you weren't such a bitch he'd still want to be around you," I say to her.

Lightning fast she produces an ice knife and plunges it into my shoulder. I scream, my vision going black. My head throbs as blood and fire flow to and away from the knife embedded into my flesh and bone.

Again Ashley just laughs.

"Do you remember when I thrust the knife into your friend? Do you? Because I'm going to do it to you, too."

I kick and thrash trying to get Ashley off of me, screaming in frustration when I get nowhere. She stays sitting on my back, my feet firmly planted on both sides of me. That's when I get an idea. I reach around behind me, my shoulder shrieking in pain as the knife in my shoulder shifts as I do. But I need to get her off of me. So I reach my arm for her leg, grab ahold of her ankle, ignite the burning flames from under my skin and scorch, scald, blister, incinerate the person I hate most in this entire world. She cries out in pain and pulls her leg away from me but I hold on tight, pushing the flames further out of my body, further up her leg. She kicks at me and lashes out at me but I hold on. Until she grasps the hilt of the knife and twists it in my shoulder. Muscles and tendons are shredded and ripped apart in my shoulder. My grip on her leg slackens until I can't even make a fist with my hand. I try and try but my hand is useless. If I could heal myself this wouldn't be an issue.

Suddenly the weight on top of me is no longer as Ashley's body is pulled off of mine. I try to push myself off the ground but with only one working arm it's more difficult than I would have anticipated. But my savior grabs me and pulls me up. I'm light headed from blood loss and my hanging arm but I stay on my feet.

"Casslyn," Cohen says. He looks as though he wants to say more but what more is there to say? Are you okay? Because obviously I'm not.

"Is everyone still alive?" I ask him, knowing he will know who I mean.

"Yes. We're winning. Some of the griffins have taken off. The others realize they are losing."

"Good," I say, my head throbbing. My vision blurs and spins. I feel on the verge of passing out. My body hums with constant pain. Pain from everywhere. My face, my head, my shoulder, my back. I hurt everywhere. It thrums through me alive and demanding. I want to give in to it. I want to close my eyes and rest and forget about the pain.

But this fight is not over yet.

"Casslyn," Cohen starts again, pulling me away from the worst of the fray of fighting bodies.

He simply stares at me. His eyes bore into mine, staking a claim, marking me. His brows furrow and settle deep onto his face. His lips are a thin red line.

"What?" I ask him, needing to get back to the fight,

needing to protect those I love.

Whip fast Cohen pulls me to him and slams his lips against mine. He kisses me hard, pleadingly, fierce, desperately. His lips part, forcing mine to do the same. His tongue invades my mouth, tasting me, devouring me. His arms wrap around me, pulling me tighter to him, as if he could somehow join us as one. He kisses me hard and fast, a man without air, breathing for the first time. It is frenzied and wild. Like he's losing control of something. I let him kiss me because he seems to need it, like it's the only thing sustaining him. I'll find out why later, but for now, I give in to him.

When Cohen finally pulls away I can see Logan over his shoulder. He is shocked and hurt, but there is understanding underneath.

Cohen grasps my face with one hand, looking deep into my eyes. Tears trail down his cheeks when he breathes out heavily and says, "I could have loved you. I'm so sorry."

"No," someone screams from behind him.

But it's lost on me as a searing pain punctures a hole in my chest and slides slowly passed my rib cage and into my heart.

Nineteen

Wind rushes through my hair, whips it behind my head then throws it into my face. Back and forth. Back and forth. The crisp air feels nice on my heated cheeks. I throw my head back and watch clouds pass slowly by. Back and forth.

Warm wetness seeps from my nose and enters my mouth. It tastes like salt and rust. I reach up to swipe it away but my arm won't obey. It won't move from my side. So I use my other arm. I swab at the stickiness running from my nose. My fingers are red when I pull them away. Like any child in a playground with a bloody nose I wipe it on my shirt. But when I do so more sticky wetness covers my hand. Covers it and continues to run down my front.

"You're dying," Nash says from the swing next to me.

My head swivels over to him. Like the last time I left

him, he looks sad. His cheeks are tight to his bones. His eyes are sunken in.

"I'm sorry for the way I acted last time. It's just hard."

"Why haven't you moved on?" I ask him. I'm glad he hasn't. I need him. I can't lose him.

"You haven't let me," he says, shrugging his shoulders like the answer is obvious.

"What do you mean I haven't let you?" I ask him.

Nash doesn't answer. Instead he pushes the swing back with his feet and lets go, slowly swinging passed me then back. I want to know what he means, but this Nash scares me, and I'm afraid to push him.

Blood continues to run down my nose, my chest. My right arm hangs limply at my side.

Cohen betrayed me. I trusted him, and he betrayed me. I can still feel the slide of the knife through my flesh and organs. I can still feel my fire seizing up, fleeing the ice. I fell for Cohen's trap so perfectly I'm ashamed of myself. I'm embarrassed. I'm mortified. I let my people down. I led them to the attack. I led them to their end. I can only hope that some of them make it out alive. I can only hope one day they will forgive me.

I will miss Tucker and Xander. I will miss my parents, all three of them. I will miss my new friends and my old friends. Mostly, I will miss Logan and the time we could have had together. At least, if this is my end, I have Nash with me. We can both move on together.

"Heal yourself," Nash says.

"I can't," I snap at him. I've tried and failed to heal my-self several times over the past five months. "You know I can't."

"Because you won't let go," he snaps right back at me.

"What are you talking about? There is something wrong with my power. I can't heal."

"There is nothing wrong with your power. There is something wrong with you," Nash says, practically spitting his words at me.

"That's the meanest thing you've ever said to me," I say, recoiling from his words.

"No. It's not. This is," Nash says. "You are scared. You are weak. And you are failing."

"Yup. You're right. That's meaner."

Silence descends as Nash's words settle around me. Maybe he's right. No. He is right. I am scared. I'm scared of losing the people I love. I'm scared of failing. I'm scared of everything.

"Tell me what to do," I say to him.

"Heal yourself."

"I can't," I say through ground teeth.

"Just let go," he tells me. It's cryptic and I don't know what he means.

While he waits for me to figure it out, which I won't, we swing back and forth, our rhythms out of sync. We are out of sync. For sixteen years it was like we were the same person. Always together. Always knowing what the other thought. Always knowing when the other was hurt or scared. Always there for each other. Now, it's like he's not even my brother, but a stranger.

"You know how they say twins are two halves of one soul?" Nash asks, leading me somewhere. "That's what we are, Cassie. Two halves. When I died my half was somehow sucked into your body. That's why I'm here. That's why I can't move on. Because you won't let me. Because you still need me. *We* are two halves, Cassie. *You* need to be one whole."

"I can't lose you," I say. "I need you."

"Not anymore," Nash says. "I promise you, you can make it."

"I'm not strong enough."

"You are. You just have to believe it."

Tears flow down my face, unchecked. My heart clenches, sputters, broken. Blood pumps through it and out the hole in my chest.

Heal myself.

I can't.

I can't lose him. Not again.

"You are my other half, Cassie. You always will be. But now you must let me go. I love you."

We're no longer swinging. We stand in the grass facing each other. Nash brings his hand up to cup my face. His skin is warm and soft against mine. He smiles at me, his best smile, one I haven't seen since before the accident.

Heal myself.

I swallow hard.

My chest hurts so much.

Heal myself.

I reach inside myself and pull at my power. My fire burns, but deep inside. The ice knife Cohen plunged into my chest forced it to recede. It's scared, just like me. But I coax it up, drag it from the depths of me, will it to fill my veins. When it answers my call, I focus, sending it to three spots specifically; my nose, my arm, and to my heart for two reasons. The cartilage in my nose snaps and pulls and grinds jerking back into place.

My head whips up to look at Nash. I healed myself. I did it. Not well, but I did it. But when I look at Nash, I can nearly see right through him. He's fading.

"Keep going," he prods me on.

I'm scared, but I pull at my power again, moving it to my arm, stitching the tendons back together, stretching them over bone, repairing the damage done by Ashely. Again, it is painful, and not perfect, but when I'm done my arm is in working order, practically brand new.

Again, Nash is fading, the fine lines of him blurred, the details that make him Nash, no longer visible.

"Keep going," he says, his voice soft, reverent.

"I can't. I won't see you again."

"One day you will. I promise."

"I love you, Nash," I tell him, the salt from my tears burning my lips, filling my mouth.

"I love you too, Cassie," he tells me.

One last time I pull at my fire, asking it to do my biding. It is mine and we are one. Fire races through my veins, courses through my body, flows under my skin. Flames wrap around my heart, inspecting it, looking for damage. When they find the hole my fire surges in, roars to life, knits my broken heart back together.

I gasp from the burning in my chest. I gasp because I feel alive for the first time in over a year. I am alive. I am whole.

And Nash is gone.

I stand in the park alone.

Despair fills my chest.

I've lost him again.

"I'll see you again," Nash's voice calls out to me.

It is enough to keep me moving. It is enough to force me to wake up.

And wake up I do.

To a destroyed house.

I lie on my living room couch. I can feel burn marks in the fabric. It's to be expected I suppose. Voices sound around me. Feet shuffle over the floor. Weight shifts on the couch near my feet.

I look up to see my father seated at the end, my feet cradled in his lap.

"You're alive," he says. The look in his eyes tells me he wasn't expecting me to come back. The tears filling his eyes tell me he's mourned the loss of another child but can breathe again now that I'm awake.

My right arm moves to my nose. My right arm moves.

I really did heal it. My nose is no longer broken. My arm moves. That can only mean my heart has healed as well.

"How?" my father asks, awe in his voice. "How? I couldn't heal you." Sobs wrack his throat.

"I healed myself," I tell him, saying a silent goodbye to Nash.

"How?"

I don't answer him. It's a story for another time.

The shuffling feet from around the house move into the living room and crowd around me. I look up to everyone, spotting familiar faces, going through a checklist of names to see who made it and who didn't.

Anna leans down close to me. Thomas is there. Nathan stands next to the window like before. Aspen sits on the arm of the couch above my head and plays with my hair. She's got tears in her eyes. Maybe she too thought I was gone and is happy to see me awake and alive. Even Lydia stands around the circle. Two things occur to me as I look around at my friends and loved ones.

One. "Where's Logan?"

Two. "Where's Tucker?"

Laci Maskell grew up in Northeast Nebraska. Her love of reading began when her sister handed her the Harry Potter books. Laci spent her childhood telling hour long stories on half hour TV shows. She began writing not long after. Laci attended Wayne State College where she earned a degree in English Writing and Literature as well as Editing and Publishing. Laci has worked as a secretary for a physical therapy department, a tax firm, and a computer repair company. She currently works as a Subway sandwich artist and for a daycare when she is not writing her books. In what little spare time she has, Laci enjoys spending time with her family, listening to music, watching movies, and reading.

Follow Me:

Twitter:
Laci Maskell

Facebook:
Laci Maskell

My Blog:
Laci Kay With Words To Say

Snapchat:
lacikay7

Made in the USA
Columbia, SC
14 July 2017